TAXICAB TO WICHITA

A NOVEL BY
AARON LOUIS ASSELSTINE

Booktrope Editions
Seattle WA 2014

Cover Design by Majanka Verstraete
Edited by Stevie McCoy

This is a work of fiction. Names, characters, places, brands, media, and incidents are either the product of the author's imagination or are used fictitiously. Any resemblance to similarly named places or to persons living or deceased is unintentional.

Print ISBN 978-1-62015-233-1

EPUB ISBN 978-1-62015-336-9

DISCOUNTS OR CUSTOMIZED EDITIONS MAY BE AVAILABLE FOR EDUCATIONAL AND OTHER GROUPS BASED ON BULK PURCHASE.

For further information please contact info@booktrope.com

Library of Congress Control Number: 2014906564

It is life's strength, the wings by which we fly beyond the further reaches of the sky.

— *The Conference of the Birds,*
by Farid-ud-din Attar

CHAPTER 1

Where the driver meets his passenger and they decide on their trip.

WE BOTH HAD OUR SECRETS: I owed a king's ransom to a pill pusher and he robbed a bank with a urine sample. We needed each other. But I was unaware of this mutual need as I reached into my shirt pocket and grabbed a bent cigarette. The ritual of pulling it out and putting it back, in favor of a better specimen, had finally come to an end; it was the only one left. And as I held it I understood what it was telling me...

My options had finally run out.

My hand trembled as rain-beaded windows kept us dry, and worn out upholstery exuded the dirty perfume of a thousand little spills in various states of decay. It was a persistent whiff of street level hustle and bustle.

My passenger was counting out a thick stack of cash and shooting me glares. His paranoid eyes kept my left foot hovering over the brake. Half of me wanted to pull over and boot him out, but the winning half was welcoming the sight of his pristine bills. My misgivings were simply no match for the magnetic force of all that crisp green.

As the cigarette dangled between my chain-smoking lips, I squirmed at the thought of raising a lighter to my face; I hated advertising weakness to customers, and my shaking hand was a neon billboard.

You see, as a taxi driver I'd come to terms with the unsettling fact that most folks were thinly veiled apex predators. Seeing anything that resembled fear could turn them downright bloodthirsty downright quickly.

Now, right about here, I should clearly state that my unsteady hands weren't the sole product of weakness. I knew this because I'm aware of the vast ocean that sloshes about between benign character traits and the ever pernicious Achilles' heels.

Not that I wasn't heavily afflicted at this time by my own badly manufactured mythology.

I most certainly was.

In fact, I was deeply flawed.

My shaking, however, was—and is—mostly genetic. Unfortunately, when it's compounded by a bad case of nerves and chemical dependency, like it was on this particular day, I could easily pass for an alcoholic with delirium tremens.

My mom, my older sister, and me, all tremor. We tremble like dry oak leaves. My older sister has it the worst, and for some reason she went through college to become a medical laboratory technician. I used to call her a technical vampire, because she stuck needles in people's arms and drained them of their plasma five days a week. She filled and labelled dozens of vials of dark red syrup each day, then stashed them away in a refrigerator for other more educated, more behind-the-scenes vampires to examine.

Suffice it to say, she didn't last long at that job.

But back to the unlit cigarette in my mouth.

I stole another quick glance at my passenger. He was fully immersed in his money, so I reached into my jeans, grabbed my lighter, and brought it up to what I thought was the end of my cigarette. Missing by a few inches, I looked away from the road and went cross-eyed trying to close the distance. Finally, I made contact. I snapped it three times with a weary thumb and got nothing but spark. At this point, my hand was betraying me in the worst possible way. It was careening back and forth like a hopeful drunk staggering to the next bar.

Then the car hit a frost-heaved sewer grate, and the lighter knocked the smoke out of my mouth. It fell down onto my crotch, bounced forward, rolled back, and disappeared between my legs. On better days I would've managed a smile right then, but my mind was heavy with gloom. Instead, I looked up, grim faced, at the road, as I felt around. Gradually I worked my way along the inside of both thighs until I was cupping my balls.

The distinct clink of a Zippo seized my attention; I jerked my head to the right and stopped what I was doing. My passenger's face was smirking beyond the flame.

I found my cigarette.

He pushed the flame underneath, and I filled my lungs.

"So where you goin'? You got in, and told me to drive like they do in the movies, and that's cool and all... I get that... Everyone wants to do that. But I need to know so I can call it in to dispatch," I said, while regaining composure through a slow exhale.

He shut his Zippo, and returned to his stack.

"You always shake like that?"

"Yah... Well not quite this much... It's been a rough day."

He stopped sizing up his wad, which I noticed was split into Canadian and American bills, and looked over at me with eyes that had a little too much white in them. Eyes that reminded me of guard dogs on choker chains.

"A rough day, eh?" He looked away, then outta the corner of his mouth said, "I don't know where I'm goin' just yet, but yer comin' with me."

"Umm... I'm the cab driver... So yah, I'm comin' with you."

"No, I mean yer gonna take me to *wherever* I decide I'm going."

He waved his cash like it was bribe money. I didn't much appreciate his attitude, and I was thinking of saying so, but the soft flutter of the bills distracted me as it zeroed in on my ear canals and found a suitable nesting place deep inside my skull.

"Look... I got a call to wait at the corner of Range and Sterling, and I don't normally take corner calls but I did this time... I sat there for ten more minutes than I usually would. You're lucky to even get a cab in this rain."

He laughed.

"Are you desperate? You need money?"

He ran his finger along the edge of his bills like a card shark. I looked away. He was right on both accounts but I wasn't about to say so.

"Of course I need the money, but I'm not desperate... I'm a cabbie... We're not millionaires... Now where're you *goin'*? I'm not askin' again."

"You got an extra smoke?"

"No."

"You *are* desperate," he said, with that glare I'd already come to hate.

"Tell me where you're goin' or you can get out right here."

"Wichita, Kansas," he said, without missing a beat. "There's an abandoned amusement park there called Joyland, take me there."

"Wichita?"

"Wichita," he repeated, as he peeled off a fresh half-inch of hundreds and stuffed them into my shirt pocket. The new weight against my chest set every jangled nerve in my body on fire. My mouth twitched at the thought of rubbing fingers over fresh serial numbers but I resisted, and instead adjusted the rear-view mirror so that I could admire it secretly. I was wearing my favourite cab driving shirt: a vintage Steely Dan concert shirt that I'd bastardized by sewing a front pocket onto. The pocket was for holding my float, which of course, I rarely ever had.

"Can I ask you why?"

"In the Caddoan tongue, Wichita means a *shady* place... I need some proper shade to lie down in."

I'd never heard of the Caddoan language, but it was as good an answer as any; and not only that, the way my day had gone, I was in need of some shade, myself.

"Okay... You better be serious 'cause I'm gonna call this in."

"Do it," he said, as he leaned back in the seat.

CHAPTER 2

Where the driver finds out who his passenger really is and vice versa.

IT WAS THE WAY he said, "Do it."

There was something about it that gave me pause. It was as if it was a dare or something. I decided I needed to know a little more about him before I committed.

"Hey, you know... We *are* strangers and Wichita's a pretty good clip from here. I know what it's like to be trapped in a small space with someone you don't see eye to eye with."

He shifted in his seat and turned to face me.

"You're not only desperate... You're afraid."

"Look. Stop saying that, and *stop* testing me. This is a completely normal thing to wanna suss out before we hit the open ro—"

"The name's Carl. But *you* can call me Rocky," he said, cutting me off.

"Rocky? Seriously?"

"Yah... You gotta problem with my name?"

He reached over and flicked the bills poking out of my shirt pocket. I took the hint.

"You don't look like a Rocky, that's all... I mean you're—"

"I'm what? I'm a middle-aged Asian man and I can't have a name like Rocky? You're a bloody racist."

I played with the coiled mic cable and tried to come up with the words to avoid a crash landing with this guy. Then outta the corner of my eye I saw him moving in an odd way. I looked over to see him undoing his shirt collar and searching for something around his neck.

"I should probably take this off... For the benefit of the both of us," he mumbled.

"Take wh—"

I didn't finish what I was about to say, because what he did next shoved the words off my tongue and back down into my voice box. I sat there not believing my eyes as he grabbed hold of his skin at both collar bones and peeled it up over his head.

I remember thinking his skin looked a bit off, and his eyes bulged a little too much, but nowhere in my awareness did I even remotely consider the possibility that he was wearing a mask.

A freaking mask.

The top of my skull was blown clean off.

"Holy fucking shit man! A mask? Why were you wearing a—"

I stopped myself again as I connected the dots and realized the significance of the crisp stack of cash. He grinned a sickly sweet smile and filled in the blanks.

"That's right… I robbed a bank bro… Actually, it was that little foreign exchange place over on Rankin Street."

I was incapable of speech. Suddenly there was this twenty-something white kid sitting beside me.

"Every man needs a hobby and mine just happens to be special effects. Go on YouTube. You'll see my work there. It's all pretty fucking mint, if I say so myself." He paused as he looked down at the heap of black hair and flaccid skin on his lap. "This—this is my finest foam latex yet… Spent a whole year designing it just for this occasion. Just for today. By the way, we need to burn it somewhere."

"No fucking shit!" I blurted.

I couldn't make sense of my failure to notice that he'd been sporting a mask. But then I put it down to the fact that I always made a point of not looking too hard at my passengers. They were money first, and people second.

I let go of the cable, brought my hand up and rested it back on the mic. He followed my movement with his eyes. He even licked his lips in anticipation. I couldn't help it. I had to take it away again just to bug him.

"Aw fuck man. Make up your mind, *dude*... This money needs to get the hell outta this dreary little town, and if you won't do it someone else will."

He started rocking back and forth a little. I was turning the tables.

"Okay let's back up here for a minute," I said. "Number one, I'm not a racist. Rocky's a funny name no matter who you are. Number two, what makes you so sure we won't be swarmed by police at the next intersection?"

I rolled my window down a little and flicked the butt of my smoke outside. The rain spattered my face.

"You're desperate... You're afraid... And you think I'm stupid."

"Answer the question," I barked. I was willing to admit to myself that I was desperate, but I was *not* afraid. I knew full well that if the police had swarmed us at this point, all I had to do was give him back the money and feign ignorance.

He cleared his throat and blinked slowly.

"I planned this right down to the short and curlies, my friend. I cased that place out for two months. I could set my watch by the sound of the door opening at 5:01 p.m. every night. I even went in to change some money a few times, so I could get a good look at the security system and let me tell ya, it ain't no corporate bank over there. The cameras are all badly placed and they're dusty and old... *And*... The two employees who work there leave at different times, one fifteen minutes before the other. Why? I don't know, and I don't care, but it made my job easier."

He stopped to scan our surroundings. We passed a toddler throwing a tantrum in front of a store. On the other side of the street, a professional looking man laughed into a cellphone while running a hand through thinning hair. I hoped in vain that my skepticism had made inroads on his bravado as he looked furtively over his shoulder, and continued in a lower voice.

"That's just the technical stuff. The real artistry came in with the mask and the rest of the costume," he looked down at himself, "Notice the stained silk button up and the wrinkled flannel slacks. Notice the cheap cuff links with Japanese lettering. Notice the scuffed up fake leather shoes. I was a desperate Asian man with a gambling problem, you see. I even dropped a receipt from that Indian casino on the way out. Hell, I even had dinner at the cheapest dirtiest little hole in the wall sushi bar just so the smell of fish would be overpowering. Let's just say I left a lasting impression."

His smile was straight from Cheshire.

"Very nice... But how clean was your getaway?"

He laughed like he was waiting for that one.

"Let me paint the picture for you. There I was across the street smoking a cigarette. The first employee left fifteen minutes before and the one with the thick glasses was due to come out any second... Then *BAM!*" He struck the dash with his hand, "The door swung open and I stepped on my smoke and walked over to her while she had her back turned fumbling with the keys. I leaned into her ear so she smelled the fish... *Let's go back inside all calm and slow like,* I whispered. I also told her I had a little bottle of my piss and that it wasn't normal piss. It was piss with blood in it. Infected blood... *And I know you're thirsty,* I said. She gasped a little but obeyed me. Back in we went, and then we went farther in through the security door and behind the counter." He stopped and scratched the side of his head, "Keep in mind I did my best broken English all that time. Then I told her to give me ten grand, three thousand in Canadian and the rest in American. She did it like a well-trained Shih Tzu, and I stashed it in my trusty satchel here." He held it up for proof before continuing. "Then I sat her down in a chair, tied her up and taped her mouth shut. And for the record I didn't hurt her. Scared the hell out of her but didn't lay a finger on her," he said, with a hint of shame weakening his appeal. "The only thing left to do after that was to turn off the lights and leave as quietly as I entered. All this was half an hour ago."

I sat there turning his story over in my mind, looking for holes, for anything that could compromise the feasibility of us getting to Wichita unchecked. After all, my only concern was getting my cut before he got caught, not whether he would get caught eventually.

"If you were that close don't you think she noticed your mask?"

"Nope. I told her not to look at me, and I also took her glasses off."

"What about the cameras?"

"The lenses were dusty, and besides—this brilliance," he stretched the latex so that it made a sharp punctuated slap against his palm as it snapped back into shape, "looks absolutely mint on camera."

My Sherlock instincts had been shot down in flames, but I was still unwilling to commit. He started fanning himself with his wad of money as he waited. I took a deep breath in, and rested my thumb on the button of the mic, teetering on the edge of commitment.

He smiled and nodded.

"Not so fast there driver."

I turned and looked at him—confused.

"Now what?"

"Well, you forced a confession from me, so now it's your turn. I wanna know more about the rough day you've had," he said, with narrowing eyes.

He had an odd sort of power, this guy. He was seeing into me somehow. I felt it right from the moment he got in the cab.

The half inch of hundreds in my shirt pocket tugged on my peripheral vision and tipped the balance in his favor.

"Fine," I huffed. "Cabbies don't make a lot of dough in this city, but we do make a shitload of connections if we pay attention. Unfortunately not all of those connections are beneficial..." I paused and looked down, "If we let curiosity get the better of us, and if we have a sweet tooth. We can wind up in the wrong place at the wrong time. Put it this way... My sweet tooth and my curiosity have backed me into a corner that's gonna cost me two grand to get out of, and two grand might as well be a million right now."

I stopped as I let the events of the morning scribble over my mind. His unblinking eyes egged me on.

"I quit the day shift a long time ago, but today was a special day, because of a delivery I had to do."

My voice warbled with residual anxiety as the ugly truth forced me to stop again. He just sat there with the beginnings of a smile on his face.

"It was the kinda delivery that'd make any normal person shit their pants. I—I was moving a couple thousand dollars' worth of product for a guy I know."

His smile was now fully formed. I kept going in spite of it.

"The package was about the size of a hardball," I said, as I made a circle with my hands, "And I was supposed to deliver it to this other guy over on the east side."

I stopped once more and looked out the window. The rain blurred the sight of the moving road. I was having serious doubts about how much sensitive information should be laid on this kid. We were headed in the direction of Wichita, but I was by no means committed to the job. After all, the cash in my pocket was stolen and therefore un-spendable; but I also knew there were ways to get around this inconvenience, and besides, I could tell he wasn't going to let me off the hook that easily. He had trusted me, and now it was my turn to reciprocate. I respected the code being leveraged. Not to mention, I was deep in a hole that only money could fill. And where was I going to find that much cash if I chose to bail on him? Nowhere. I had to play along.

"C'mon now," he coaxed.

I tapped the mic a couple times and proceeded.

"After picking up the package I hopped back in my cab and what d'ya know, I get a casino call. The one you were just talkin' about. I took it because I wasn't told there was a rush on the delivery, and it was a chance to make a few extra bucks. *Anyway*," I said, rolling my eyes, "it took me an hour, or so, and as soon as I got back I headed straight to the east side. I pulled up about a block from the dude's house and walked to this little cut through thing. It's like an alley way that leads right to the guy's back door. When I got to his door I knocked, and about thirty seconds later a fucking cop appears. He tells me to stay put and walks back down the hall. Now... Remember... I'm holding enough morphine to put me in federal, so I take the opportunity to toss the bag off to the side in these bushes. Thing is, it didn't quite make it to the bushes. It fell just short, and sat there like a dirty secret, winking at me. Then the cop comes back with a plain clothes detective type who starts right into the questioning: Who am I? What am I doing there? How do I know the guy who lives there? That's when I saw a body get carried out in a black bag, behind them."

I stopped to search my pockets for another cigarette, then gave up.

"It wasn't hard to figure out that the poor bastard got his ticket punched because I took that call to the casino and showed up late.

Somehow someone knew the pills were supposed to be there, and they weren't gonna leave without them, or at least not without sending a message. Anyways, after a few more questions the detective realized I wasn't involved and let me go. I walked away trying real fucking hard not to turn my head back around."

"You feel lucky?" he asked.

I let my head fall back against the seat, and then rolled it slowly to the left side, hiding my face from his eyes. I didn't feel lucky at all because I couldn't stop kicking myself for throwing the dope away, like I did. *All you had to do was play it cool*, went 'round and 'round inside my ears like a chorus of grade school bullies. And then it finally hit me. All at once, the gravity of my situation tapped me with an icy finger as I lifted my head and faced the paranoia imposed by three unanswerable questions: *What if they find the package? What if they connect the package to the guy who showed up at the back door? Wouldn't that tie me to the murder of a well-known drug dealer?* These merciless doubts whipped my anxiety up into a malicious froth as I stewed in the heat of my self-disgust.

I was about to break into a sweat when an even darker thought wormed its way into my brain and flicked on an evil little air conditioner. I cooled myself back down a little by realizing that I could use Rocky like a bargaining chip—a pawn. With cold calculation I prepared to capitalize on a situation if it arose. You see, for all I knew the detective found the morphine in the bushes, and quite naturally connected it back to the name he wrote down in his little black book while I stood in front of him with knees knocking together. If this was my lot, then I was definitely willing to roll over on Rocky because at this point he meant absolutely nothing to me. He was just another idiot punk with too much time on his hands. No amount of money could've bought my silence if I eventually found myself in the interrogation room down at the cop shop, over a ball of pills that was covered in my prints. And furthermore, the dealer I owed the big bucks to was way scarier than this scrawny nut job sitting beside me. *If I could cook up a deal that made me untouchable, then that's exactly what I was going to do*; at least that's what I thought I would do at this particular moment.

With my mind and heart galloping toward mutually assured destruction, I answered his question.

"I feel pretty bad for being the cause of a murder. Not to mention I owe two grand to a guy who won't hesitate to break my arms, legs, and teeth."

The windshield wipers slapped out a less than perfect time signature. One of them had seen too many seasons—too many extremes of hot and cold.

"What's your name anyway?"

"Quinn," I said with darting eyes.

"Well, Quinn. You should feel lucky. It's a choice you know. There's always a choice." He took a black bandana out of his satchel and wrapped his wad of bills with it, as he spoke. "They probably woulda killed that guy anyway. Even if he had the pills to give them. Come to think of it they probably woulda killed you too if your timing was a little different. So don't feel guilty. Guilt is useless. Besides, there's no rules to the game we're in. Do you really think God would dish out free will to everyone, and then as an afterthought send us a big book of rules to live by? Do what you will, man. Have some balls."

"Don't get too deep on me, here. I don't have the stomach for it right now," I said, as I tried pushing the remnants of my plan to roll over on him from the forefront of my mind. Here he was doing his level best to prop me up right after I had contemplated ratting him out to save my own worthless ass.

"My point is... You live and learn... We're all made by how we handle our mistakes. If mistakes even exist. I'll tell you one thing for sure. Guilt and shame will shove you in a cage and throw away the key faster than a fat kid on cake."

He still had the mask resting on his left thigh as we hit a busy intersection.

"Are you wired?"

"Wired? What... Like an undercover cop or something?" I asked, with insult reflecting off my voice.

"No... Hardwired. Addicted. You're shakin' like crazy and your eyes got that cellophane shine."

Once again he was spot on. I'd been a full-blown addict for a couple years.

"I need a smoke," I said, as I looked past the traffic lights and saw a convenience store.

"I'll take that as confirmation. You on the draw? Y'know... Dope sick?"

Part of the reason why I'd been shaking so bad was because I hadn't taken my share of the pills out of the package before tossing it away. And now the dread of having only one left with no easy way of getting more was gnawing on my insides. I suppose I could've surgically removed my cut beforehand; I'd done it a few times before. But that kind of sneakiness never sat well with me. My preference was for keeping things above-board, and on the level. There was always enough treachery floating around to sink a battleship, so I did everything in my power not to get mixed up in it. I kept a deliver first policy. Not to mention, the guy on the west side who gave me the pills for the guy on the east had done his "preventative maintenance", as he called it. He sealed up the package so expertly, I was literally forced to deliver in order to get what was mine.

"You're good. You got me figured out."

"It wasn't hard."

"Thanks," I scoffed.

"Look at me. What do you see?" he asked.

"I see a young guy with a whole whack of stolen money." I played it safe. I could've told him I saw a young punk risking major time for armed robbery. The kind of young punk that lifers like to shower with.

"What else? Describe me."

"I see piercing eyes that make me a little uneasy. I see pale skin. I see hands that don't look calloused. And I see no hair."

"You see this?" he said, while leaning in sideways and pointing to a spot on his head, just above his left ear.

I strained my eyes and made out a small mark of some kind.

"What do you think that is?"

"A tattoo? I don't know."

"It's a tattoo all right," he said, "I'll tell you more about it later."

I shrugged off the mark on his head. It didn't matter nearly as much as getting cigarettes.

I pushed on the pedal as the light turned green. Just past the intersection I turned off into a large parking lot and found a spot near the back of the store.

"You have any scissors, or a knife or anything?"

"For what?" I asked, as I took the car out of gear and leaned back into my seat again.

"Before we burn this piece of art here..." He lifted the mask a little. "I wanna cut a piece off for a keepsake. A trophy."

"Hold on." I reached down under my seat, lifted the carpet up and felt around. "Here, use this."

I raised up my most prized possession for him to see. He grabbed it, and immediately started turning it over, opening it up, and closing it.

"A straight razor. Is this a gold handle?"

"Yeah, its gold plated and it's old. I got it from my grandfather. He was a barber." My grandfather suddenly chastised me from the mirror of my mind as I remembered sitting in his barber's chair as a young mischievous kid.

"A barber, eh? Now there's a *real* job... Everyone needs a haircut," and he ran his hand over the stubble on his scalp, "Kinda like being a cabbie when you think about it. Everyone needs a ride sometime or another. Not only that, have you ever noticed there's a cab in every movie?"

"Nope." I said. "I see 'em every day in *real* life... And I ain't much of a movie buff."

He shot me a look of contempt before admiring his mask again.

"I'm gonna cut the eye outta this face. Which one do you think I should take?"

"I don't know." Aren't they both the same? I thought and noticed him delicately caressing the latex.

"I'm gonna take the right one."

He opened the razor up and spread the mask out beside him.

"Be careful," I warned, and not for his safety.

"Oh, I will... This is my baby."

"I meant be careful of the seat."

He ignored my concern as he started cutting with laser-like precision.

"This is a fine blade. You keep it for protection, don't you?"

"If things go south in a cab you got no one to help you," I said, then realizing my only protection was resting in *his* hands, not mine.

"Very true...Very true... You know, speaking of protection. Did this face look familiar to you?"

He pointed at the mask.

"No."

"Not surprising. You're a white man like me, but the difference is I have an eye for detail. This—this my friend, is none other than the late, great *Bruce Lee*... Well, actually it's a middle-aged Bruce Lee. A composite sketch, if you will."

He grinned with perverse satisfaction.

"Bruce Lee... Huh... Neat." He must've been expecting to bond over Bruce Lee trivia or something, because my lack of interest seemed like a slap in the face to him.

"Dude! You just don't get it do you? White people can't tell the difference between Asians. When the lady at the foreign exchange gives her description to the sketch artist, she's gonna do her very best. She's gonna be like, this is my chance to get this bad man," he said, in a haughty falsetto. "But she's gonna miss by a country fucking mile. And even if she doesn't. Even if she gets it somewhat right, the idiot keystone cops are gonna wind up broadcasting a picture of a forty-five year old Bruce Lee!"

He started laughing.

I thought about what he said as he kept cutting. Then I started laughing too.

There we were in a taxicab, behind a convenience store, laughing uncontrollably as Rocky performed surgery on Bruce Lee's middle-aged face.

We laughed until Rocky held up the one eyed mask and dug out his Zippo.

"Have you ever seen *Eye of The Dragon*?" he asked.

"No. I've heard of it, though."

He looked around, then opened his door.

"There's a clip cut from the original 35mm print in 1973. It's during Bruce's final battle with Han, in the hall of mirrors. During the sequence you hear a voice say, '...*the enemy has only images and illusions behind which he hides his true motives. Destroy the image and you will break the enemy'*."

He punctuated his recitation with a flick of his flint. An orange flame shot up as the smell of burning rubber filled the car, and a plume of black smoke whirled about in the wind.

I watched as Bruce Lee melted down into a pile of black sludge.

"That was the last movie he made. He died two weeks before it came out. He was only thirty-two... How old are you?"

"Twenty-seven."

"You look older... Must be the dope."

"Yeah I know. But when I'm sufficiently medicated my shakes are barely even noticeable, which makes this job way the hell easier. And besides, if I'm gonna get you to Wichita in one piece... I'll need enough dope."

"So you're telling me you don't have enough to get us there?"

"No... I can make a call but it could take quite a while, and there's no guarantees."

He clinked the brass lighter shut, and shook his head slightly.

"Don't have time. We need to get the hell outta here... And from what you've told me, you're a wanted man now, in the illustrious underworld of Grey Grove."

"That I am, but necessity is necessity."

"We can stop along the way. I'm sure Toronto can hook you up."

"That's a pretty big gamble," I said.

"Just—just don't worry about it *all right*... I've got a plan."

I gave him a quizzical look as I wondered what kind of a plan he actually had. His little bank heist seemed pretty well thought out though, so I stayed quiet for the time being.

He shut the door and sat there for a moment. He looked deep in thought. Then he snapped out of it, grabbed the eye of the mask and held it up over his own eye.

"This is my magical eye for detail, Quinn... With this I can see every tiny crack and fissure you have."

I looked at him and chuckled a little. He just sat there looking back at me.

"So what do you see then?" I asked.

"I see a bunch of you... But one's killing all the others."

"Haha. Yup. Junkies and their alter-egos."

He shook his head slowly.

"Destroy the image," he said, with a deepened voice.

I couldn't hold his gaze. I looked around aimlessly, then glanced up into the rear-view and caught my reflection. I wanted to look away from that too, but couldn't.

CHAPTER 3

Where the driver bargains with his passenger for the fare and they hit open road, after a few details are taken care of.

THE FACE IN THE rear-view mirror was sunken eyed, tired, frazzled, nervous, irritated, slightly paranoid, and broke. But mostly it was nostalgic for long lost things like ex-girlfriends who once cared but out of futility packed up and left; acoustic guitars that purged emotion through wooden veins, and cathartic grains, but got pawned; worried pets that exposed soft underbellies while wagging tails unconditionally at my blatant self-destruction; thirsty plants perched behind north facing windows in dreary apartments, exasperated, and brittle from neglect.

The face had an hourglass countenance that changed drastically, once a day. When the medicine was scored, the hourglass was turned, and the face became imperturbably serene. Twelve hours later, however, it was a twisted knot of fear.

I saw somebody walk behind the car with a bag full of junk food, and it brought me back to awareness. I glanced at the mic on the dash and reconsidered my options.

"Hey, you know that eye for detail you have? Well I think it's rubbing off on me because I just realized I should call this trip in directly, so nobody with a scanner can hear it... cops included. They scan our frequencies all the time."

"Excellent," he said.

I pretended to pat myself on my back.

"I'm gonna go get a map and some smokes."

Rocky nodded at me as I popped the door open and headed off to the store like he was giving me permission to be dismissed. What I really wanted to do was drive the car around front so I could keep an eye on him from inside, but I resisted. I told myself that the only real way to determine whether or not I could trust him, was just to trust him. Better to find out sooner, rather than later.

I stared at my feet as I walked toward the front side of the building. The rain was still coming down pretty good. There were puddles here and there on the cracked asphalt; and I had to hop over them, or skirt around them, because my shoes were in bad shape. The soles were almost worn right through on the heels and the right toe had come unglued, so that if I walked fast enough, it'd make a slapping noise.

I'd been meaning to buy a new pair for about six months, but drugs came first.

"Hey!" Rocky called, from behind.

I wheeled around to see him tapping his shirt pocket and then pointing at me. I got the message. I put the cash in my jeans and kept going.

"Quinn!"

I stopped again and turned to face him.

"You can't spend that here, you know that right?"

It hadn't crossed my mind but I pretended it did.

"I know... I got a little bit on my debit," I said, not remembering how little that bit was.

He nodded as I disappeared around the corner. When I got to the front of the store I pulled open the door and headed directly for the cigarettes. A display of windshield wiper fluid caught my eye for some reason. It was a brand I'd never heard of called *Knight Watchman* with a jaunty advertising slogan, *keeps your windshield clean so danger is seen.* I grabbed a bottle and continued on toward the teenage boy behind the checkout counter. He was probably about sixteen or seventeen by the looks of his smooth face and rail thin physique.

"Can I get two packs of those ones over there? The blue ones..."

He grabbed the smokes, scanned them, and then placed them on the counter top in front of me in a stack.

"Do you have maps?"

"Uhhh... Yeah... The other side of that rack right there," he droned.

I stepped to the side and picked out a map of the United States and another of Ontario. He scanned them and put them on top of the smokes, making a little tower of stuff beside the two-litre jug of wiper fluid.

"Uhhh... You wanna bag, bro?"

I looked outside. It was still raining. "Yeah. Sure... And this'll be on debit."

I punched in my numbers and waited nervously for the screen to tell me the transaction was approved. When it finally went through, I grabbed the bag and walked away without saying thanks.

"Steely Dan kills it!" The kid said, as I walked.

I wheeled around, surprised.

"You've heard of them?"

"Totally, bro... Sick jams."

"Nice... And thanks." I said, as I quickly turned and kept going. I didn't want him getting too good of a look at my face. I was, after all, now guilty of harbouring a criminal.

Back I went to the driver's seat of a getaway car.

When I got to the taxi, I paused at the trunk to open it up and put the wiper fluid in. The trunk always had a key in it so that I didn't have to get out of the car every time a customer with groceries or luggage showed up. I wasn't the only one who did this. Most of us in Grey Grove did. You see, when cabbies are lucky enough to tap into the elusive rhythm of a city and the money starts piling up, superstition prevails and we balk at the thought of breaking the flow. *Make hay while the sun shines* is every cab driver's golden rule. For the record, however, I always got out from behind the wheel to lend a helping hand to elderly folks and frazzled single moms with too many kids.

When I was at the driver's side, I could see Rocky was slouched a bit in his seat and rubbing his head. I opened the door and handed him the bag.

"Smokes and maps," I said.

He smiled but it looked forced.

"You okay?" I asked just to fill the silence, but immediately regretted it.

"Yeah... I'm okay... Got a headache, that's all."

"So you *are* human," I joked, my nerves twitched as I sensed his declining mood.

"All too human, my friend... All too human."

He sounded weary.

"You ever gonna tell me about that mark on your head you showed me?" I couldn't stop myself from just blurting out the question, very much aware that his responses were getting shorter and fading in intensity.

He turned and glared at me like he was trying to suss out whether or not I was implying something.

"*Just fucking drive man...* The sooner we get outta this shitty little town, the better."

He kept rubbing his temples. It looked like he was wincing in pain, but his head was turned the other way so I couldn't see.

"Where's the nearest coin laundry, Mr. Cabbie?"

"Umm... Five or six blocks from here, why?"

"'Cause we're gonna launder some cash."

"Very funny... Are we gonna fold it too?"

"*Listen smart ass...* We have ten grand in marked bills here... We can't just take a fucking eraser and get rid of those serial numbers... Now *drive*."

I backed out of our parking space realizing that Rocky was apparently prone to mood swings. I put it down to the headache and didn't react.

"Sorry man... I was just trying to lighten things up..." I looked at him but he was still turned away. "If you don't mind me asking though, how exactly does a laundromat launder money any better than anywhere else?"

I was trying my best to sound as matter-of-fact as possible, like I had done this all before.

"Coin laundries have change machines don't they? Those machines are always kept full... As long as we mind the security cameras we can break our bills down into spendable money."

"But won't that mean we'll end up with a shitload of coins?" I envisioned the seats covered in a sea of coins.

"You got a better idea?"

I racked my brain.

"No."

"Those machines will buy us a lot more time than any store, and it'll be easier to not get noticed." His patience seemed to be wearing down, and I was starting to get a feeling that changing the bills wasn't as thought out as his meticulously planned robbery was.

"What about the train and bus stations? They have those machines, but you get bills from 'em."

"True," he said. "But those are the first spots the cops are gonna look."

That shut me up. He was right. It also reminded me that the police would be visiting all the local taxi companies.

I had to be very, very careful when I phoned the fare in to dispatch.

It was 6:30 p.m. when we rolled into the parking lot of the laundry over on Walton Street, which wasn't far from the main highway. The sight of flowing traffic seemed to lift Rocky's mood. It must've relieved some of the pressure in his head as well, because he was sitting back up with that glare of his firmly returned to his eyes.

The laundromat was in a plaza so I pulled off to the side in front of a store that was closed. I took the car out of gear and watched as he emptied out the contents of his satchel onto the seat. The first thing he held up were a pair of latex gloves.

His eyebrows went up.

"I almost forgot about these, *shit*."

"Fingerprints?"

"Yeah... that, and I didn't bother to colour the skin of my hands to make them look more Asian. These gloves did double duty."

"You really did think of every last little detail, didn't you?"

"I'm no Nancy Drew, but I'm pretty good."

He said that while reaching back into his satchel. This time he brought out a little action figure. The corners of his mouth curled up into a tight smile. I couldn't tell what the figure was supposed to be because it was old and weathered looking.

"What's that?"

"A scarecrow... I've had it forever... It's my talisman."

I thought it was kind of funny for him to be all wistful like he was about his toy. But his use of the word *talisman* added a darker tinge, forcing me to suppress the chuckle that'd threatened to bubble up. I stayed silent as he put it in his pocket, reached back in and pulled out a tattered paperback.

"Reading material?"

"*The Stone Angel*," he said.

"I think I read that in high school... That's the one about the old lady who fights against being put into an old age home, right?"

"Yep. She can't abide the horrible indignity because she's a proud woman. She's a fighter, as you say. A true desperado... A survivor."

His description of her made me realize that in his mind desperation was some sort of heroic rite of passage. I thought about his earlier insistence upon calling me desperate, and suddenly I didn't feel so shamed. In fact, I felt rather honoured to be called that by him as I watched him neatly arrange his things on the seat. Then he grabbed the gloves, put them back in the satchel and put the satchel 'round his neck. "Sit tight," he said, as he stepped out of the car.

This is the point in my story where everything could change, isn't it? It's the point where deception could lay its well-moisturized hand on the plot line like a meddling governess. It's the juncture at which goodwill could be taken advantage of by a less than noble opportunist—by a ruthless exploiter of credulity and desperation— by a cold blooded manipulator.

As I watched Rocky disappear inside the coin laundry, paranoid thoughts swarmed my permeable brain like a cloud of heckling bees.

In an effort to smoke them into docility, I opened a pack of cigarettes and lit one up. I inhaled deeply as I unfolded the map of America. I knew it was about 600 km to Windsor. All I needed to do was figure out how far it was to Wichita from Detroit. As I dragged my finger across the Midwestern states, I remembered snippets of stories my mom had told me about growing up on the Great Plains. She was born and raised on a farm outside Omaha, but left at eighteen after being accepted into the prestigious university at Grey Grove. My finger slid by Michigan, then Indiana, then Missouri; where it paused as my eyes judged the distance from south Kansas to eastern Nebraska. I briefly considered making the jaunt up to Omaha to see the homeland of my relatives on the way back, but decided against it. The less I spent on gas, the more money I'd have to pay down the sky high interest I knew would be accruing on my debt, the longer I was away.

I checked the scale of the map and did the math. Detroit to Wichita was about 1,500 km. I also saw it was pretty much a straight line right through if we took the HWY-401 to its end and hooked up with the I-94 at the border.

Looking at the map conjured up some wanderlust. I'd travelled before with great results. I loved the feeling of being on the open road—in a constant state of newness, where every passing second presented some strange and beautiful foreign landscape.

It'd been a while since I had been outside the oppressive confines of Grey Grove, and the timing felt right for it to happen again.

As my mind spun a web with the borders, roads and rivers on the map, my cigarette started to burn my knuckles, snapping me out of my reverie.

Rocky still wasn't back yet.

It wasn't long before a grim scenario ran through my head:

Rocky says he'll be right back. I wait in the car, oblivious to his devious plan. He goes into the laundromat that he knew had a back door and leaves by that very door, quickly making a well-rehearsed escape into the sheltering darkness of nightfall. He gets a safe distance away and makes an anonymous phone call to the police, tipping them off to a cab driver with fresh and crisp one hundred dollar bills that he thinks were the result of a robbery at the foreign exchange. He gives them my description and cab number, and not too long after that I get convicted and sentenced to ten years in the big house for a crime I didn't commit.

The most remarkable part of this horrible little fantasy was that it ended with Rocky huddled in a phone booth somewhere, peeling off a second mask. At which point, he becomes who he really is—a little old lady.

"Absurd!" I said to myself, as I lit up another cigarette.

I looked up and there was still no sign of him. It'd been ten long minutes.

With the nerves of a wet cat, I sat there smoking furiously.

As I tapped the steering wheel, the gauges on the dash drew my attention. The oil level was fine, even though a small leak around the gasket was a constant source of worry. But getting the hole sealed up wasn't worth the expense, considering the age of the car. So I dealt with it the only way I could. Every time I pulled into a gas station I religiously checked the dip-stick. If the engine was thirsty, I topped it up with one of the three quarts of oil I kept in the trunk at all times. This was the only sure way to prevent the unforgivable sin of an engine seizure.

The brake light was on but I knew that was due to a corroded sensor.

The mileage was mildly shocking like always: 400,000 km.

It stirred something inside me. Would this old steel beast get us to Wichita and then be ready to turn around and do it all over again?

I had a glove box full of receipts that said almost every replaceable part had been replaced in the last two years: brakes, shocks, radiator, solenoid, alternator...

The tires were from the wreckers, but they were a good name and came off a brand new car that'd been in an accident the day it left the lot; at least that's what the man said.

The battery was three weeks old and still had the sticker on it.

The transmission had never given me a problem and wasn't likely to, because I got it checked every time Soldier was in the shop.

Yes.

Soldier was the name of my taxi. His dependability demanded a name.

He'd been my bread and butter and home away from home for almost four years. And I happily repaid this constancy by making sure I had enough money, or at the very least enough credit with my mechanic, to ensure that any problem was dealt with as soon as it reared its head.

As for the upholstery: a forensic investigator could've lifted the disintegrating remnants of my tears, blood, sweat, and sperm—sperm that set about trying to find the holy grail amidst the synthetic fibres of a seat cushion, after having been coaxed out by a lusty girlfriend in a conservation area.

I did my best to maintain a clean office, however. Every Sunday I'd pull into a car wash and scrub the cab down, outside and in. We were a team. Man and machine. Each an extension of the other.

There was a tap on the passenger window. It was Rocky. His satchel looking much heavier than when he left.

As usual, I'd forgotten the handle on the passenger door only worked when it wanted to, so I reached over and let him in.

"Well *that* went better than expected," he said, breathing heavy. "Not only was there no camera above the change machine, there was no attendant and no customers either... And I got rid of the gloves," he added.

"How much did you get?"

"I did a hundred bucks worth... I figure that'll be enough to get us to Chinatown in Toronto... Right?"

"Yeah... Why Chinatown, though?"

"I wanna spend a few crisp bills and leave a predictable trail if ya know what I mean... Plus you have your little issue that needs to be dealt with."

"True..." I paused and reached into the little coin pocket of my jeans with my index finger. "Speaking of which, I need to take this now... Just wanted to let you know," I said, holding up my last little grey pill.

"So that's your medicine, eh?"

His sarcasm was palpable. I changed the subject.

"Hey, you see that dollar store over there..."

He looked up but didn't stop running his fingers through the coins.

"Yeah... What about it?"

"It's still open... I'm gonna go get some of those coin rollers so we can tidy this up y'know? It'll make buying stuff a lot easier."

"Good thinkin'," he said, as he handed off a half dozen loonies.

I jerked open my door and jogged over to the store. I knew Rocky was in a hurry to split town so inside I quickly found what I was looking for, all the while keeping my eyes peeled for anything else we might need. Nothing on the shelves stood out but something popped into my head. It was a song. Not even one of my favorite songs or anything. It was "Me and Bobby McGee," a song I pretty much loathed hearing due to overplay. I started humming it softly as I met eyes with the clerk.

I was still humming as I got back in the cab and tossed the coin rollers over.

I was *still* humming when we merged onto the highway and headed west into the rain misted sunset.

There were four exits in Grey Grove. By the time we hit the third one, the morphine was kicking in and the lyrics started to come. They weren't the right lyrics, though. They weren't even close.

And I knew what that meant.

As the wipers sashayed back and forth, beating out rhythm like an industrial printing press, I sang under my breath.

Windshield wipers made you blind, crashed up by a railroad line.

That was it. Just that one altered lyric over and over again in my head, like a mantra.

I glanced up into the rear-view mirror and saw the fleeting angles of a familiar face, before the bright lights of an oncoming car forced my eyes back to the road. My heart reacted first. My mind followed. Rocky was rolling up coins, completely oblivious to my inner turmoil, but he heard me singing.

"Those words ain't even close, man." He held up a twenty-five dollar tube of loonies and inspected his handy-work. "Listen... I was thinking... Maybe you don't even *have* to call the trip in. Whaddya think?"

I registered what he said, but my mind was churning with hidden meanings. It all came to a rapid boil when the last sign for the last exit flashed itself like the tail of a disappearing deer.

"I'm turn—"

My throat was bone dry. I had to swallow hard to finish.

"I'm turning off here," I said, as I veered to the right.

"*What the FUCK.* What're you doing!?"

"I have to... I forgot something."

"What! You forgot *what?*"

I hadn't cracked the code of the lyrics yet, and so I couldn't just tell him that the wipers needed to be changed. In hindsight this was good because it put everything on the table. At least on my side of the table.

"The guy that drives this cab during the day. I—I need to call him and there's no time on my cell phone... There's a payphone at this gas station over here..."

I couldn't have said anything more offensive to Rocky's ears. He threw his hands up, jerked his head around and laid one of those face melting glares on me.

"There's another bloody driver!? This *totally* fucks everything up man! I mean he's gonna wanna know every last detail about our trip and guess what? That's gonna *compromise* things."

"Don't worry about it, I'll fudge the details... I'll take care of it."

"Oh, I'm worrying all right... I'm not *fucking stupid*... Go to wherever you're going and call this guy... I'm gonna stand right beside you so I can hear everything you say... On second thought, I'll tell you exactly *what* to say."

I was trying my best to block his voice out so that I could keep concentrating on the lyrics, but he was getting more and more irate with each curse he hurled at me from under his breath. I decided the only way out of the mess I'd created was to gamble on the truth—the crazy truth.

"It's not like that," I said.

"What do you mean *it's not like that?* What the hell's going on here?"

"I—I can't call him."

"Oh, yes you can... All this cash *SAYS* you can."

He grabbed his black bandana full of bills and slapped the dashboard with it.

"And you better sound perfectly fucking normal when you talk to him too... Not like you do right now..." He rubbed his face. "What... Is your *medicine* not agreeing with you?"

"You don't understand... I really can't call him."

"*What? You just said you had to!*" He shouted. "What're you hiding from me?" His voice turned low and hissed through his partially bared teeth. I had the urge to stop the car and get as far away from him as possible. But then I started to get angry.

"Just shut the fuck up for a second and listen," I said.

I went quiet as I searched for the right way to put it, but there *was* no right way. Finally I just sucked it up and told him.

"Look... I can't call him because he doesn't... He doesn't exist."

"Huh? So he's not the day driver?" His eyes were black with suspicion and his jaw was clenched.

"No. You heard me... he's not real."

"Are you *nuts*?! Like are you *loony tunes?* I wanna know now because this could be a deal breaker."

I took a deep breath.

"I have a friend that sends me messages through song lyrics. Wrong song lyrics. It sounds absolutely crazy I know, but it's the truth... I first met him after busting my head open when I was a kid and since then... Since then he's helped me out... He's—he's like a guardian or something. I don't know really. He just looks out for me from time to time. Gives me warnings about things."

"Are you serious? Or are you shittin' me?"

I didn't say anything to him. I just looked him straight on.

"Ok, man... Okay... I'll accept your little imaginary friend. Actually I'm oddly relieved to know you have one," he laughed. "Does he have a name?" He asked.

"Frank... Frank Bastion."

"He's got a last name too does he," he drawled, rolling his eyes. "Do me a favour and tell Frank I'm glad he doesn't really exist, and that as long as he stays that way we won't have any problems."

"Sure thing... But just remember, I ain't any crazier than you. Mister rob a bank with a Bruce Lee mask and a urine sample."

I saw him grin as we pulled into the gas station. I took it as a good sign.

I pulled up to one of the pumps as Rocky finished rolling the last of the coins. We had a hundred bucks all neatly packaged. It made me feel better. I always got embarrassed counting out a pocket full of change for a disgruntled clerk. It was stupid of me, I know.

He handed over the four rolls.

"Here. Put 60 bucks in gas in and buy some chips or something. Get salt and vinegar if they have it. *Oh*, and some pop and some water."

I was still feeling a bit out of sorts for having to reveal such an intimate secret to him.

"Uh, okay... I need to get wipers too... That's... That's what Frank warned me about," I said, with shyness muffling my voice.

"Then you better get some *mother-fuckin' wipers*!" he said, as he handed me another roll. "And before I forget... What I was saying before you dropped that freaky shit on me, was... Do you really even need to call this trip in?"

I hesitated but not for long.

"No... I guess not. I own the cab."

"How much then. To Wichita?" he asked, point blank.

"Well, I looked at the map and it says it's just over 2,000 km if we head west down the 401 and jump on the I-94 in Detroit."

He went to open the map up.

"Look. I'm willing to cut you a deal and charge a dollar a kilometer. You'll be saving close to 700 bucks considering the flat rate to Toronto from Grey Grove is almost 400 and it's only 280 kilometers."

He stopped.

"I don't really care what the price is... I just want you to get your fair share... How 'bout I spring for gas the whole way too. Think of it as a tip."

"You really don't have to do that."

"I know. I *want* to."

Normally, I would've felt an old twinge of suspicion after such a grand display of generosity. I had deep-seated trust issues, you see. But there *was* no twinge this time. And I knew it was because he didn't judge me after hearing about my drug problem, and then, of course, about Frank. I had the feeling that he was comfortable around me, and for having just met me, well, this gesture of fellowship was highly disarming. I decided right then and there to take a chance; I fully committed to the trip.

"All right... Let's gas up and get outta here," I said.

I popped open my door and went to the pump. With my back against Soldier I looked up at the racing clouds and felt free.

More free than I'd felt in long time.

First Intermission

There's a canteen for your eating pleasure. There's also a fully stocked bar. Get up and stretch your legs, or stay seated, and do some eavesdropping on the couple making out behind you.

CHAPTER 4

Where the driver and his passenger hit the open road with plans to spend a few hours in Toronto.

AS I FINISHED FILLING the tank, I saw Rocky spark his lighter in order to read his book. I also noticed two surveillance cameras spying on us.

I turned my face away and kept my head down as I walked toward the kiosk.

In just under two hours I was already thinking like a fugitive.

The attendant was leafing through a magazine as I entered. He glanced up but didn't say anything as a small array of windshield wipers announced themselves along the wall, just inside the door. The pair I needed were pretty common. Almost every place carried them and as it turned out, this little gas bar was no exception.

With wipers in hand, I grabbed two bags of chips, a bottle of ginger ale, a bottle of water and two chocolate bars and put everything on the counter. The guy rang it up without looking at me. When it came time to pay I paused, as a clip-strip of battery powered reading lights drew my attention.

My hesitation made him look up at me.

I saw a tiny flash of fear emanate from somewhere inside the circumference of his pupils. It was as if the usual sequence of events had been interrupted just long enough to elicit a pop-up warning, behind his eyes.

Maybe it was just another opiated flight of fancy on my part.

Speaking of which, around this time the morphine was busy working its reliable magic, cleaning and dressing my psychological wounds like a Florence Nightingale. I was thoroughly enjoying a recursive sense of well-being. The same sort of well-being you might enjoy while digging your toes into the sand of a tropical beach at sunset. Or maybe not right on the beach but more inland, where you float in the bathtub warmth of a secret lagoon, and count the early evening stars as the soft white noise of an ocean is pierced by the distant cry of an albatross.

I felt high and fortified as I stood there in the kiosk, cloaked in opiates. I was newly resilient to my surrounding environment's weaponry of heavy weather. Morphine never failed to dress me up in a Kevlar flak jacket and render me invincible to the advancing artillery of life.

You see, my dalliance with dope was always more about protection than it was simple pleasure.

At least that's what I told myself.

But let's be honest.

The days of dalliance were long gone.

By this time my daily excursions with the bitter alkaloid mistress had bloomed into a passionate affair, undertaken whenever possible — however possible: gas station bathrooms, lobbies, mid-step on my way to the mailbox, after dinner, before dinner, breakfast, lunch, or snack time.

All I really needed was a beverage to wash my precious little pill down with. If I had a gulp of liquid I could be anywhere.

Wrapping my lips around a filthy gas station faucet was not out of the question.

My preference, however, was to wash it down with coffee because coffee was hot and therefore dissolved the pill faster. Not to mention the added pick-me-up of the caffeine.

All things considered, I was actually a fairly responsible user. I paced myself and I had foresight. Normally, I made sure I had, at the very least, a three day stash.

"Sir?"

He'd closed his magazine and was straightened up a bit on his stool. His eyes were in limbo; not knowing quite where to look and not wanting to look at me. His face was a blooming bud of apprehension.

"Can I get one of those reading lights," I said.

He plucked one off the strip and rang it through. He looked relieved. And I was relieved *for* him. I even felt a spark of compassion as I determined he was obviously fearful of working the night shift at a gas station by himself.

Then a darker thought entered my skull.

I was struck by the idea of him falling prey to a self-fulfilling prophecy. Lending his worst case scenario more credibility with each passing night. Like a pack of feral dogs, I saw the sum of his anxieties were circling around him and slowly closing in.

I watched him fill the plastic bag with my stuff and silently wished him luck with a small directed burst of goodwill. I thanked him and left—hoping that somehow, in some small way, I'd helped him.

On the way back to the taxi I saw two more surveillance cameras. They were attached just below the fluorescent lamps above the pumps; hidden in the glare. Their edges gleamed as they gathered evidence like two crows sizing up a picnic. I made sure not to look up as I rounded the car, opened the back door and placed the bags on the seat.

"Here."

Rocky turned around and saw the reading light I was holding.

"This'll work better than your lighter."

"Cool," he said, as he turned it on and shined it at the bag I was holding. "Where's the chips? I'm starvin'."

I kept the wipers and passed him the rest of the stuff.

"I'm gonna put these on, then we can go."

It took me less than five minutes to make the switch. As I made sure everything was secure I remembered the first time I attempted to replace a set of wipers. I made the mistake of throwing the packaging out without reading the instructions and spent three quarters of an hour in sub-zero temperatures trying to prove to myself I could do it.

I was never good at puzzles, but I was excellent at being stubborn.

Eventually a teenage kid who'd been skateboarding around the parking lot, stopped what he was doing, coasted over to where I was and offered his help. Within two minutes he had both wipers installed. I shook his hand and offered him a few bucks but all he wanted was a smoke, which I happily parted with.

I put the packaging and the old wipers in the garbage container, then got back in the cab, sucking the top of my index finger.

"Cut yerself?"

"Ya... Nicked it a bit."

"You better go get that stuff you just threw out," Rocky said, between mouthfuls of chips.

"Why?"

"Think about it Quinn... If the cops manage to pick up our trail they'll be at this gas station at some point in the next few days examining the playbacks on the security cameras... They'll see you throwing those old wipers in the garbage and sucking your finger and instantly smile big shit-eating grins..." He took a swig of pop. "Now go get the eviden—"

"*What evidence*?" I blurted, cutting him off. "If they pick up our trail they'll already know who I am, simply by calling the taxi stand and asking them who was driving cab number 17."

"D-N-A evidence, Quinn. It'll *prove* without a doubt it was you on the camera."

"Yeah well so will the attendant over there... He got a good look at my face."

"Look. It's a matter of fucking principal, that's all. If we don't get careless then the thief gods will be kind to us."

He said that without any self-consciousness at all.

"Thief gods?"

"Yeah... You ever heard of Loki?"

"Wow... So you're a Norse pagan," I chuckled.

"It's no joke. The less we tempt fate, the better... Now go get that stuff and let's *hit the damn road*!"

I glanced over at the attendant, and remembered his pack of feral dogs.

"You know... If you believe in Loki you should also believe in the laws of attraction. The more you fear something the more it seeks you out," I said, still looking at the kiosk.

"Exactly. And that's what Loki is for... He's our protector... Kinda like your friend Frank is."

He had a point.

"All right... Be right back," I sighed.

I skipped over to the garbage can, reached in and pulled out the old wipers and packaging.

The attendant still had his nose in his magazine as we disappeared into the night.

We closed in on the 401 with a full gas gauge and a clean windshield. Rocky had moved from the chips to the chocolate bars and was washing it all down with generous guzzles of pop. He was either a junk food addict or he hadn't eaten in a while; his bony frame suggested the latter.

The on-ramp to the highway was visible in the distance when we hit one last intersection. As we sat there waiting for red to turn green I noticed yet another surveillance camera. It was perched off to the side of a traffic signal, like one of those fake owls you see on rooftops. The sight of it brought me to words.

"I've never really noticed before, how many surveillance cameras there are everywhere..."

Rocky was oblivious as he finished the last of his chocolate bar.

"You ever read any sociology stuff?" I asked.

He held up his index finger, then let out a series of huge belches. With the first one he said, "Nope." With the second, "I." And with the last and longest he managed to articulate, "Have not read any sociology stuff." I was duly impressed and told him so, before continuing on with my deep thought.

"So *anyway,*" I drawled. "There's a guy named Foucault... Michel Foucault... He wrote a book called 'Discipline and Punish' that talks about how power and control are maintained in prisons and things."

"Is it captivating stuff? *Get it... Captiva*ting," he joked.

"Pretty funny," I said, while realizing that he had a playful, if not downright dorky side. Then I thought about his mask making hobby, his fascination with Bruce Lee and his action figure, and it became very clear to me that I was indeed sitting beside a bit of a nerd. A decidedly dark nerd.

"Don't you mean, pretty *punny?*"

I was getting a little annoyed at this point.

"Seriously. It's very interesting stuff."

"Okay, sorry... Go ahead," he said, as he stared off at the red line of tail lights that stretched down the highway.

"All right. I'll make it simple. He talks about the surveillant gaze and how it's an essential part of every power structure. He says it's used to promote self-discipline within the general population..."

"You mean like a scarecrow... in a cornfield?" he said, holding up his action figure.

The accuracy of his metaphor surprised me.

"Yes! Like a scarecrow." I nodded and smiled, then continued. "He presents his theory by describing a panopticon, which is a big dome-shaped prison. Sorta like a stadium but with cell blocks where the bleachers would be. And right in the middle there's a big tower."

I stopped talking as I turned toward the on-ramp. I did a shoulder check and saw Rocky looking back at me in rapt attention. We merged into the river of red lights as I checked my mirrors and got up to speed.

"This tower in the middle of the prison... What do you think it's for?" I asked.

"I dunno."

"Okay. Who do you think is inside of it?"

"Guards?"

"No. That's the whole thing... There's nobody inside and this is the take home point. There doesn't have to be anyone inside because what do people do when they think they're being watched?"

"Umm, they act different? More normal, I guess."

"Yes. They act normal. They self-regulate. They discipline *themselves...* They follow the rules."

There was a brief silence as we passed a slow moving transport truck. The wipers were on full blast and made short work of its wheel spray.

"That's what the scarecrow does... It tricks the crows," I said, as we got around the truck.

Rocky twirled the scarecrow around with his fingers. I could tell he was charmed.

We passed a small herd of vehicles, then settled into the smooth groove of the open highway. Darkness had fallen firmly all around as the digital display on the dashboard announced the time: 8:00 p.m. Beside me, Rocky was testing out the reading light I'd bought him. He'd clamped it to his book so that a miniature spotlit stage was resting on top of his lap. Under the spotlight he made his scarecrow dance around. I smiled as I lit up a cigarette and puffed away — enveloped within the soothing hum of the engine.

"Something that frightens without harming," he said, as he grabbed the pack of smokes and lit one up for himself.

"What's that?" I asked.

"I said, 'Something that frightens without harming....' That's how the dictionary defines it."

"Defines what?"

"A scarecrow."

"Oh."

I looked over as he turned the action figure around to face me so that it was backlit and silhouetted. Then he exhaled into the reading light, shrouding everything in a dramatic haze.

"What frightens you but hasn't harmed you?"

He said that in a scratchy voice. The voice of the scarecrow, I presumed. I couldn't help raising my eyebrows at him while I played along.

"Well... *You* haven't harmed me yet and you definitely frighten me a little."

I smiled at him. He kept a straight face.

"Do I give you the *creeeps, Quinn*?" said the scarecrow.

"Yes... There's something mildly disturbing about talking to an action figure," I chuckled.

His straight face remained.

"What about death, Quinn... You've never experienced it and yet it frightens you doesn't it?"

I exhaled the last of my smoke, flicked it out the crack in the window and slouched in my seat a bit. I wasn't sure where he was going with this little performance of his.

"Yes, death scares me, but as of now I'm alive and I'd like to keep it that way."

"Me too. But I can't afford to be afraid of death. Fearing the inevitable is a recipe for disaster."

He switched back to his normal voice when he said that, and it left me feeling strange. It was as if he was alluding to something.

"What do you mean exactly?" I probed.

His face got real serious looking. Or maybe it was real sadness. I couldn't tell.

"Nothing... I'm tired. I'm gonna sleep for a bit," he said, flicking the reading light off.

Just like that everything came to an abrupt halt. I shook my head slightly in the silence that followed, watching the oncoming road like a hawk, as he struggled out of his jacket to use it for a pillow.

The blue glow from the dashboard reflected off the lifeless and now forlorn looking scarecrow beside me.

The rain was still steady.

Farther on to Wichita we rolled.

I remember feeling like I was behind the wheel of a ship, navigating an asphalt river as Rocky slept. I was driving a rusty car in the third dimension, but sailing a pristine crystal ship in the fourth; strange ideas like this were par for the course when I was high.

Then suddenly I was overcome by a sense of fragility. Our ship could fracture and shatter at any moment. I grew anxious.

Luckily my fear gave way to the calming effects of logic.

Fragile? Was it really fragile? I took geology at the university, so I knew very well that crystalline structures were almost always extremely hard.

I decided to make our ship out of quartz crystal.

Quartz is the second most prevalent mineral in the earth's crust and as such is the equivalent of a hardy plant or animal. The word itself, quartz, comes from the German word *quarz*, and before that from the middle/high German archaic *twarc*, said to have originated from the Slavic *tvrdy*; meaning *hard*.

So why then do most of us think crystal is synonymous with frailty?

Allow me to suggest that it's because we've divorced ourselves from nature so extravagantly that we first think in terms of man-made things and then as an afterthought, in terms of those that naturally occur.

When people think of crystal, usually a picture of a precious heirloom behind the glass doors of a heavy mahogany cabinet will pop into their heads. What they won't think of is the rugged rock cut just outside of town, boasting an ancient layer of amethyst.

And so it goes that our quartz crystal ship wasn't fragile at all. It was a durable, light refracting vehicle of the seafaring variety. Able to withstand even the most relentless of eroding forces. And it suited us. Because its toughness was attained under extremely high pressures and temperatures, in the hellish depths of the earth's core.

What doesn't kill you makes you stronger. And necessity is the mother of invention.

I knew what I'd been through and I could pretty much guarantee that Rocky had his own substantial cross to bear. It was safe to say we both had our sea legs. We may have taken different paths, but we were now travelling the same road as slightly different incarnations of the same basic archetype—the deviant. It wasn't a complex thing. It was simple adaptation. It was a necessary step in our evolution, and its identity lived in our eyes.

Mine were evasive. His were slightly maniacal.

But we were both desperadoes. And desperation can make you tough. It can make you capable. It can fuel you up and drive you forward when you know damn well that you're running on empty.

I lit up another cigarette and glanced over at Rocky. He was sound asleep. Something made me think about my straight razor. I couldn't remember what I did with it. With one hand on the wheel, I felt all around me and in between the seats, but there was nothing. It was too dark to see on the floor so I gently removed the reading light from the book and flicked it on. I shone it down by my feet, then over by Rocky's. There was nothing there but his satchel.

I flicked the light off and worried that it might've fallen out of the taxi at some point. Then his satchel started tugging on my imagination. I knew it was wrong of me, but if he didn't know then it wouldn't be a problem. Besides, he may have just put it in there by accident. I looked over at him again to double check. He was breathing deep sleep breaths. I leaned over, got hold of the strap with my fingertips and eased back to my sitting position, setting it down, ever so softly, between us.

We were doing 120 km/h in the rain. I had one hand on the wheel, and the other resting on my right thigh, hesitating. I really didn't want to second guess Rocky at this point, because as I said earlier, I was fully committed to the trip. But it was a now or never situation. I didn't want to believe he might've purposely lifted something so precious to me, but more than that, if he did have my razor then that meant I was defenseless. If he could rob a bank, then what else could he do? The only way to mollify the grip of paranoia I was in, was to trespass. I looked over again. His jaw was completely relaxed and his head lolled with the contours of the highway. He was out cold. For his benefit as much as mine, I proceeded with my transgression. Keeping my eyes on the road, I slid my free hand under the top flap and down into the main belly of his satchel. There was a front pocket as well but it was buckled shut and I already knew it held the money.

A car sped by us in the left hand lane doing almost twice the speed limit. The wheel spray obliterated my vision for a couple seconds as I watched its tail lights shrink down to little red pin pricks.

The first thing I felt was a chocolate bar wrapper. The second, was something cold and heavy. My heart sank. But then as I turned it over in my palm I realized it wasn't my razor. It wasn't long enough and I could feel multiple blades under my fingertips. It was a pocket knife. The third and final thing I felt was a thin booklet of some sort. This piqued my curiosity because I couldn't think of what it might be. I pulled it out and saw it was his passport. I was about to put it back when I was seized by the desire to check out his photo. Again, I looked over to make sure he was still unconscious. He was, so I brought it up in front of the dashboard and opened it. The glow from the gauges was enough for me to clearly see his face. But there was something very different about the guy sleeping beside me and the guy in the picture. The guy in the picture looked to be about thirty or forty pounds heavier and at least five years younger. It made me wonder. I sat there examining the facial features of the photo, every now and then glancing over at the real Rocky.

I came to two conclusions: either he was an addict like me, or the picture was outdated.

If it was outdated I knew we were in for problems at the border.

I suddenly got nauseated as the faces of trigger-happy border guards crowded my mind.

I went to put the passport back and that's when it happened.

All at once the sky opened up and dumped a flood right on top of us. I looked up, switched the wipers back to full speed with the outstretched fingers of my left hand and saw a tangle of tail lights in the distance. The wipers were doing sixteenth notes but were still barely offering me visibility. As we got closer I saw a bridge above the mess of red lights. It dawned on me that there'd been a multiple car accident under the bridge and more than likely there was no way through. I let the passport drop back into his satchel at the exact moment I started pumping the brakes to avoid skidding out of control. The deceleration pushed us both forward — Rocky more than me. He woke up being held back from the dash by his seat belt as we came to a stop 500 feet from the pile up, and about 50 feet from a turnoff.

The rain hit the hood like a thousand tiny hammers as I checked the rear-view but didn't see any approaching vehicles. We were stopped in the middle of the right hand lane so I pulled over to the shoulder and gathered my wits as Rocky rubbed his eyes. Neither of us said anything because the scene before us was unfolding quickly.

A man had jumped out of an expensive-looking car near the back of the accident, holding a newspaper over his head. We both watched him run over to a smaller car that was crunched up against the center bridge support between the east and westbound lanes. He knocked on its roof and leaned in. It looked like he was talking, which meant somebody inside was conscious. He nodded his head a few times then ducked under the bridge and pulled out his cellphone. He was obviously calling 911.

At that point I turned toward Rocky.

"How many cars do you think are involved here?"

"Fuck... I don't know. Half a dozen at least... That little car the guy was just standing beside looks like an accordion."

I glanced back up into the mirror. It was still black.

"We should do something," I said.

"I can't go up there, Quinn... I just can't. I'll be useless."

I sized him up. He looked paler than usual and his eyes were avoiding the wreckage.

"You gonna be okay?" I asked.

"Just go... You're right, we should see if they need help. But don't tell me anything when you get back... Especially if there's dead people."

I didn't respond to him. I just yanked my door open and ran to the crunched up car. As I got closer I could see smoke billowing up from the front end. I slowed down as I rounded the driver's side and prepared myself for the worst. The window was smashed out and both air bags had been deployed.

"You okay in there?"

"*My legs*... They're stuck."

"Don't try and move 'em," I said. "Just stay—"

I cut myself off when I heard a weak moan emanate from the passenger's side. The deflated air bag was hiding whoever it was.

"Who's beside you?"

"*My wife*," he cried. "Christie? Chris? Oh god... *Oh god.*"

The man was trying to raise his voice but he couldn't. I ran around to the other side and pulled the remains of the window out of the door. I reached in and moved the air bag to the side, then winced at what I saw. She'd been thrown against the dashboard and was now being held up by her seat belt, limp as a rag doll. Her face was completely red, due to a deep cut on her forehead that was swollen and purple and bleeding so bad the blood was streaming down off her chin in spurts and pooling up on the seat. I didn't think. I reacted. I ripped off my shirt, rolled it up, and then tied it as tightly as possible around her head, all the while doing my best not to move her. I glanced up to see her husband watching with slow blinking eyes.

"Thank you," he murmured

"You're welcome... You're both gonna be okay," I said, trying to keep the doubt from my voice.

I put my fingers on her neck and felt a pulse. It wasn't a strong one but it was there. I stood back up into the rain. There were five or six people huddled together and staring at me when I turned around. None of the other cars looked that damaged from what I could see.

"Is there anyone else that needs help?" I shouted at them.

They all looked at each other for a second then shook their heads. I nodded. The guy with the overcoat was still talking in a rapid staccato on his phone. I went over to him and listened in. He noticed and looked at me with wide eyes as he continued describing the accident to the operator.

The skewed headlights of the smashed-in car, the drifting smoke and the pouring rain all made him look like an actor on the set of a film. I bet he felt like an actor too, because there's nothing less real than the unexpected explosion of ultra-violent events. An unreality emerges in the aftermath, to cover everything in a merciful layer of otherworldly ash.

I turned and ran back to the woman in the car. Her bleeding wasn't nearly as bad with the added pressure of my tourniquet. She still had a pulse.

"You're gonna be okay... They're on their way," I said, as I touched her back.

She whimpered as she felt her coagulating blood on the seat with her fingers.

I started to shiver. Then I remembered I had two road flares in the trunk of the cab. I looked around once more, ran back to where we were parked and yelled in at Rocky. My door was still open.

"*Gimme your Zippo!*"

He shoved it at me. I grabbed it and sprinted back to the trunk, popped it open and took out the flares. When I saw them I remembered I didn't need a lighter; they were button flares. I ripped off the plastic caps and struck one after the other so that within seconds I had two bright orange plumes in my hands. The heat they threw singed my skin as I turned around and wiped the rain out of my eyes with my shoulders. The afterimage of the twin flames was partially blinding me, but I could see there were still no cars coming. I pushed them both into the wet gravel, then ran back to the taxi and jumped in.

"Here," I said, as I handed his lighter back.

When I held it out for him I saw there was blood on it. I wiped it on my pant leg and held it out again. My hands were back to shaking like they were earlier in the day. He took it, still looking drained and frail.

"They'll be all right... But we should get outta here before the cops show up and start questioning us."

"Yeah... Probably should," he mumbled.

I slammed the car into gear and headed down the turn-off.

We needed to find a way back onto the highway.

Halfway down the off-ramp we both saw something that vanquished all doubt. It was a black and yellow road sign for a rail crossing. We looked at each other as we passed it by. When we got to the tracks I stopped the cab for a minute to look back at the accident scene. The man who'd been on the cell phone was over at the smashed up car again tending to the couple inside, along with some of the others. It gave me hope. I did a quick check for trains then hit the gas.

"Can you—"

"So Frank was right..."

I was about to ask Rocky to grab the map and find a way back onto the highway, but we had started talking at the same time. What he said carried more weight, though. It hung like over-ripe fruit in the brief silence that followed. I picked up his thread.

"I guess he was... And it wouldn't be the first time."

Rocky smiled a little.

"I gotta say, I didn't *really* believe you before... I mean you have to admit that kinda stuff's hard to swallow."

He grabbed the map and started unfolding it.

"Do you wanna know what I thought?" he asked.

"What?" I said, as I realized he was doing exactly what I was about to ask him to do.

"I thought you got scared and made up an excuse to find a phone so you could rat me out before we made it too far outta Grey Grove."

"Nope... Frank's as real as your thief god *Loki*... Maybe more so..." Saying that forced me to extrapolate the line of thought I was on. "Come to think of it, Frank's more real for me than God is in a way. He's helped me out many times with his little transmissions. I can take his wrong-headed lyrics to the bank every time."

Rocky pursed his lips and rubbed his chin like he was considering what I said very carefully. Then he turned the reading light on to illuminate the map he'd spread across his knees.

That's when he noticed his satchel lying beside him. He immediately froze.

"How'd my bag get up here? I put it on the floor."

I scrambled to find words that just weren't there.

"How'd my fucking bag get up here, Quinn? Did you do what I think you did?"

"Look... Shut up for a second." I decided to fight fire with fire. "I couldn't find my razor and I got paranoid... That razor means a lot to me... It was given to my father by his father and now they're both dead *okay*... It means a lot to me."

He went quiet and looked down at the map.

"I put your razor in the glove box when you were in the dollar store."

He leaned forward, popped open the glove box and handed it to me.

"Did you go through my *whole* bag?"

His tone was peculiar - more curious than accusing. But his eyes were unmistakeably challenging.

"No... I didn't," I said. "Just the main part... And I didn't look inside or anything... I just felt around with my hand."

When I said that to him I immediately started wondering what else might be in the front part of the satchel, which he had picked up and put back down on the floor, this time between his feet and the door. I got the urge to ask him about his passport but fought it off, of course. Obviously it wasn't the right time.

He went back to focusing on the map. Then he stopped and looked over.

"When did your old man die?"

"I was twelve."

"Sorry."

"Thanks."

We continued down a small paved side road, hardly big enough for two vehicles. It ran almost parallel to the 401 but the farther we drove, the farther we veered away. My mind returned to the accident and then to Rocky's reluctance to help out.

"If you don't mind me askin', and don't take this the wrong way or anything... but why were you so afraid to get out of the car back there?"

"I knew this was coming."

"Sorry... I'm just wondering, that's all... I understand if you're squeamish... Lots of people can't look at blood and stuff."

"It's not that... You really wanna know, eh?"

"Well... Yeah, I guess..."

"I was in a bad car accident when I was five... Both my parents were killed instantly right in front of me... I was in the back in my car seat, covered in their blood and holding a He-Man action figure when the cops found me. Still can't watch those old He-Man cartoons."

A viscous silence oozed out between us. I wasn't expecting to hear that, and I felt awful for asking.

I resolved to do what I always do in awkward situations. I changed the subject.

"That Steely Dan t-shirt was my all-time fav', it was an original from their '74 Pretzel Logic tour... Their last real tour... I found it at a second hand shop a few years ago."

I started humming their song Deacon Blues, and tapped along on the steering wheel, as Rocky adjusted the reading light so that it lit up the outer edges of the map and by extension, part of my torso.

"Right now you look like a junked out version of He-Man with that seat belt across your chest and the blood and everything."

I let out a laugh as I looked down at myself. I didn't know what to say. What he said was funny on the surface, but just underneath lurked a sadness that peered out from inside a lock box of tragedy. I didn't want to open that box any further than it already was.

He kept on with the He-Man thing and I felt relieved.

"Y'know... In the original TV series He-Man had telepathic powers. That's how he sensed the presence of the Sorceress."

In my peripheral I saw him turn his head toward me. I glanced over and he looked away.

"You and Frank communicate telepathically," he said, as he looked off into the darkness of the roadside. "Who'd'ya think Frank really is anyway? I mean maybe he's just you... Maybe he's the voice of your intuition or your ESP or whatever it's called."

"I think it's more than that... Sometimes I think I can actually see him in mirrors... Like when I'm in the cab for instance I'll catch glimpses of him in the rear-view just before or after one of his songs goes through my head."

"What's he look like?"

"He's shadowy... Black hair... Black eyes... That's all I can distinguish really... He's like a silhouette."

He picked his scarecrow up off the seat, turned it over a couple times, and then put it back in his shirt pocket. If he had had a notebook to write in, I'm pretty sure that's what he would've done right then. He would've jotted down some important clue that pertained to whatever secret investigation he was in the middle of.

"I was supposed to be a twin when I was born," I added.

"What happened?"

"The other one... My brother... He stopped breathing just after birth and they couldn't revive him."

Rocky started nodding his head.

"Well that's him then isn't it? That's Frank... It has to be... You have those dark features too."

"Maybe... Maybe it is. Maybe my parents were gonna call him Franklin. I've never asked my mom... It's a tough subject..."

"You should... You should ask her when you get back from Wichita... Ask her before it's too late."

He dropped his head back down and continued squinting at the map under the reading light.

"You never know when it's gonna be too late," he added.

I took another cigarette out and sparked it up as the truth of his words flew over and perched on my left shoulder.

CHAPTER 5

Where the driver and his passenger discuss the vicissitudes of being 'on the road', as Toronto awaits.

ROCKY TURNED OUT to be a champion navigator. He got us back to the highway within twenty minutes of leaving it. His prowess with a map wasn't all that surprising though, considering his inhuman capacity for detail.

I started pondering his firm command of brass tacks and soon found myself dissecting an old idiom that everyone's heard before:

The Devil is in the details.

I let it ricochet around my head for a while. I even entertained the idea that Rocky might be some sort of real-life Faustian character sent from a cavernous abyss to tempt me into iniquity. I came quite close to believing he *was* an incarnation of Mephistopheles until I remembered another idiom:

God is in the details.

So which is it then, God or the Devil? I thought to myself.

Bam!

I was instantaneously mired in the Velcro fuzz of my own opiated stitch up job, which then forced me into some dubious deduction work.

This was, of course, a fool's errand, and it went something like this:

If lawyers are as morally bankrupt as they're said to be, then it must be the Devil who resides in the details.

I based the above rather clunky equation on common knowledge. For everyone knows that lawyers, especially defense lawyers, pride themselves on their ability to root out overlooked and often highly ambiguous details that can be presented with a certain artifice, so as to bolster the plight of whatever client they happen to be representing.

I marked this down in the Devil column.

In God's defense I dug up some interesting ideas. But the main one - the one with the most relevance for me, was this little piece of blackbird pie:

God is said to be the creator of the universe, and so it follows that everything in the universe is the copyrighted diaspora of his intellectual property. In other words, God made the damn details so the Devil is his bitch when it comes to the fine print.

Not surprisingly, it also crossed my mind at the time that maybe God had a small royalty claim on the character development of the Devil himself. He most certainly had bragging rights based on the brilliant authorial rendering of the Devil's precursor, Lucifer. But to properly hedge my bets I had to first consider the possibility that the Lucifer to Devil transformation was part of a meta-narrative that even God's own postmodernist sensibilities had failed to incorporate. The rebellion was, after all, your basic bastard child of free will. The more I thought about it, however, the more it seemed in God's best interest to have a fall guy. Or a terrorist, if you'd rather.

And so it goes... I came to this lofty conclusion:

It is God, not the Devil, who inhabits every last tiny detail of every last little nook and cranny of every last dust ridden corner of the entire fucking universe.

Warning: Regular morphine use may lead to profuse pontificating.

Oh, and as for Rocky, well he just seemed too vulnerable to be truly devilish. From what I knew of him so far, he was just as torn and frayed as I was.

Maybe even more so.

Before I go any further, I have to mention the blink-and-you'll-miss-it town we went through to get back to the 401.

Rocky said it wasn't even named on the map.

It was around nine o'clock and we looked for anything at all that might sell coffee or doughnuts or have a bathroom but there was nothing. The whole place had closed up shop for the night. There was one street light blinking on and off next to an unlit sign for a general store, creaking back and forth in the wind. Several Stephen King novels came to mind as we noticed a chubby kid walking by himself up ahead, smoking a cigarette. He couldn't have been more than twelve.

We slowed up as Rocky rolled down his window.

The kid was staring at his feet and cupping his smoke so it wouldn't get wet from the rain. He was about fifteen feet from the cab, and either didn't hear us approaching or was ignoring us. I tapped the horn and he looked up, taking earphones out as he did. Rocky asked him if there was anything open. The kid took a big haul off his smoke and looked us over before answering.

"What does it look like to you?"

His face was a perfect sketch of pre-adolescent sarcasm. Rocky glanced back at me, then out of nowhere ripped into him.

"What're ya listenin' to? An audio book on how to be a little *prick*?"

The kid spat on the ground.

"Slayer," he said, after taking another drag and flicking the butt into the wind so that it bounced off of our windshield and tumbled on down the street.

Rocky watched it hit the car, then did something that made me re-evaluate his sanity. He popped open his door, jumped out, grabbed the kid by his coat and pushed him hard up against a pole.

"Listen you little redneck, I don't like you *or* your backwoods family. If you think you know *anything* about life you're mistaken... I might just be the kinda guy who'd throw you in the trunk right now, drive you out to the middle of nowhere and make you do things you don't wanna do."

He looked around, then seemed to come to his senses a little. He let go of the kid, reached into his pocket, took out the other pack of cigarettes, and shoved them in the kids face.

"Take these you little shit... Have 'em... And remember what I told you. You can't trust anyone. You can't trust the friendly farmer, the fat-faced cop, the wannabe cool school teacher, the whistling postman, the bald headed barber, the old guy behind the counter at your general store over there, the local half-wit mechanic and most of all..." He paused as his face scrunched up into a ball of hatred. "*You can't trust the fucking priest or the pastor or whatever the hell he's called here in this perverted little place.*"

The kid was white with fear when Rocky backed away from him and returned to the cab.

"I'm telling you this for your own good kid, so don't go running to anyone after we leave... They're all sickos underneath the masks and uniforms... *Every last one of 'em*." He stopped and shut the door. "Now go smoke those and think about what I told you."

The kid looked down at the cigarettes, but didn't dare say anything.

I hit the pedal and got us the hell outta there as fast as possible. The shock of what he'd just done rendered me speechless until we got back to the highway where I felt a little safer—far enough away from the posse of 4x4, gun-racked trucks, that I was sure would be in hot pursuit of us once the kid's smokes ran out.

I let ten kilometres of asphalt pass under the cab before working up the nerve to acknowledge what'd happened back in the ghost town. It was the very last thing I wanted to do, but it had to be discussed because outbursts like his were anathema to us flying under the radar. We'd simply never make it to Wichita if he was gonna make a habit of getting unglued in public.

I didn't know whether to confront him directly or not. I shifted in my seat and fidgeted like a kid staring down algebra homework, before deciding on the long way 'round. My front line training on the mean streets of Grey Grove demanded I do so. In my experience, it was better to give my infirm and unstable customers a chance to prove themselves, rather than test them and risk winding up on the receiving end of mouth-frothing insults and no pay.

Or worse, the receiving end of a knife and stolen pay.

At this point you might be wanting to point out to me that I was just as infirm and unstable as any customer. Allow me to scratch that itch with a resounding, *YES*. I was indeed very infirm and unstable at this time. But that's what gave me my diplomatic edge. I knew how to deal with people like myself, because I wasn't in denial and I was highly allergic to hypocritical bullshit.

I was also dead set on getting to Wichita.

Because I needed the money, of course.

Now, as I said before, customers were supposed to be money first and people second. Even though I'd learned a lot about Rocky's pathos, and I felt the tendrils of compassion entwine themselves within my ribcage upon witnessing it, I was very much opposed to breaking my policy of not crossing the line between friend and client. At this moment however—at this stained, wrinkled, and unwashed shirt of a moment, I needed to admit something to myself. I needed to admit that I hadn't just crossed the line, I was in the process of erasing it altogether.

But how could I not? If what he told me was the truth, then at five years old he was forced to watch his parents die under extremely violent circumstances. No kid survives that and remains a kid. At least not in any normal sense.

It's safe to say, that at this stage, I was no longer just his taxi driver. We were officially acquainted. And part of me felt the beginnings of a friendship. I couldn't help it. His brokenness, fragility and desperation all conspired to loosen the cynical seams of my morphine flak jacket. Only three hours had elapsed since we met, but I felt oddly willing to step up to the plate for him. The real fucked up thing was, this was all in spite of the fact that I knew in my bones there was something even bigger and more pressing he was keeping from me. It was a gut feeling I couldn't shake. I didn't know what it was exactly, but it was hovering between us like a spectre.

I could feel it.

I lit up a smoke and offered one to Rocky. He took it and turned toward the window. He didn't light his. He just let it dangle from the corner of his mouth. Then he started whistling. It bugged me. It was as if what he did to that kid was no more noteworthy than taking a piss. Speaking of which, I really had to take a piss around that time, and it was making me edgy in the way that a bulging bladder would. I was also cold, and starting to shiver.

I turned the heat on, and decided to break the silence that'd congealed around us.

"I need to find a shirt somewhere."

He glanced over.

"Yah, but if we can stay on the highway we'll be in Toronto in less than an hour."

"Yah? Well I need to take a leak too... We're gonna have to stop at some point."

"Just use the pop bottle... I'll hold the wheel."

I was no prude. But the idea of holding my dick out in front of him wasn't all that appealing.

"What're ya afraid I'll look?"

"No... It's just pulling over would be easy enough."

He picked up the empty bottle and handed it to me. His face was perfectly expressionless.

"Just piss in the bottle."

He grabbed the wheel.

"What the fuck? What is this...? Peer pressure?" I joked, half serious.

"Would it help if I whipped mine out too?"

That got under my skin.

"Fine... Keep your eyes on the road."

I unzipped, pulled out, and placed the tip against the plastic mouth. The relief that washed over me as the bottle started filling up was awkwardly juxtaposed. I associated it somehow with Rocky, which made me a little uncomfortable. Especially since he was leaned over like he was.

"I bet the girls like you," he muttered. I looked up as he looked away.

"What? What the *hell, man.* I said keep your eyes on the damn road... *Jeezuz.*"

The self-consciousness that ensued choked off my stream, and I had to concentrate to get it back up to full flow. I took the opportunity to divert the attention back to him.

"Why'd you do that to the kid back there?"

He finally lit his smoke with his right hand, still steering with his left. The bottle was half full.

"He was a little prick. He deserved it... Anyways, I gave him a pack of smokes, didn't I?"

"Yeah, well you can't do stupid shit like that. You're a fucking fugitive, remember? We're both pretty much fugitives at this point, and if we're gonna make it to Wichita then you better think twice before goin off on people like that."

He exhaled and grinned a little.

"That lady I tied up won't be found until tomorrow morning, which gives us plenty of time to get across the border."

"How do you know she doesn't have a husband or something...? If she does he'll be wondering where the fuck she is, and the first place he'll go is to her work."

"Quinn... Quinn... Quinn... I took care of the details... I built us a fire proof disco, *man*... I called the place more than once and talked to her specifically... Put it this way... If you ask the right questions under the right pretext you'll get all the information you need, and the person will be none the wiser. She told me she was single and lived alone. End of story."

I finished my ridiculously long piss, did my best to shake it off, screwed the cap back on and set the warm bottle down in the back before taking the wheel.

"I hope so...," I said. "And you better be tellin' me the truth about all this. So far I've been takin' your word for everything."

"Scout's honour," he chirped.

"And no more outbursts... That kid could easily go home and tell his parents we're a couple of child molesters or something; and if he did, it won't be long before we get yanked over."

He reacted to my child molester comment with some overly hollow laughter.

"We'll be fine, Quinn... The kid was a rebel. The last thing he's gonna do is go tell his mommy."

"I wouldn't be so sure if I were you... Just to be safe we should take the top sign off the roof."

"Yeah, okay... Pull over at the next turn off."

His voice changed. I detected a hint of doubt. He took a big drag off his cigarette, then got a bit confidential sounding.

"What I said to that kid was the bloody truth. I know all about the wolves in sheep's clothing... I kno—"

He changed his mind about telling me whatever it was he was about to tell me.

"Just trust me," he spat. "Everything about this nanny state we live in is a lie. It's all a big protection racket... The religions, the bylaws, all of it. Besides, I'll never be a wolf or a sheep 'cause I'm a bird."

His bird comment left me in a lurch once again, but somehow I knew that asking him to elaborate would only confuse me more. Instead, I flicked my butt out the window and kept my eyes peeled for a good spot to pull over.

At the next crossroad we pulled off just long enough for me to unhook the bungee cords that held the top sign on the roof of the car. I threw it in the trunk and we got right back on the highway. We were no longer driving a taxi.

I turned the radio on and dialed in some FM college station playing "Seven Nation Army" by The White Stripes. When it got to the last verse Rocky surprised me by singing along.

I'm going to Wichita... Far from this opera forevermore... I'm gonna work the straw... Make the sweat drip from every pore. And I'm bleeding, I'm bleeding, I'm bleeding right before the lord. All the words are gonna bleed from me and I will think no more.

His voice was high and pure with a naturally pleasing timbre. I was compelled to tell him so when the song ended.

"You can sing, man."

"It's a good song... It's the scarecrow's theme," he said, patting the shirt pocket that held his action figure.

I felt the urge to roll my eyes, but resisted. And thinking back now, I'm positive it was this seemingly insignificant gesture that fully tipped the scales in his favor. In one conscious instant he went from being the surreptitious miscreant to being no more strange, weird, odd, untoward, troublesome, awkward, disturbing, perverse, or hapless than I was. I remember smiling to myself; a ventilated smile.

"You ever watch any of those road movies?" he asked, out of the blue.

"Like... which ones?"

"How 'bout *Butch Cassidy and the Sundance Kid*?" he asked.

"Yup... seen that."

"What about *Thelma and Louise* or *Bonnie and Clyde*?"

"I've seen those too," I said, catching his drift. "Do you think we're like that?"

There was a silence, filled in by the radio.

"Of course we are... Rocky and Quinn. It's got a ring to it."

I grinned. I couldn't help it. But it dissolved pretty quickly when I thought about the way all those films ended.

"All those movies have the same ending," I pointed out.

"Yeah, but they all died heroes."

"I think the proper term is anti-hero."

"Naw, they were all heroes, Quinn... They mighta killed a few people but they sacrificed themselves too... They're fallen soldiers in the never-ending war against mediocrity."

His angle intrigued me.

"How do you mean?"

"Think about it. They were all rebelling against the soul crushing bullshit we call civilized society. They were desperadoes extraordinaire my friend. Nobody's fools. Collars and leashes were unbearable to them." He suddenly got animated. "*God bless the wild ones and may all the willing slaves be damned.*" He lowered his voice back down. "The wild ones are the ones who risk it all for *real* freedom. Not that dumbed down processed shit you buy from stores and schools, but the natural stuff. The stuff you earn on your own with fearlessness and stoicism... The wild ones are the trail blazers."

He stopped his rant and started humming *Seven Nation Army* again. I let the words ramble through my mind as he did.

"I bet you can't name another song with Wichita in it."

He stopped humming just long enough to ask me that, then started back up. I thought about it for a minute or two, but came up empty.

"I got nothin'," I told him.

"Jimmy Webb's your hint."

"Who?"

"Jimmy Webb."

I thought some more, but still drew a blank.

"Jimmy Webb wrote 'Wichita Lineman'. Glen Campbell made it a hit in '68."

"Cool," I said, as my thoughts returned to the films we talked about. "So who's who in those movies? Like which one's you and which one's me?"

He seemed to think about that question pretty hard before responding.

"Well, Butch was your basic womanizing good time guy. Bad with money and even worse with a gun. Remember when they're in the stand-off with those Bolivian bandits and he admits to Sundance he's never actually shot a man before? That goes to show he was only robbing banks as a means to an end. All he really wanted was the ladies and the poker games the money brought. Sundance on the other hand, was a lot darker. I'm not even convinced he was all that interested in women *or* money. I think he just wanted freedom at any cost. I mean, he sure gave up his girl pretty easy when she wanted to go back to the States. Also, remember when he tells Butch he's from New Jersey? An outlaw from New Jersey? You know what that means eh? It means he cut loose. He couldn't abide the restrictions of society. He was the *real* rebel. Why he always deferred judgment to Butch, I'll never know. For some reason he thought Butch was the smart one, but time and again Butch fucked things up for them."

"Maybe Sundance left New Jersey because he didn't think he was sophisticated enough. That'd also explain his need to rely on Butch's charm."

"You could be right, Quinn... Or maybe he was just plain shy."

Rocky went quiet. He looked like he was really contemplating Sundance's inner workings.

"So who's who then?" I repeated.

"I don't know you well enough yet, Quinn... But with all due respect I'd have to say I ain't nothin' like Butch."

"Fine... I'll be Butch." I paused for a few seconds, "Now how 'bout Thelma and Louise?"

He burst into laughter.

"Well you're the brunette and you're older so that makes you Louise."

I remembered looking at his passport and noticing he was twenty. Funny enough, his hair in the picture was much longer and it looked reddish blond, like Thelma's.

"Okay so you're the lusty housewife who's had enough of her pig husband?" I joked.

"Yep... But I learn pretty damn quick, and before long I'm knockin' off banks and stores like nobody's business."

The game of one-upmanship was on.

"And I'm the aging one with the brains who saves your sweet young ass by blowin' that fucktard away in the parking lot."

"Much appreciated *girlfriend*. And thanks for lettin' me get it on with Brad Pitt by the way," he said, batting his eyelashes.

I played along.

"No problem... But you got my money stolen you dumb bitch."

"But I made up for it by locking that douchebag cop in the trunk when he was about to bust you."

"Okay, okay... You're forgiven."

We both had a good laugh, then gradually drifted back into the business at hand.

"You know anyone in Toronto we can visit? Preferably someone who lives near Chinatown."

I did know someone. She was a good friend.

"I know a really cool girl who runs a punk and hard-core speakeasy there... It's not that far from Chinatown."

"Nice, Quinn... Hook it up when we roll in."

He settled down into his seat like he was relishing the fact that his plan was coming together. I felt good and relaxed too. The inner echoes of the laugh we had over *Thelma and Louise* and the idea of having a couple beers at my friend's were mellowing my mind.

We retreated into ourselves for the remaining stretch to Toronto. Our laughter had tilled the soil of camaraderie just enough for an easy meditative silence to bloom between us.

A silence infused with crunched numbers and imagined landscapes that all related to Wichita.

For the better part of an hour we followed our white rabbits wherever they chose to go. I don't know what Rocky was mulling over in that head of his, but I was thinking of Glenda Lancaster and all the times we spent dancing on the silken edge of a romance.

It was a romance that never quite came to fruition. We were a frostbitten, early spring bud of passion, special in its undeveloped purity for never having donned the saffron garments of a full exposition. We were destined to shun the harsh light of day. We were a night blooming lily decorating the darkness with a sweet bouquet of river silt and roses.

Glenda grew up in a small town not far from Grey Grove. She was a year younger than me, and shared my astrological sign. She was blessed with an electric mane of ebony threads that when teased by the western winds, or a long night of dream heavy sleep, melted the defenses of anyone who laid eyes on her. It was as if her ready smile had rubbed up against her beautiful brain to create a static buildup of raw energy that zapped out through Tesla coiled filaments of hair.

The first time I met her she wore day-glow army boots, and a beat up leather jacket. I was instantaneously smitten. Somehow I knew just by looking at her, that she was the remedy. I knew she could change me if I gave her the codes to my heart, but I was reluctant to do so. They were burdensome codes. I wouldn't have wished them upon anyone. Especially not a rare, crackling with life incarnate, such as her. I purposely held myself just far enough away so that the mental and emotional distance would absorb her innocent charms and protect me from falling hopelessly in love. I wanted to shield her from the intergalactic disease I felt I carried. And so naturally she became more like a kid sister to me, which ended up being the perfect working arrangement.

We *did,* however, sneak into the trellised garden of lust one night to make five course meals of one another. But the next morning we both had the sense to re-draw the line in the sand. Together we took a graceful step back from the edge.

Glenda lived on the lower-east side of Toronto. She moved there when Grey Grove no longer matched her own level of inner combustion. It wasn't long before she attracted a core group of like-minded souls who helped her start up a street level music venue for punk and hard-core bands.

It'd been a few years, but in my head she still danced with the same holographic vibrancy.

I was already smiling in advance of her blue-eyed brilliance.

SECOND INTERMISSION

The chicken Parma Rosa is excellent, by the way. And they're now serving cocktails, along with some other lesser known mixtures. Don't look now, but the frisky couple behind you seem to be on the verge of something...

CHAPTER 6

Where the driver and his passenger roll into a sprawling metropolis and make their way to some much needed downtime.

WHAT IS IT ABOUT driving into a massive city at night? Is it the thousand billboards selling themselves like so many garish hookers? Is it the skyscrapers scraping at viral sky, vying for the best view by thrusting upward into the defiled loins of the lower troposphere? Is it the sudden onslaught of agitated, at wits' end, flat broke and berserk, plum crazy, deranged, distraught, foaming at the mouth, hectic, hot under the blue and white collar, in a tinkering tizzy, keyed up for chaos, cracktastic, unglued, wigged out, tweaked on designer street drugs → *energy?*

All of the above, I think.

And I was glad for the extra padding I wore: my trusty morphine force field.

We turned south onto the Don Valley Parkway, rolling downhill through electrified blocks of night kissed industry. We hadn't said a word to each other in almost an hour and the sights, sounds and smells around us kept it that way for a while longer.

As we zeroed in on the famously provincial but multicultural heart of the city, we started catching passing slices of life.

The first street level evidence of sentience was the graffiti that shone forth from a never-ending maze of walls. Some were Gordian codes only to be broken by the initiated and others were stenciled images of Banksy-esque brilliance.

After that it was the people—the real people:

Old men with leathery skin, dressed up in ill-fitting rags, pushing rusty shopping carts full of empty bottles and cans, and lice infested blankets that warmed bones on frigid northern nights.

Old women with eyes like spies, sizing things up before hording them away.

Young folks, with their fresh meat providing the lion's share of dividends for business men and women, pursuing lifelong ambitions under fastidiously manicured agendas.

Stray cats, and dogs, and rats, and cockroaches, and bedbugs, and maggots conspired in the festering twilight as the odd song bird chirped from a tree branch overhanging a polluted stream that bobbed with dead fish.

We passed Suicide Bridge.

It wasn't such an impressive piece of architecture, but it did have the dubious distinction of being the second most visited feat of engineering in the world for those lacking the will to live. It loomed in the trash dotted foreground like an unabashed monument to hopelessness, defeat and despair—silently calling out to all those who lost themselves somewhere along the way.

Down, down, down we drove into the concrete and asphalt belly of confusion where people sought out and more often than not, found what they were looking for. Where people lived fast lives in the midst of plenty. Where people lived lonely lives in the midst of plenty. Where people suffered and starved in the midst of plenty.

Where people were born in the midst of plenty. Where people died in the midst of plenty. Where people made love in the midst of plenty and for a brief while transported themselves and those they were loving to a better, warmer and happier place.

There were so many people walking and running and talking and driving and slowly making their way toward a yawning abyss that promised them nothing but notions.

A little awestruck and a little weary, we drove into the darkening heart of Toronto.

I've always been amazed by how quickly people could adapt to new situations and surroundings. It gave me hope. For instance, I'm sitting here at my new kitchen table, looking out the new window of the new apartment I just moved into, and it already feels like home. It already feels like I've lived here forever, eaten off this table forever, and looked through the glass of that window over there, forever. To really put this into context, though, not only am I sitting here at my new table, in my new apartment, on my new street looking out my new window, but I'm also writing this new book about a chapter of my life that was jam packed with newness, from Grey Grove to Wichita.

As I sit here examining a short, life-changing journey, I snap back and forth between co-existing worlds. Back and forth between a new apartment with a new window over a new street, and an old world that rides the line of an event horizon just beyond the glass, darkly. I'm snapping back and forth like the alternating current that feeds this computer. I'm spelunking into the past, firmly tied to the present, and bringing back whatever dusty gems I can quarry and carry. I'm doing this now like I've been doing it forever. I sit here under an off-white ceiling with my feet on a thin grey carpet, commuting betwixt the new and the old like Hermes dressed in jeans and sneakers.

I'm wet-winged, and gifted with the everyday power to peruse co-existing worlds.

I put bread in the toaster, and come back to the keyboard to look out my window into the past, and type what I see. The toast pops, and I stand back up into the present. I fetch the toast, then walk back over to the keyboard to gaze out my window, and describe what's waiting there. And maybe what I see wasn't there before. Maybe my old world had decided to offer up something new just as my new world became old.

People get used to things so fast sometimes that they don't even realize how much they've accomplished in a day, or how far they've progressed in a year. They don't realize they're time travellers, and astronauts, and expedition climbers, and moms, and dads, and teachers, and fools, and wise men, and killers, and victims, and sexual deviants, and virgins all in the span of a day. Maybe in the span of an hour. Maybe in a minute, or a second, or even possibly a micro-second. Time is naught. Time *is* a knot. And if this is what time is, then so is space.

My new apartment, my new table, my new window that opens up over my new neighborhood, all make up but one small setting in a kaleidoscope of settings nestled inside my head. Some of those settings

I've actually been in, and others I've only read about, but nevertheless, they're all vying for my attention.

I can feel the velvety skin of a girl who kissed me on my eighteenth birthday in a high school corridor, just as plain as the grain of this wood my keyboard rests upon.

Glenda Lancaster had lovely skin too. And she had perfect breasts; small, and in no need of support, and always right there poking out from beneath tattered cashmere sweaters.

As I slowly grew accustomed to my new metropolitan setting, I could feel her naked chest against my own.

It'd been a while since I had my desires quenched.

Not that I was expecting anything. But I could daydream. She wouldn't mind. She'd encourage it with her sublimely subtle flirtations. She enjoyed being enjoyed, and *that* was an affirmation of life — a brave celebration of liberty. It was always refreshing. It was always un-precious. It was pure Glenda.

We turned off the Don Valley Parkway and headed west on Queen Street East. Rocky was still absorbed in the cornucopia of life that drifted by beyond the glass of his window. Then suddenly he spoke up.

"Wait... There's a coin laundry... We need to do a couple hundred dollars' worth of washing," he said, with a wink.

I hit the brakes and pulled over to the side as he dug into his satchel for some bills.

"I'll go this time," I offered.

"Okay, keep your head down... away from any cameras."

"Gotcha," I said, as I pulled the door open a little.

"Hang on a sec... Can you pop the trunk? I wanna keep my satchel in a safer spot while we're here," he asked.

I popped the trunk, took the bills from his hand, and then dashed back to the laundromat.

The rain had stopped somewhere around the time we turned south toward Glenda. It still wasn't a clear sky, though. It was pregnant and waiting on the next thunderclap contraction. I was about fifteen feet from the car when Rocky called out to me.

"Quinn!"

I stopped my trot, and spun around to see him bare chested and holding his shirt. I looked down at myself and shook my head at the oversight. Walking around shirtless was a damn good way to draw unwanted attention.

As I buttoned up, I jogged back toward the laundromat, praying to whatever God of convenience I prayed to, for the door not to be locked.

I got to the handle and pulled. It opened. I glanced at the hours posted and chuckled to myself as I read the words, TWENTY-FOUR HRS. I hadn't fully adjusted to being in the big city yet. In Grey Grove, last loads were to be in by 8:00 p.m. because the laundromat, and by extension the entire business sector of the city, locked up at 9:00 p.m.

I located the change machine near the back, but halfway there I saw it was out of order, with a little handwritten sign taped to it. That threw me into Macgyver mode. I turned around and headed for the slightly greasy looking attendant who was tucked behind a yellowing Plexiglas partition inside a dingy little hole-in-the-wall office space, looking both bored and alert at the same time. My mind raced with possible verbal disguises. About five feet away I settled on my version of a southern accent. I knew it sucked, but it was the only thing I had that could even remotely be deemed convincing.

"Howdee pardner. Ya'll gat chaynge fo a cupla hunrids?"

The guy looked up from his paper and gave me one of those flitting glances that said everything in split-seconds. It said: *we don't get your type around here very often and I feel sorry for your ridiculous sounding accent.* I felt my face turning a little red but I went with it, figuring the shy southern boy thing might actually make me seem more authentic. I decided to throw in a stutter or two, for good measure.

"I—I gotta get me a phone cawd and that lil' shap up a holla thayre don't have nare 'nuff ta brayk thayse hayre bag bills."

I did my best aw-shucks grin, then waited for a response

"So what you want? Twentees?" he half shouted through a thin, mustache dampened smile.

"Shore. Thad bay jus swayl."

I knew I was overdoing it at this point, but I was starting to have fun. He counted out 10 twenties, slapped his hairy knuckled hand down and pushed it all toward me. I handed him the 2 hundreds.

"Ya'll run a rayle daycent 'stablishment. And may tha gud lawd hisself come down from ova yonda ta wash up his own shurt an trowzahs right hayre!"

I flashed one last toothy grin and walked away with a slow, Mississippi half step of a gait.

I stopped at the door of the laundromat and counted my cash twice in quick succession. It was a habit I had formed after getting burned by grifters' sleight of hand routines one too many times while working. I stopped counting pretty quickly when I remembered I was in downtown Toronto.

I stuffed the bills in my back pocket, yanked the door open, stepped out onto the sidewalk and let a new wary eye survey my surroundings. Across the street and half a block down, huddled on the steps of a slowly disintegrating brownstone, were three dudes just kinda sitting there, smoking and joking. They looked a little too sly to me. A little too pleased with themselves. I knew enough about the bold hustle of dope pushing to pick up on their vibe.

It was just a hunch. But a hunch is a hunch.

And crack is crack; the most addictive substance known to man.

I smirked to myself as I headed up the big city street in the other direction, back to the car. I was no stranger to cocaine, you see. And I knew a thing or two about its jittery younger sister, crack. Grey Grove was a garden variety hick town, but that didn't mean it couldn't play host to the same chemical glitterati of king-pins, dealers, pushers, junkies and weekenders.

Cocaine is an interesting drug. Depending on the form it takes it can represent two completely different socio-economic statuses. In powdered form it tends to be found among the upper classes and upper middle classes. Doctors, lawyers, businessmen and women, judges, professors, politicians and teachers all do it, but they usually squirrel it away for Friday or Saturday night; the two nights where Hyde is permitted to usurp Jekyll.

Jekyll, as we all know, maintains a gleaming, non-threatening appearance by stuffing all the socially inappropriate ideas and urges he accumulates throughout the work week, down into a little black box that sits in the corner of his cellar. The cellar has a thick bank-vault type door secured by a dead-bolt. Hyde, of course, is the only other one with access to this door, and come the weekend he pads softly down the stairs in silk slippers, whispering to himself the precious digits of a security code. When he comes to the door he pauses for a second or two, straining to listen above the pounding heartbeat in his head for any signs of interlopers. If the coast is clear he ceremoniously opens it up and creeps in. Once inside he sticks a palm-moistened key into the black box. His blood pressure rises at alarming increments as the box pops open to expose its many treasures. After choosing the most tantalizing, he indulges like a boss. A mind bending blur ensues. Come Sunday morning, he wakes up feeling a little disgusted with himself. Just disgusted enough to want to return to the comforting drudgery of a day job for the next five self-flagellating days.

Okay, okay, I'm willing to admit that the above paragraph was unnecessarily cynical of me. But at least I threaded in a literary trope.

I remember getting stopped by a cop one time. I'd just come out of my dealer's house after breaking one of my cardinal rules, which was: *never get high until you get home*. I was entering the tail end of a crack buzz. The edged out and psychotic part. The part that makes you wanna hit yourself in the head with a hammer for being so fucking stupid in the first place. That's right! I dabbled in crack. Although in Grey Grove it was usually freebase, which is crack's purer, more skill demanding ancestor. Crack, you buy all done up. It's already 'cooked' and full of a few random chemicals that probably all eventually cause dementia. It's the fast food of street drugs. Freebase on the other hand, demands some real technical know-how.

Freebase comes with a little cue card recipe, much like the ones you or your mom might keep in that old cookie tin in the bottom drawer of the kitchen. It looks something like this:

1. Grab your already blackened stainless steel tea spoon and a filthy glass of tap water.

2. Frantically rifle through your cupboards for some leftover baking soda.

3. Put a light dusting of baking soda on the spoon.

4. Add a half gram of cocaine into the spoon (or, if you're feeling gluttonous add a full gram and hope to hell that it's of decent quality because if it's not you're gonna blow a gasket in about five minutes.)

5. Dribble a small amount of water onto the spoon so that it doesn't overflow and cause you to start licking it up off the floor like a dog.

6. Take your lighter and start cooking it (hopefully you thought to get a lighter or you're gonna start smashing shit before you remember you have a stove upstairs with one working element.)

7. Gently cook the mixture until little white chunks form.

8. Scrape out the white chunks (the pure crack that is) and presto, your recipe for disaster is complete.

9. Go smoke it on an old pop can and get extremely high. So high, you think your head's gonna pop off and scurry away out the front door. I hope you locked all the doors by the way. Because in 45 minutes when your crumbs are all gone and you've scoured the revolting carpet, frantically smoking everything from old rice to random pieces of crusted lint that cause you to hack up your lungs and retch until your face is dotted with burst blood vessels, you'll be tearing your hair out wanting more. But, of course, you'll be too fucking paranoid to leave the house on account of all the undercover FBI and DEA agents hiding in the bushes and trees.

Anyway.

Back to the cop that pulled me over. I walked out the alley to the street and looked both ways. The coast looked clear to me, but I *was* high remember. I started walking home with that driven step that crackheads get, when a cruiser pulls up and rolls down its window. I almost froze, but miraculously managed to slow down smoothly so as not to arouse immediate suspicion. The officer inside was about 30 years old and was smiling that sickly sweet smile that cops get when they're two or three steps ahead of you. He asked me where I came from. I hesitated as I tried to invent something. He pounced. He had me. He asked me if I had anything on me. I said no rather weakly and he smiled again. He then told me to give him whatever I had or he'd simply drive me down to the station and have me strip searched. He said: "Strip," with his canines fully exposed. I was fucked and I knew it. I reached into my coin pocket, pulled out a little baggie of white powder and handed it to him while stating my case. I told him I wasn't a junkie. I said that "I was just tryin' to have some fun with my girlfriend." I don't know why I said that, but it surprised the shit out of me when his eyes suddenly grew less predatory and he smirked a little. The next thing he did threw me for one hell of a loop. He laid the baggie down on his metal clip board, looked me right in the eye and said, "You never saw me." He said it as calmly as anything. Then he drove off and left me standing there. I was a man just spared the gallows as I watched him disappear from view. I was also empty handed and out eighty bucks and that stung a little, but eighty bucks was pretty cheap as far as second chances go.

As I navigated the sidewalk, swerving around the spit, gum, dog shit, fermenting vomit, piss and blood stains, I felt small. The cluster of skyscrapers above me loomed like the shoreline of a pimped out Easter Island. I wondered how many janitors were scrubbing the halls of those towering erections, cleaning up after paper pushing civil servants and sneaking hilarious peeks at neurotic keepsakes and awkward family photos.

I wondered how often they found white stains in the bathrooms.

I walked along and my attention was drawn downward by the weight in my shirt pocket—Rocky's shirt pocket. It was his scarecrow. I reached in, pulled it out and looked it over. It was your average looking scarecrow, made of straw and smiling a vacant smile. A mildly disturbing smile. As I traced its miniature plastic contours with my fore-finger I thought about the ever popular straw man fallacy that so often gets deployed in polemical debate.

Tinder box issues and straw men seem to get along famously.

But what's the proper protocol for a straw man deployment?

I'm glad you asked.

To successfully wield a straw man, you must first commit to attacking him mercilessly at some point after he's been fabricated. You must attack him with all the ideological certainty of a lead pipe on a glass piñata. Microscopic bits of stuffing should be floating about on sunbeams and gathering in corners, weeks, months, years, decades, centuries and even millennia after the assassination has been carried out.

You must also know the proper ceremonial sequence of events. Which is as follows:

You must conjure up the illusion of having refuted a proposition by substituting it with a superficially similar yet non-equivalent proposition (the straw man). Then you must artfully refute the straw man, without ever having actually refuted the original proposition. This dandy little bit of black magic has been used throughout history to further the agendas of many a regime, religion, corporation and/or government. If you don't believe me ask any Jewish person. Any black person. Any Asian person. Any gay person. Any woman. Any drug user.

Any minority at all, for that matter.

Any *sinner*.

In plain speak: To build a straw man, simply turn someone into an easy target by rendering them one dimensional with half-truths, exaggerations and conflations. Then raise your crossbow and squeeze them out of the picture.

I turned the scarecrow over and around in the darkness, squinting at it, trying to absorb some sort of meaning from its moulded countenance. I passed under a streetlight as I looked at its feet. The sodium glare was enough to reveal one small word that looked to have been written in ballpoint pen on the sole of the left boot. It said: Ray. I then looked at the right foot and saw the word: Mond. Thus, I was introduced to *Raymond* the scarecrow. I thought about his name for a bit as I continued back to the car. I knew that in French it meant wise protector. It was a fitting name and I silently commended Rocky on his ironic choice.

I thought further about scarecrows and became intrigued by the idea of them being crucified figures. I wondered why I was thinking about all this. My mind felt pregnant with some sort of bastard child kicking at the walls of my skull. Then it hit me. I remembered Rocky saying, "destroy the image and you will break the enemy." The scarecrow *was* the image; a sacrificial distraction; the blood red cloth of the matador. He was also the uncontested idol. The immortal icon glowering down. And he did his job well. He scared the brains right out of billions of people.

I got back to the car and all my thoughts dispersed like so many sophomoric butterflies. I put Raymond back in Rocky's shirt pocket and opened the door.

"I think I'm gonna start whispering."

That was the first thing he said as I got back in the driver's seat.

"Ummm... Okay."

"No really... I'm gonna start whispering when I talk to people. It's more effective than speech. The whisper is louder than the scream, my friend."

As usual, I had no idea where he was going with this.

"Did you get the bills changed?" he whispered.

"Yer funny... And yes, I did but the machine was down so I had to ask the guy behind the counter."

I handed him the ten twenties then took his shirt off and gave it back to him.

"Thanks," he whispered, again.

"Are you seriously gonna whisper? You're already crazy enough, you don't need to advertise it."

I started the car while he put his shirt back on.

"Can you reach in the glove compartment and get my phone and charger?"

He popped it open and handed them to me. I plugged the charger into the cigarette lighter.

"I need a phone card," I said, thinking out loud.

"And a shirt," he added, still whispering.

"*Please* stop whispering. It's too creepy... Just be your normal fucked up self for the next little bit. No whispering okay? Glenda doesn't have a lot of patience for creepy types."

It was true. Glenda was open-minded, but she shut people down pretty quick if they tried messing with her head. She was a bit of a freak magnet so she'd had her fill of sociopaths.

"Glenda?"

"Yes, Glenda... My friend... The one who lives in Toronto. The one who'll put us up for a couple hours. It was your idea to stop here remember."

"Does she have a wand?"

"What? Yeah, she's got a wand and a set of wings."

My sarcasm was in vain.

"Is she good or bad?"

I just shook my head as I pulled the car out into the street and headed for the nearest convenience store. He kept at it.

"She must be good... She's northern," he muttered.

"I have no idea what you're going on about. Just keep an eye out for a store, would ya."

He turned his gaze outward and slouched in his seat like a frustrated child. Apparently Glenda's name had some sort of meaning for him.

The phone charged as we made our way past the neon signs and the pan handlers and the tipsy revelers on their way to the next club. Whatever he was hinting at would have to wait. I didn't feel like humoring him right then.

Glenda was only minutes away and the more I thought about her, the more I wanted to ditch Rocky for a couple hours. I felt bad for thinking that way, but it was the truth.

Within a few blocks we passed what appeared to be a variety store. As I pulled over we got a better look. It was a head shop. The front window displayed the usual assortment of stuff: hookahs and pipes.

Pipes of every color. Pipes of every shape. Pipes for every use. Glass pipes. Aluminium pipes. Steel pipes. Wooden pipes. Corncob pipes. Pipes, pipes, pipes, and more pipes.

I've always found it interesting that there's so many illegal drugs, but so many *legal* drug implements.

You can't be caught dead with crack, but you can go buy a little glass crack pipe for the same price as a bag of milk.

Oh, the wonderful Janus-faced hypocrisy of it all.

One hand giveth as the other taketh away.

There were t-shirts hanging in the front window as well, decorated with varying degrees of witticisms. One said, I'M SO GREAT I'M JEALOUS OF MY SELF. Another said, WHERE ARE WE GOING AND WHY AM I IN THIS HAND BASKET? Another one proclaimed, I GOT ENOUGH EXERCISE JUST PUSHING MY LUCK. They were all pretty funny actually, and I couldn't help laughing when I got to the one that read, I'VE BEEN ON SO MANY BLIND DATES I SHOULD GET A FREE DOG.

Rocky was toiling with his buttons. He'd done them up wrong.

"So... I guess I'll go in. I'll pick out one of them funny shirts for you."

"It says they have phone cards," I looked down at my phone to make sure it was still charging. "Can you get me a fifty-dollar card?"

I reached into my back pocket, took out a hundred and tried to give it to him.

"It's on me," he said, as he popped his door open and hopped out before I could politely refuse.

I watched him walk into the store. It was the first time I really took note of how skinny he was. He couldn't have been any more than 130 pounds and he was as tall as me, 5'10" or thereabouts. A strong wind would've knocked him over if he wasn't holding on to anything. With his extremely short buzz cut, his bony frame and his slightly sunken eyes and cheeks he easily looked twice his age. Something was up with him. It was obvious to me. I made up my mind to gently broach the subject at some point before we hit the border. Preferably a reasonable distance *before* we hit the border so I could make the necessary adjustments if I found anything out that might jeopardize us getting across.

Border guards are a jumpy lot. They don't get paid enough to be doing all those prostate exams. They also carried loaded guns and tended toward trigger happiness when processing the cagier reprobates of the world.

A nervous hunch forced me to crane my neck so I could monitor Rocky, but there were too many things hanging in the front window. You see, even though I'd come to like him a hell of a lot better than I did a few hours previous, I still didn't fully trust him. I mean who would? He was just too much of a loose cannon. For all I knew, he could've burst out the store with a bunch more stolen cash in his hands.

I was no stranger to loose cannons, that's for sure. Grey Grove seemed to be inundated by them. But my powers of placation only lasted for as long as it took to complete the average inner city cab ride.

Not for 2,200 kilometres.

In all fairness, though, Rocky's looseness was more of a refusal to kowtow than it was a legitimate psychosis. He simply wasn't interested in authenticating other people's preciousness. In fact, I don't think he gave a rat's ass about protocol. He certainly didn't hesitate to point out my own moments of recherché.

All in all, I appreciated his particular stripe. It's just at this nascent stage of our friendship, I wasn't about to let my guard down. Letting my guard down was never an easy thing for me to begin with. Suspicious turns of mind were commonplace for me. It was a built-in character trait, bolstered by endless gritty nights perched behind the wheel of a taxicab in a demented little town.

One thing I *will* say, is that after a certain number of years all cab drivers should be given honorary degrees in sociology and psychology, because the time I spent working for the human delivery business saw me take a whole lot of shit directly on the chin from everyone and their dog.

I would've been far more jaded than I was, if I hadn't of come to the conclusion after years of hack research, that people are always willing to let their humanity shine through, when given half a chance.

Unfortunately, savagery can shine through too. It can lurk like a contagion beneath the sweetest of exteriors. It took far too many bastards licking my windows and kicking my tires, seconds after appearing like the nicest people in the world, before I realized that you can never invest without first hedging your bets.

When it rains it pours, as they say, and sometimes it pours down with belligerence so hard the sewers back up and you're forced to dig the hip waders out of the trunk.

My phone beeped at me to tell me it was completely charged. I picked it up and scrolled through my directory, looking for Glenda's number.

There it was, right underneath *Frog Man*.

Frog Man was the dealer I owed the two large. He was the west end kingpin who somehow maintained a veneer of inscrutability.

Maybe it was because he never stomped on his own stash. Maybe it was because he seemed well read and somewhat cultured. Maybe it was because of his genuinely sweet girlfriend who was always right there with a tension-breaking joke when the details of a dope deal were being laid out like land mines.

She was an odd character. She was agoraphobic and barely ever left the posh apartment they had. I ended up being her personal delivery driver as well as Frog Man's. She was always giving me lists. Grocery lists. Personal beauty product lists. Movie lists. Thai food take-out lists. Pet food lists.

You name it, I held it in my shaky hand.

I thought about calling Frog Man as soon as the phone card was applied, but then put it off. I wasn't in the right head space to tell him I wouldn't have his cash for another couple days, at the very least. Nor did I want to be on the receiving end of his menacing brand of disapproval.

Rocky walked by the front of the car with a bag of stuff clutched in his hand and a troublemaking smile pasted to his face. I took a deep breath in and let it out slowly as I imagined all the horribly inappropriate things his impulsive streak might've caused him to acquire.

I lit up a smoke as Rocky opened the door. I was glad I did too, because right then he let out the biggest fart I've ever heard. He did a little dance outside the car that involved spanking his own ass, followed by a surprisingly graceful pirouette.

"That's the sacred fart dance," he said, as he put the bag of stuff on the floor in front of his seat and got in.

I shot him a raised eyebrow.

"You say that like it was chiseled in hieroglyphics on the inside of Ramesses' tomb."

"Good one, Quinn... Good one, but *noooo*. I invented it." He turned and looked at me. "You should feel honored, because I only perform it for the deserving. It exorcises the stink from the pants."

His voice was a mock-up of reverence and diplomacy.

"Thanks Rocky, I'd do the same for you. Did you get the card?"

He handed it over to me and I immediately started going through the motions of getting it applied. It was the usual frustrating process of trying to read tiny numbers while punching them into the phone after being prompted by a sultry-voiced robot. I was oblivious to what was being laid out with meticulous care beside me. When the card was registered I turned to see the extent of his shopping spree.

On the seat between us were:

One box of *Fundies,* which had as a slogan, *the underwear for two.*

One four inch long shiny blue hash pipe.

A box of vibrating condoms.

A tube of something called *Lust Lotion.*

An X-rated comic book.

Two packages of Beedi Indian cigarettes.

One pouch of chewing tobacco.

One hookah (complete with four woven tubes and a big brass bowl)

I think my eyes were dangling from their optic nerves.

"So... Whaddya think?" he said, with a perfectly executed tone of false innocence.

I rubbed my face with my hands a few times, then took a big drag off my smoke and blew it in his direction.

"The border guards are gonna poke us like a couple piñatas... That's what I think."

"No, no, no... These are all gifts for your friend, Glenda... Housewarming gifts. Everything except the comic book. I haven't looked at it yet."

"That's *great* Rocky! She's not a freaking call girl you know. Or a hillbilly...," I said, holding up the chewing tobacco. "But you're lucky, she'll probably find all this shit pretty funny."

We both started laughing.

Then I remembered he said he was gonna get me a t-shirt.

"What about the shirt?"

"I was saving that for last... Here."

He had it hidden on the far side, between him and the door. I took it, unfolded it and read the caption. My eyes rolled like marbles as I tilted my head back against the seat.

"*I'm with stupid!?* You seriously got me an *'I'm with stupid'* t-shirt? I've managed to get through 27 years of life on earth without ever owning one of these things, then I meet you and within..." I looked at the clock on the dash. "...within four hours I've got no other options."

He turned toward the door and grabbed something else.

"You could wear this one if you want..."

He held up another t-shirt with a woman's naked torso and a large pair of boobs silk screened onto it. It was so well rendered anyone who saw it from a distance was bound to do a double take.

"No thanks... I'd rather be with stupid," I shot back.

"Excellent. That suits me *just* fine... Glenda can have this too then. Or maybe..." He held it up to himself. "How do I look?" he asked, batting his eyelashes and doing his best duck face.

"Like an ugly chick with a boob job."

I picked up the phone, found Glenda's number and dialed.

CHAPTER 7

Where the driver catches up with an old friend.

THE PHONE RANG about five times, but I knew her place was big and she could've been busy somewhere within its reaches, so I let it go.

Hers was a large studio apartment. The main room was about half the size of a school gym, and there were three small rooms along the back wall hidden by an old heavy-velvet theatre curtain. I'd only been there once before and from what I remembered it had no windows, but what it lacked in natural lighting it more than made up for with a raw inner city charisma. It was perfectly suited to its function, which was to provide an all-ages venue for up and coming punk rock bands— bands that were either from the Toronto area or were looking for a gig on their way through.

Glenda herself was a musician. And it was her taste in music that created the high energy, sweat pouring, devil-may-care deliciousness that saturated the air and vibrated the foundations on any given night.

She was also a gifted actress.

Her natural ebullience was perfectly suited for any stage. From the time she was a budding teenager with a knack for well-timed histrionics, she'd been winning lead roles in small to medium budget productions. She hadn't broken through to the illustrious wings of the big rooms yet, but it was just a matter of time.

Not surprisingly, her place doubled as a street level theatre that featured everything from Samuel Beckett to Shakespeare to Tennessee Williams—all of which were interpreted through her shoot-from-the-hip eye for style. Often times she'd hold soirees that opened with one of her plays and closed with two or three bands. At the very end of these nights, the thunderous roar of a fully expended crowd would ring out the room until the next gathering. It was all very artistic, utterly unpretentious and splendidly life affirming.

On the eleventh ring she picked up.

"Hello?"

"Lancaster... It's Quinn."

There was a rustle in the background, like she was moving stuff around.

"*Quinn baby! How are you?*"

Her voice was as sweet and clear as it ever was.

"I'm in town..."

"*Well c'mon over then...*" She reined in her surprise a bit. "C'mon over... I've got a great band here tonight I know you'll love."

"I'm there for sure... But listen, I'm working... I'm drivin' cab, so I got my customer with me. He hired me to take him to Wichita."

"*Wichita? That's a good gig! Are you sure you're able to?*"

"Well, yeah... He's cool with it if you are?"

"Just get your butt over here... And I hope he likes it loud."

"I'm almost positive he does."

I turned to look at Rocky when I said that. He was reading his comic under the book light. There'd be enough distraction at Glenda's to keep him safely occupied even if he didn't, I told myself.

"They're just setting stuff up now so it'll be another hour probably... They're called Blunt Fiction by the way... They're really good."

"Cool," I said. "See you in ten or fifteen... Is there still parking out back?"

"Yes—" She stopped talking when the drummer slapped out a few fills in the background. "*Oooooh, I'm so excited to see you Quinn, hurry up!*"

"Me too... There's a big hug comin' yer way. See ya soon."

"*Byyye,*" she lilted.

I glanced over at Rocky as I hung up.

"All right then, let's rock 'n' roll."

"Giver," he said, without taking his eyes off the magazine.

I started the car and checked the mirrors, lingering for a few seconds on the rear-view. It was a pathetic attempt at emotional blackmail. I wanted to guilt Soldier into making me look at least somewhat presentable. It didn't work. He was understandably defiant.

He'd seen too much.

I accepted defeat and merged into traffic with a tiny flame burning somewhere beneath my ragged sternum.

As our wheels rolled over cracked asphalt a hush fell upon us. I was indulging in the sweet memory of making love to Glenda. As for Rocky, Well I assumed that his X-rated comic book was engaging him sufficiently.

It was a dark and stormy night.

Really. It was.

I'd just popped the cork on a big bottle of cheap wine when the power flickered, then went out altogether after a huge bolt of lightning lit up the sky. We sat for a while in the dark with the windows open, listening to the rain wash the dirt from the city.

We were hanging out at her house, about to watch a movie. But it didn't really matter what we did. We just liked wasting time together. I found it easy to be around her, and she found it easy to be around me. It's because we didn't keep much from one another; we weren't afraid to speak our minds. We had no fears. We weren't possessing each other, so the afflictions that come with ownership had no meaning for us. There were no rules—no sacred vows. It was just easy and fun.

Sometimes it felt like we were brother and sister, because sex was never on the radar.

In fact, there *was* no radar because we had no need for early warnings.

On this particular night, however, that all changed.

The strange thing is, I'd always found her attractive, but never once did it occur to me to act upon it. She loved to laugh but knew when to be serious. She was rugged but nicely refined. And her skin was absolutely perfect. She had the kind of skin that genetically repelled the wear and tear of life. Not to mention her tits were immaculate and her ass was divine. I'd never actually seen them, but I could tell.

And that's how it started.

We were lying across from each other, her on the futon and me on the floor with a pillow. The rain was rushing along the gutters outside.

You could hear it draining down through the grates. It was dark except for the muted glow of a cloud covered moon in the window. I'm not even sure what made me say what I said. It could've been the wine. Or maybe the desire had simply taken root somewhere within my subconscious and on this night chose to unfold itself, blooming out the corners of my mouth like a crocus of curiosity.

Without design or motive, I asked her if she might show me her body. It was an informal request born out of a boyish thirst for visual proof, more than anything else.

It ended up being the only thing said between us until the flood of dammed up energy had subsided.

As her face reflected the half-light she answered me with dilated pupils, and a shrug that said, *why not?*

She eased her sweater up and over her head, drawing back a mane of electric hair from her face. Then she paused, as if to adjust the crown of succulence I'd just placed upon her. Our eyes locked. The hem of the mystical union had been reached. She removed her jeans and shimmied out of her underwear, silently announcing her full exposure. She was naked, and beautiful, and bold. Her nipples, sharpened. Her hips hosting a small black rose.

Her downward glance commanded my response. I stood up. I could feel the heaviness and pressure of my arousal, as I did. I unbuttoned my pants and slid them down. My desire leaned on the same silver dusted darkness that caressed her skin. We looked at each other as time retreated from the counterpoint passion we anticipated. She walked toward me and stopped. I could feel the heat of her blood radiating. She kissed my cheek, then slowly knelt down.

I don't think I'll ever be able to describe the pure sensation that her hot mouth inspired, but if there's a God it revels and dances with the same abandon.

As veins transformed into thick cables, she turned and beckoned with a backward glance. I obeyed. I approached and entered the ancient chamber with a slow push. A drawn out sigh escaped the gloss of her lips and we started in on our feast, moving like holy animals, swaying like supple trees, and doing our best to honor each other's bravery before the heavy web of reality fell back upon us.

I kissed her spine as she approached the inner summit. She took my hand in hers, and we ascended together.

Our Siamese spirit took flight on western winds as one last rumble of thunder acknowledged the embers of our fire.

Remembering my secret night with Glenda was a little dangerous because it ramped up the usual mix of emotions that accompanies reunions. I knew anything could happen, despite the fact that we both realized the habit forming fruit of paradise could never be plucked again without risking our platonic threshold.

Then again, the past is the past.

Rocky finished the last page of his comic book as we pulled down into the alleyway that led to the parking spots behind her place. He grumbled a little.

"Is this what they call an adult graphic novel? There's nothing *graphic* about it."

"What do you mean?"

"It's all so damn tame... I want something that assaults my indoctrinations. This just masquerades. Just like everything that tows the line to make money."

"Huh?"

"Everything that makes money becomes a whore, and whores don't have the time or the need for real art."

"Wow... How wonderfully cynical of you."

"You know it's true, Quinn... All the great artists were dirt fucking poor for most of their lives. Even if they did get lucky and come into money at some point, they still drew upon their years as poor wretches for inspiration. Money and art make very bad bedfellows."

"I'll agree with that... Vincent van Gogh never sold a painting in his lifetime. But I think you have to be careful not to romanticize the starving artist thing... Y'know?"

"I hate romance. That's exactly what I'm saying. These career types all end up courting the image, the money and the system. They depend on comfort and nice things. They ride the fucking gravy train and make filthy love to the trademark of their own empty projections. The only thing worse than them are the imitators. Imitators make me wanna hurl.

They're merchants of mindlessness. They're phony through and through and wouldn't know innovation if it bludgeoned them in their feather beds."

His scorn was airborne and condensing on the windows of the car.

"You're being a bit harsh... I don't think most of those people would call themselves artists. I think they realize they're more like entertainers."

"Well let them entertain then. But it's all bullshit distraction... Sugar coated poison. It's merely giving people what they want and that's the very last fucking thing anyone should ever do. No one does the Devil's work better than the manufacturers of insipid fucking crap."

I decided it'd be best just to let him rant for a bit. And rant he did. He was still spewing his rancor as we locked the car and made our way up to the back door.

There were two beat-up metal doors without handles facing us. In the dark it was hard to tell which one was the entrance, because the last time I was standing where I was standing was almost five years before.

Scrawled above the door on the left, in a chalked cursive, was the name: *Edvard Munchie House*. I remember Rocky staring up at it, trance like. I don't think he blinked for a solid minute. Not until we got closer and the sound of a muffled guitar chord and a few random bass notes broke the silence. I took my phone out of my pocket and texted Glenda to tell her we were outback.

We waited. Me, with my *'I'm with stupid'* t-shirt on, and Rocky with his bag of housewarming gifts. He was standing on my right, but then looked down at the arrow on my shirt and went to the other side.

"What... Are you purposely gonna avoid being on my right side now?"

He cracked a smile.

"I could only do that if you let me drive?"

His tone was hopeful, but I had to shut him down.

"Not gonna happen, Rocky... I'm the driver."

"All right... But you know what'd be fun?"

"What?" I said, keeping my eye on the door.

"It'd be fun to take pictures of you standing beside people wouldn't it? Does that phone have a camera?"

"Yep," I said, squinting at him with mild annoyance.

The thought of him snapping pictures of me for the remainder of the trip made me want to break out in hives.

"This'll be a trip to remember, Quinn... You're gonna want some pictures to look back on so let's start right now. Gimme your phone!"

I ignored him. Or at least I tried to ignore him, but he just kept standing there—his hand outstretched, his eyes as plaintive as a hungry dog. I kept up my refusal until something small, but important, changed within me. Maybe he was right? I thought. Maybe this *was* going to end up being a trip of a lifetime. It'd already seen its fair share of sterling moments: the bleeding woman with my favourite shirt wrapped around her head, buying her time; and the beefy country kid with his I'm-too-intense-for-this-town attitude, getting owned by Rocky's rage.

These two incidents already smelled of campfire mythology. They were already bronze sculptures in a private hall of fame and there were bound to be more where they came from. Rocky's abhorrence for everything trite was a sure-fire guarantee.

Alas, I succumbed.

I handed him the phone. He nodded and smiled then scooched up beside me.

"*Saay stu-pid!*" he said, with the obligatory rising cadence.

Then he pressed the button.

I'm looking at that picture right now. Our first picture. There we are shoulder to shoulder in the darkness of the parking lot. My shirt's calling some invisible person on my right, stupid. He and I are calling me stupid, and maybe you too, if you're seeing what I'm seeing. And then there's Soldier, my favorite car of all time, in the background.

The car with a heart of an ox. I swear it had a heart sometimes— the way it never let me down.

Oh, and Glenda's about to poke her head out.

Right as we both said, "stu-pid," Glenda poked her head out and beamed us a warm grin as the music splashed around her.

I stepped forward and gave her the hug I promised.

Hugging her was tantamount to smelling something good. She smelled of vanilla and sage with background notes of cinnamon; it was like a whiff of Christmas at a Sufi gathering. It wasn't contrived. There were essential oils and a flavoured cigarette involved, but the essence of her bouquet was natural. It could've easily been the raw by-product of her cellular activity.

She was wearing a black three-quarter trench coat with a thin navy blue wool sweater. Her hair was cropped and boyish and her grey eyes were charcoal lined and smoky. It was perfect 1960s Parisian parlance. On her feet were a pair of well-worn blue tennis shoes and her skinny legs were tightly bound in faded, ripped-at-one-knee jeans.

"You're looking as fine as ever," I said softly, as we embraced.

She pulled back and gave me the once over. Her eyes were surprised by what they read in between the new and strange lines of my face. She couldn't hide her suspicion, it leaked out around the hematite rims of her irises like hot lava.

"You look like you've been hittin' the highways a little hard, Quinn..." she said, as she singed me with a laser beam of concern and compassion. "And who's this?" she asked, looking back to Rocky.

I waited for him to say something, but he stayed silent. He was arranging the items he bought. Then he looked up, and with a courteous purse of his lips, a ceremonial flourish of his left hand, and a slight bow of his head, handed her the bag.

"My name is Carl, but *please...* call me Rocky. And here are some housewarming presents we've picked up for you."

Glenda, of course, appreciated his dramatic embellishments.

"Pleased to meet you and thank you both for your chivalry," she said, with an elegant English accent and a quick curtsy.

She extended a swan-necked hand and ever so gracefully received her gifts. A formal grin floated across her face as she took stock of her winnings.

"I see you've gone out of your way to please a lady... Dare I say you've outdone yourselves...? Thank you so very kindly and welcome to the Munch... Please, do come in."

She gestured for us to follow. Rocky shot me a contented smirk as we trailed behind her.

The band was set up in the far corner of the room. The lights were dimmed and a few people were already hanging out—smoking and sipping on cans of beer. Blunt Fiction's banner was hung on the wall behind the drum kit.

"Make yourselves at home... The middle room along the back wall is free if you wanna chill for a bit, Rocky... And there's beers in the fridge over behind the bar. Help yourself, but don't get hammered if ya can't hold your liquor."

She shot Rocky a direct look. She must've sensed the roiling crosscurrents just beyond the surface of his skin.

"If you wanna come with me, Quinn... I wouldn't mind catching up with you for a bit."

Her smile was tight lipped. I knew she wanted to get to the bottom of things.

As Rocky made his way to the fridge, I went to face the music.

Remember that unglued sole on my shoe I told you about? Well, it came back to haunt me as we walked through the shadows along the back wall toward her bedroom. The flapping sound it made bounced off the bricks and mocked my every step.

"That shoe says it all," she said, as we paused at her door for her to get out the keys.

I took a deep embarrassed breath.

Inside, she flicked on her light and went over and sat on her bed, placing her bag of gifts down as she did.

"Have a seat."

She pointed at the green Edwardian chair in the corner. It was stiff and perfectly suited for my imminent interrogation.

"I like your short hair... Suits you." I avoided eye contact after saying that by looking at her posters. Most of them were for past shows at the Munch.

"Thanks, I needed a change." She let that statement hang in the air between us, then took off her trench coat and started in on me. "Toronto's a great place... It's full of the best and worst humanity has to offer, and as you know, I see a lot of people come through these doors... *A lot* of people, Quinn... They either sparkle with life, or they're in the process of imploding... The imploders are like black holes of misery that come in here to either forget about that misery for a little while or spread it around like some communicable disease."

She stopped to light a cigarette. She offered me one and I took it. It was vanilla flavoured.

"I've seen my share of junkies, and you look just like all of them right now, sitting over there with your shame face on, probably neck deep in denial... You've changed quite a bit since the last time you were here... You're imploding."

She exhaled while burning holes into me with her eyes.

"I'm not in denial," I muttered.

"Oh *really*? *Really*? Wake up! Wake up before you wake up on the floor of a prison shower with a bar of soap clutched in your hand."

"Very funny," I chuckled.

Her tough love didn't budge an inch as she continued corralling me.

"I've never met an addict that wasn't in denial, so don't even try and fuck with me right now!"

She raised her voice slightly and I wanted to crawl inside myself, or at least turn off the light so I wasn't so exposed. I puffed on the smoke distractedly. My hands shook.

"Let me see your arms..."

That was going too far, I felt. I thought she knew me better than that.

"Are you *serious*?"

"Dead fucking serious! Now *show* me your arms... You look that bad."

"I don't poke shit... Okay! I pop pills, that's it."

I hated the sound of my own voice. It sounded whiny and petulant. I wanted to cut out my own throat. She got up, walked over, grabbed my left arm and held it up to the light then did the same to my right.

"You know how many users start off *just popping pills*? All of them! How could you let yourself get this way, Quinn?" Her voice trembled a bit. I dropped my head down, not wanting to witness her emotion. "What are you taking?"

There was no use in trying to hide anything. I knew I was an open book before her big city eyes.

"Morphine... And... And sometimes a bit of blow to perk me up when I get groggy behind the wheel."

"*Great*... You're a cokehead too." She paused, regaining her steeliness. "Tell me something... How does cab driving pay for all this?"

"I work long hours."

"You're *fucking* lying to me... I can see it in your face... Besides, cabbies in Grey Grove don't make that kinda cash."

I sat back up in the chair and swallowed the last of my pathetic pride.

"Okay, okay," I pleaded. "I do runs for certain people and they— Well, they tip me for it."

"You do *WHAT*? *Oh my god QUINN*! You're trafficking dope?"

She got up and started pacing the length of the room. I traced fractures in the concrete floor with my worthless eyes.

"Do you know what they'll do to a pretty boy like you in federal? Holy shit you're *stupid*!! That shirt you're wearing should have an arrow pointing up!"

I wanted to laugh at that, but something weird happened. I felt a hot and cold whirlpool of neglect become dislodged from my solar plexus and rise up into my throat. I saw my mom's face and my dad's face and my sister's face and my best friends face from grade seven and then I looked up into Glenda's face. Her cheeks were lined with tears. That's when I broke. The dam that'd been reinforced by the dulling effects of opiates for the last two years, burst open in one violent gush of backed up anxiety and ignored emotion.

I got dizzy with the sudden onslaught and collapsed. I actually fainted. It was the first time I'd ever done that.

I was a straw man with his stuffing torn out.

Maybe it was because it'd been over 18 hours since I'd slept, and the last thing I ate was a chocolate bar for breakfast, but somehow I slid off the chair and onto the cold floor, dropping the cigarette as I hit. It must've rolled over by her feet, because the sight of her stepping on it was what I woke up to.

The light was harsh in my eyes. I covered my face.

"I so wanna put the boots to you right now, but I can't... I'd probably break you, you're so frail looking."

She knelt down beside me and ran her hand through my hair.

"I have a pair of shoes for you... I think they'll fit... Someone went home barefoot one night and never came to get them." She helped me up and walked me over to her bed. Then she went to her closet, pulled out a pair of red high-top Converse, came back over and knelt down in front of me. "I'm here for you, Quinn... But I can't help you if you won't help yourself... Promise me you'll start respecting yourself again... Promise me you'll help yourself," she said, while pulling off my old shoes and letting them drop to the floor.

"I promise," I said, through bleary eyes.

"Good... Now you need to tell me how deep you're into all this."

She put the right shoe on me first and laced it up.

"I owe two thousand bucks to a dealer in Grey Grove... It's why I took this Wichita job... I wouldn't normally risk such a long ride because my car isn't tip top... Fuck, I don't even know if I'll make it there and back... But I have to... I have no other options."

She put the left shoe on and laced it up.

"You'll make it, Quinn... I know you will... But you need to make some serious changes in your life when you get back... You hear me?!"

I just nodded my head as I looked down at my new shoes. I smiled. I felt better somehow. She made me feel better. I looked up and into her eyes.

"I'll do it for me... And these shoes will be my reminder."

"Good... Now come here and give me a hug, *stupid*."

I stood up and put my arms around her.

I looked down at the shoes.

They were already testing me.

We hugged, then she pulled back and slapped my face.

"*Stupid!*" she repeated.

I felt my cheek go hot and red.

"If you're hard wired you know you're gonna have to wean down slow, right? Don't set yourself up for failure."

She grabbed my old shoes off the floor as she said that.

"I can't even think about cleaning up until I get back to Grey Grove and pay off my debt, and make a few extra bucks to live on while I'm sick... I definitely won't be working for the two weeks it takes to clear it."

"Are you sure that's the best place?" she said, as she walked over to the corner of her room and held the shoes over a small trash can.

"No... Not sure at all... Too many perks for that one last dope run... Too many underworld connections all eager for my service... Too many people with my phone number and address."

She nodded at me, then let the shoes drop from shoulder height. A metallic thud reverberated around the room.

"Look... Why don't you come up here and stay with me after you do what you need to do back in Grey?"

"You mean you'll help me through?"

"Yes... I've done it before with other friends... I know what to expect."

As I stood there thinking about her proposal a knock came on her door.

"*Who is it?*" she called out.

"It's Rocky... Quinn needs to come and see this... The eleven o'clock news is about to show that accident we were at," he said, in a weak voice.

Glenda turned and looked at me.

"There was an accident on the 401 on the way up... We stopped and I... Well I got out and helped the best I could."

She walked over to the door and opened it. Rocky was standing right there, supporting himself on the frame. His face was pale.

"Jesus... You look *horrible,*" I blurted.

"It's another one of my goddamn headaches... Musta been the beer I had... I shouldn't dr—"

He stopped in mid-sentence and hunched over with his head in his hands. I went over to him.

"Glenda, can he lie down on your bed?"

"I was just on the couch in next room... The TV's there."

We each took one of his arms and helped him back.

Inside, the TV was blaring and all the lights were off. We laid him down and got him some water.

Then we settled in to watch the news coverage.

Newscaster:

We're getting reports of a multiple car accident in the westbound lane of the 401 underneath the Cranston train overpass. It happened during the heavy rainfall earlier this evening. Poor visibility is said to be a contributing factor. Two serious injuries are listed... Now this is where it gets interesting folks. A woman who's recovering in the hospital from a severe head injury, has told reporters she owes her life to another driver who tended to her by removing his shirt and using it as a tourniquet, which stopped the bleeding until the paramedics arrived... Talk about giving someone the shirt off your back! And that's not all!! Apparently this same driver went on to light road flares, alerting oncoming vehicles to the pile up... The woman has issued a statement regarding her mysterious rescuer... She says, "If you're out there listening I want to thank you for saving my life. I can go home to my children because of you. You're my hero... And I'm sorry for ruining your shirt."

The Newscaster laughed at that last bit, then made a crass joke about getting stains out of shirts, before moving on to other stories.

I got up from the couch and turned the TV down. I wasn't feeling heroic in the slightest.

"That was too close for comfort... It's *channel five*... If she hadda mentioned I was a taxi driver, or if one of the bystanders saw the top sign on the car, who knows what would've happened... We don't need that kinda publicity right now," I said, looking at Rocky.

Rocky nodded, then widened his eyes and tilted his head toward Glenda—warning me about giving away too much information. Glenda looked confused. I thought for sure she was about to ask me what I was getting at.

Nervousness rattled through my body as she opened her mouth.

"What are you talking about?! You *saved* someone's life, Quinn... Take a second and pat yourself on the back would ya?"

She was seeing me through different eyes—much less scornful ones than those she wielded in her bedroom.

But I didn't feel worthy of any praise so I downplayed everything.

"There's a lot of people out there who'll probably never know they've saved a life... I don't mean to get all melodramatic here, but if Rocky hadn't of hopped in my cab today I don't know what would've happened.. This morning I was convinced that driving to the old quarry outside Grey Grove and slitting my wrists with this, was the answer..." I pulled my straight razor out of my pocket and held it up. Then I turned and looked at Glenda. "And you... If you're willing to help me avert this fucking disaster..." I looked down at myself. "Then you'll have saved my life as well..." I felt like I was onto something. "When you think about it not many of us get noticed for our everyday rescue efforts... It really is the small things, y'know... It's the little daily sacrifices people do out of love and respect that in the end add up to be much more profound than all the over the top, Johnny-on-the-spot shit that hogs the limelight in our society."

Rocky had rolled over while I was talking so that he was facing me.

"Very nice, Quinn... That's a Nobel Prize-winning speech if I've ever heard one... I knew I picked the right man for the job... By the way, *nice shoes!*"

"I know, eh?"

I did a little two-step dance and grinned.

"Ray likes 'em," he said, holding up his scarecrow.

I looked over at Glenda. She was giving Rocky the raised eyebrow of dubiety.

"Thanks, *Ray*," I chortled.

Glenda got up off the couch and came over to stand beside me.

"You can stay here 'til you feel better, Rocky... If you need anything just let me know."

"What I need right now is a picture of you two."

He pulled out the phone and held it up. Glenda fixed her hair and put her arm around me.

"*Saay stu-pid!*"

We did as we were told and he snapped the second picture of the Wichita trip.

There she is in all her glorious radiance—her intelligence beaming forth like a lodestar. Just minutes prior, her bright eyes had diagnosed my disease and pulled from me a promise to get clean. It was to be the promise that eventually saved me.

I think I'll take a break from writing and give her a call.

Stay with me. We're usually pretty brief when we talk on the phone.

She's about to put on a production of *Streetcar Named Desire*. She'll rock that one.

Now back to the story.

Glenda and I left Rocky in a shaft of blue TV light and closed the door behind us. As we walked along the back wall the band struck up on the other side of the velvet curtain. They were indeed loud, but it was a thick pulsating loudness. The kind that feels good against flesh and bone.

She leaned in. "I need your help for a bit," she shouted.

"For what?"

"I'm doing another Shakespeare play here in a few days."

"Which one?"

"*Antony and Cleopatra*... I need you to be Antony in the last scene of act four so I can get my lines down."

We came to her door, then slipped inside her room and shut the music out.

"Funny," I said. "I did a bit of acting earlier at a coin laundry."

"Really?"

"Remember when you taught me how to do a Mississippi accent? Well, you were on my mind, and I was about to ask the attendant for change, so I took the opportunity in your honour," I said.

She laughed.

"If'n thayre's one gal that can teach ya'll 'bout Mississippi hayre in Teronnah, it's maay," she drawled.

"Ha-ha... Someday me and you gotta go down there and paddle through the swamps in that cedar canoe you told me about... You remember the pact we made?"

"How could I forget...? It was the night we fucked each other's brains out."

There was a brief silence as we remembered.

"I've always said I'd go back to Oxford... Ten years was long enough for it to get into my blood, and I know you wanna see Faulkner's place..."

"Totally wanna see it... I wanna see the room where he cooked up all those hard-luck characters."

"Speaking of hard-luck characters..." She dug through a drawer and plucked out an orange covered copy of *Antony and Cleopatra* and tossed it to me. "Page 185," she said.

I flipped through the book as Blunt Fiction ripped it up out in the main room. The walls throbbed as the cheering crowd inspired the singer to scream out more of his beautiful angst.

"I call them the Munchies."

"Who?" I asked.

"The kids that come here for the bands and the party... They're all about ten years younger than us... They smoke weed like crazy, and they're always askin' me if I have anything to munch on... Sometimes you can hardly see through the haze..." She smiled. "You definitely can't be out there for very long without catchin' a bit of a buzz."

"Nothing wrong with weed," I said.

"Maybe I'll christen that hookah you guys bought me."

"I'm down with that."

THIRD INTERMISSION

Moving to a different seat, I see. How good of you to give those ravenous lovers their privacy. There happens to be a seat right next to me, if you're so inclined. We could discuss this film together? Meet me at the bar and I'll get you a drink.

CHAPTER 8

Where the driver and his passenger have a run-in with an unexpected visitor. After taking care of business they then say goodbye to Toronto and head for the border.

I TURNED TO PAGE 185 and scanned Antony's lines. Glenda went to her bureau, opened it up, reached in, and pulled out a bottle of red wine.

"This is a prop," she said, with a mischievous grin. "Find line 42."

I found the part she was referring to.

"I am dying, Egypt, dying. Give me some wine, and let me speak a little."

I did my emotive best. Glenda looked impressed as she poured a glass of her favourite cheap Chilean and handed it to me.

"Nice projection and diction, Quinn... Keep that up," she said, as she checked herself in the mirror and fixed her eyeliner to make it more Pharaonic.

She took a gulp straight from the bottle and we got started.

"O sun, burn the great sphere thou mov'st in, darkling stand the varying shore o' the world. O Antony, Antony! Help, Charmian, help, Iras, help: Help, friends below, let's draw him hither."

She was a picture of feline grace. Her hand gestures, perfectly timed. Her dramatic flair, naturally endowed. I rose to the occasion as best I could.

"Not Caesar's valour hath o'erthrown Antony, but Antony hath triumph'd on itself," I answered.

She came up closer to me, brandishing the bottle like a pirate.

"So it should be, that none but Antony should conquer Antony, but woe 'tis so!"

She glanced at my shoes and flashed a Mona Lisa smile. I got the feeling ulterior motives were at work. It was as if she'd purposely chosen this section of the play.

"I am dying, Egypt, dying; only I here importune death awhile, until of many thousand kisses, the poor last I lay upon thy lips."

My enunciation was spot on. I was feeling it. I was in the zone. I took a healthy drink and followed along in the book as she laid herself down on the bed.

"I dare not, dear, dear my lord, pardon: I dare not, lest I be taken: not the imperious show of the full-fortun'd Caesar ever shall be brooch'd with me, if knife, drugs, serpents, have edge, sting, or operation. I am safe: Your wife Octavia, with her modest eyes, and still conclusion, shall acquire no honour demurring upon me: but come, come, Antony, help me, my women, we must draw thee up: Assist, good friends."

She motioned for me to lay down beside her as I finished my glass.

"O quick, or I am gone," I said, grimacing with the onset of the inevitable.

"Here's sport indeed! How heavy weighs my lord! Our strength is all gone into heaviness that makes the weight. Had I great Juno's power, the strong-wing'd Mercury should fetch thee up, and set thee by Jove's side. Yet come, come, come. And welcome, welcome! Die when thou hast liv'd, quicken with kissing: had my lips that power, thus would I wear them out."

She leaned in slowly and kissed me. I could taste the grapes on her bottom lip. A spark of passion illuminated some forbidden room deep within the cage of my chest.

"I am dying, Egypt, dying. Give me some wine, and let me speak a little."

She brought the bottle up and let some wine trickle into my mouth, then took it away abruptly.

"No, let me speak, and let me rail so high, that the false housewife Fortune break her wheel, provok'd by my offence."

"One word, sweet queen: Of Caesar seek your honour, with your safety. O!" I said, as I laid the back of my wrist upon my forehead.

"They do not go together," she said, lowering her head with the weight of reality.

"Gentle, hear me, None about Caesar trust but Proculeius."

"My resolution, and my hands, I'll trust, none about Caesar," she vowed, regaining some fervor.

I read ahead a bit and saw that Antony was about to die so I weakened my voice.

"The miserable change now at my end lament nor sorrow at: but please your thoughts in feeding them with those my former fortunes wherein I liv'd: the greatest prince o' the world, the noblest; and do now not basely die, not cowardly put off my helmet to my countrymen: a Roman, by a Roman valiantly vanquish'd." I let my head fall to the side with death's imminence. I motioned for her to draw in closer so I could whisper in her ear. "Now my spirit is going, I can no more."

I went limp as I shed my mortal coil. She closed my unseeing eyes with her soft hand.

"Noblest of men, woo't die? Hast thou no care of me, shall I abide in this dull world, which in thy absence is no better than a sty?" I peered out from under my closed eyelids and saw her conjure up a single tear, to let it fall down her cheek. "O, see, my women: the crown o' the earth doth melt. My lord? O, wither'd is the garland of war, the soldier's pole is fall'n: young boys and girls are level now with men: the odds is gone, and there is nothing left remarkable beneath the visiting moon."

She took her cue and fainted dramatically on top of my chest. We both lay there, feeling the rise and fall of each other's breath. I moved my hand over and ran it through her hair. She looked up with the eyes of an African queen.

We kissed again. We kissed passionately and deeply. Our blood coursed toward a final reward.

We made love once more.

There were still no rules, after all.

I know I said it could never happen again.

But never say never.

For starters, it's foolish to think that passion can be tethered. Whoever came up with the expression, unbridled lust, was obviously presuming the existence of bridled lust. I would like to say that if you find yourself able to rein in your passion, then it wasn't real passion to begin with. If you find yourself able to bridle your lust, then it wasn't real lust to begin with. If you find yourself in a laboratory coldly embracing the predictable product of a tried and true formula, then it's time to shake off that lab coat and get outside. It's time to stare into the sun, the moon, and the stars and go barefoot. It's time to dig your toes into the primeval dust and mud of death and rebirth, and wait patiently for the musk of conception.

There's no safe sex when it comes to inspiration, and oftentimes it's not even consensual.

The muse has taken me by force more than once.

I was minding my own business and the last thing on my mind was creation, but because I was out strolling under a Scorpio moon and a twinkling sea of stars, I was taken. The hypnotic rhythms of nature took me. I got caught up in the breezy sway of a silver birch. I got mesmerized by the lilting call of a red winged blackbird. I got tickled by the swirling eddies of a babbling brook. I fell in love with the dark eyes of a deer. I watched those little specks of orgone energy dance on the eastern wind. I saw the fractals in the edges of the cumulus clouds. I heard the heavy breath of midsummer as it exhaled into the spiral ears of twilight. I held the gaze of a timber wolf from across a secret creek. I laid myself down in a field of clover and followed the arc of a damselfly. I jumped up into orbit and saw dawn chase dusk around the blue girth of earth. I baptized myself in brackish water. I counted the white tipped waves of a great lake as it licked the shoreline of enchantment. I splashed in a puddle and grew young. I stood on a granite batholith and howled at the vastness of a dozen dimensions as tears stained an ancient face with silent understanding.

And then I was breached.

My muse found me vulnerable and fertile and pounced upon my flesh, working its way into my soul like a desert weed, until a visceral tornado whipped up the quicksilver of my sentience. The reaping had begun. I bore an incorrigible offspring. I carried to term an immortal orgasm. Then I rested. And of course I waited.

I waited for it to happen all over again.

I couldn't stay away from nature.

As we stretched out our satiated bodies, a song played in my head. It wasn't a Blunt Fiction song. It was a popular song. The lyrics got louder and louder until they drowned out the shouts of the sweat-dripping girls in the next room.

I've never been a big Steve Miller fan; not to say that I wasn't, at one time, like every other male teenager who discovered *The Space Cowboy* in their dad's record collection, immediately recognized his good-time potential, and then shrewdly experimented with that potential at endless drunken house parties beset by uninhibited females. But I, personally, never wore out any of his records. I simply didn't have to. His universal appeal made sure he was permanently lurking somewhere on the airwaves. It might've been from a car going by with the windows down and the volume cranked up. Or maybe it was me in a friend's car trying to dial in a radio station from the passenger's seat and having no luck because every channel seemed to be just starting or finishing a song from his nefariously contagious *Greatest Hits* album. The whole thing verged on creepy.

That's why when the lyrics came into my head as loud and clear as they did:

See Tom take the money and run, oooh lord. See Tom take the money and run.

I immediately got a strange feeling, for everyone knows these aren't the real lyrics.

I was being serenaded by Frank.

I got up off the bed and walked the length of Glenda's room so that I passed her full length mirror as I went. I didn't see anything telling on the first pass, but on the way back there he was. It was the usual fleeting glimpse of a shadowy figure billowing around the edges a little, like the blotted offspring of a paused calligraphy pen on heavy weight paper. Or was it a Rorschach? Anyway, it was him—Frank. He was back, and that meant one thing and one thing only. There was trouble brewing. I quickly tried deciphering his lyrics in my head. I sang them over and over. It obviously had something to do with money—stolen money. I checked my back pocket and my wad of hundreds was still there. I pulled them out to count them, just to make sure.

"Nice stack," Glenda said from the bed, her head propped up on a pillow.

I looked up at her and grinned as I counted the last bill. My money was all there.

"He paid in advance," I said, as I realized it wasn't my money Frank was singing about.

That left Glenda and Rocky.

"Do you have any cash lying around this place that might be vulnerable to an opportunist?"

"Haha... I wish, Quinn... I scrape by here... The rent isn't cheap."

"Then... Do you happen to know a guy named Tom?"

She looked up and away like she was searching her memory. Her eyes came back down and rested on the money in my hand.

"There is one dude... Haven't seen him in a while, but his name is Tom... He's a crackhead... I banned him from The Munch but he's been caught hanging around outside every now and then... Why do you ask?"

"What does he do outside exactly?"

My heart rate accelerated as she sat up on the bed with an uh-oh look on her face.

"He's been caught trying to break into cars parked out back..."

"Oh fuck!" I shouted.

"Wait a minute? How'd you know about this guy?"

"I'll tell you later... Is there a window that looks out to the back?"

"Yeah... Behind the painting over there," she said, pointing to a large framed Klimt print.

The print was pretty high up so I looked around for something to stand on. The trash can was the closest thing. I dumped my old shoes back out onto the floor and turned it over. I got up on top of it, gently removed the painting from its hooks, and with my eyes just above the ledge, peered out into the parking lot. I didn't see anyone right away, but I saw Soldier parked where I parked him, near the back corner. Looking at him brought everything violently into focus. I suddenly remembered Rocky stashing his satchel in the trunk, for safe keeping. In one panic-soaked split second I realized I'd forgotten to take the key out—the trunk key that stayed in the hole for the convenience of my customers... and myself.

As I stood on the trash can staring out into the gloom of imminently unfortunate events, my eye was drawn over to the far left. There was someone coming up the alley way. My veins filled with dread. He was about ten feet from Soldier when his head jerked around like he'd just seen a glinting vial of crack.

He headed straight for Soldier.

"Fuck me! Does Tom usually wear a bandana?"

"Yep... Is he out there? I'll go boot his ass out!"

"No, no... It's too late for that... By the time you get out there he'll have what he wants and he'll run... We'll go 'round the front and sneak up on him in the alley."

"You better hurry... Crackheads can sprint when they need to," she warned.

I hopped off the trash can, dropped the Klimt onto her bed and ran to get Rocky.

I burst into the room where Rocky was lying down. Papa Smurf was on the TV chastising Brainy Smurf about something.

"*Get up!* Frank just called on me..."

"Wha—Frank? What'd he say?"

"*Just get the fuck up*... Did you take the key out of the trunk when you put your satchel in there?"

He looked confused. I felt like slapping him even though it was my fault.

"What key?"

"*Exactly*... Now let's go! Your stolen money is about to get stolen again."

He jumped up like a jack rabbit as his face went from dazed to maniacal with frightening ease. I almost had to look away. It was like seeing the male version of Medusa take off his sunglasses.

"Someone's about to get *hurt!*" he said, brushing by me.

He turned around when he got to the door. "Gimme that straight razor," he demanded, as his eyes singed my pocket.

"Cool your jets. We're not killing anyone here, Rocky."

"I know *that,* now hand it over."

He stood there with dancing fingers on an upturned palm. I gave it to him. There was no time to argue.

"Glenda said the guy's a crackhead so don't underestimate him and don't fucking cut him either... That thing'll take his head right off if yer not careful."

He smiled at my warning. I didn't much like the way his teeth suddenly looked carnivorous in the darkness.

"We need to go out the front and sneak up on him from the end of the alley way," I said.

We bolted down behind the curtain to the far end, then ran out in front of the band between their monitors and the wall of dancers. We bumped our way through the crowd until we found the front door and exploded out onto the street. Outside I stopped for a second, trying to get my bearings. The Munch was pretty much dead center on the block.

"You go that way and I'll go this way... We'll squeeze him in from both ends."

"You ever been deer hunting, Quinn?"

"No!!! Fuck, we don't have time for this."

"Shut up for a second would ya! We'll do a deer drive on him. You push him toward me from your end and I'll ambush him when he gets to me, okay?!"

"Okay, okay... Let's fucking do this!!"

Off we charged in our opposite directions. I looked back when I was almost to my corner and saw Rocky already rounding his. He was fast. Around the other side I saw there was another 25 or 30 feet before the entrance. When I got to it I was completely winded and had to stifle my breath as I peeked around the edge of the bricks. Tom hadn't moved much from where I saw him before. I could see his silhouette. He had his back to the alley wall, just out of sight of Glenda's back window. The satchel was in his hands and he was wasting no time rifling through it. My adrenaline surged once more as I crouched down and moved as quietly as I could through the shadows. I couldn't see Rocky. He must've already found his hiding spot.

On I went with white knuckled fists, breathing as deeply and evenly as possible. Tom was prey in my cross-hairs. I could only hope that Rocky had the presence of mind not to slit his throat.

There was no way I was going to get much closer than I was. I could see the fear-carved hollows of his cheeks in the murky electrical light that splashed around the corner from the Munch. I could see the folds of his baggy sport clothes as they feigned casualness and obscured crack addict geometry.

I'm not sure why it is, but low end dope dealers like high end tracksuits. I call it the tweaker's tuxedo. It usually consists of a terry cloth tracksuit topped off by a fitted ball cap over a bandana. Tom's bandana was a nice touch considering it was black and white, and matched the one Rocky wrapped his cash in. It was almost as if he'd gone to the trouble.

But back to the tweaker's tuxedo.

Why?

Is it because the chronically incarcerated are simply dressing appropriately for the fight or flight situations they continuously find themselves in?

If I was constantly evading or chasing things, I'd probably dress the same way. I'd need loose-fitting apparel for evading rival dope dealers after inadvertently wandering onto piss-marked turf.

I'd need loose-fitting apparel for chasing down the money owed to me by a slippery clientele.

I'd need loose-fitting apparel for evading the cops, parole officers and bounty hunters.

I'd need loose-fitting apparel to hide the contraband.

Without loose-fitting apparel, I most definitely wouldn't have the game to *run* my business.

Running.

Always running.

Running from steel pipes, from knives, from fists, from guns, from baseball bats.

Running from surveillance cameras that never quite leave the periphery of the scene.

Running from burned friends and family.

Running for the sake of running just to make sure the running skills are up and running.

Running from nothing, from no one, from an image, from a blue scarecrow stuffed with prohibition.

Running, running, running, running.

So you see, one needs to be properly dressed for all this running. One needs loose-fitting apparel. One needs to be poised for the pop of the starting pistol. And one must never lose sight of the other runners who are all running, running, running too.

Running through endless bitter alkaloid nights.

Running fast enough to scuttle across the quicksand like a cockroach.

Running into walls.

Running into me and Rocky and my grandfather's straight razor in an alley way.

I got as close to Tom as I could. I could smell his cologne. I stood up straight and puffed myself out a little. He was oblivious to my presence—hypnotized as he was by the crisp stack of bills he was counting out while imagining all the crack and all the crack whores he was sure to make short work of.

I watched him salivate over the money for a while. It made me want to knock him out. I wanted to hit him so hard he'd wake up as a different person. Before I hit him I'd tell him so: "This is gonna hurt you more than it hurts me, but trust me, you'll wake up feeling much better."

Money.

I'm tempted to leave it at that; one word on its own line. So you can fill in all the sordid details with your own personal wealth of knowledge. But I can't. It's just too juicy. Too ripe. Too tempting.

So here it goes.

Here's my take on money:

Tom loves money because money buys him stuff. Money makes him a God for a day or an hour or a half hour or even just for fifteen fucking fleeting minutes. Money gets him respect. Tom could go just about anywhere in Toronto with that heavy stack of cash and get respect. Tom the lowdown, fall down, fuck you for a buck, twist the knife in your back, only cares about the next hit, looks fetching in a track suit, smells like trendy cologne, piece of nasty work—Tom.

Tom could shuffle step his way into any establishment in any city on the planet, fanning himself with a magnificent stack and be treated like a goddamn king. First he'd stuff a few pungent bills in the shirt pockets of bouncers to grease up their furrowed brows and folded forearms. Then he'd saunter up to the bartender, order a bottle of Grey Goose and tip with a 'you're-mine-for-the-rest-of-the-night' collection of hundreds. *Then*—then he'd spin around on his chair, eye up a whore discreetly working the room and give her the come-hither stare. She'd prance her hard expensive ass on over and be his bitch for the rest of the night.

Or until his cash ran out.

So now he's got the bouncers, the bartender, and the resident escort of the most upscale joint in town in his pocket. But in order to make the night sizzle and glimmer, he needs to dial up one of his dealers (the one he doesn't owe money to) and set up a sly rendezvous outside the bar. He'll go large and order up an ounce of uncut, then sit there waiting—his palms slowly getting moist, his mouth watering, his pupils dilating, his chest fluttering with the anticipation of a good coke binge. And I say coke because crack is just too socially awkward. His newly purchased and highly attentive female companion will gladly nose dive all night long, but if he were to suggest smoking crack she'd get very offended indeed.

She's an expensive contortionist, after all.

Tom and his money make Tom *the man* of the hour. He may be your average low life, but like any superhero, once he pulls his wad out of his designer track suit he morphs into something altogether different. And the most interesting part of the transformation is how smooth it is. He knows how to talk the talk and walk the walk of a big spender. How does he know this? I'm not too sure, but I think it comes from good study skills. I think he did his homework by watching the guys he admires—the big fish, the higher ups on the crime pole, the heavy cats that crush little dudes like him under the heels of their luxury sneakers, if he ever seriously fucks up.

Tom knows how to work it.

He knows how to pretend.

He knows how to wield the dark magic of a good swindle.

Poor Tom. He was rich for about five whole minutes. He was fabulously rich until I shattered his dreams with a question.

"Hey buddy, can ya spare some cash?" I asked him.

I made my voice as sincere as I possibly could. He looked up at me with the craziest, most absolutely insane, most completely unhinged eyes I've ever seen.

To this day they haunt me.

If I were to compare Tom to an animal, it would have to be a rat. As cliché as it sounds, the rat and Tom were quite close. This comparison is innately unfair to the rat, so let me make amends by saying he reminded me of the thuggish vermin Disney often portrays as the villain.

I was the cartoon country mouse.

After looking up at me with his stunned expression, he let his jaw drop. I still wanted to punch that jaw as I responded with a toothy smile. He put his hand up at his forehead to shade his eyes from the glare of the streetlight down at my end of the alley, and I immediately realized I must've been completely silhouetted. I decided to use it to my advantage.

"I'm here to collect on the money you owe, Tom," I said.

He'll never know how I knew his name. Never. It totally freaked him out. He stuffed the money back in the satchel and took off in Rocky's direction. I watched him run and as I did, he morphed from a rat into a botfly, headed directly for a spider's web.

As he disappeared into the darkness of Rocky's lair, I heard him trip and fall. He hit pretty hard, because the sound of his face-plant skidding along the gravel strewn asphalt lasted for a couple seconds.

When it stopped, I heard him moan. Then I heard Rocky's voice. It wasn't the happy-go-lucky Rocky. It was a new menacing Rocky I hadn't yet been introduced to.

"Have a nice dive there, crackerjack? HUH?! How ya feelin' now, eh? *Where's yer mommy when ya need her.*"

I jogged up closer to where they were and stood back a bit, making sure things didn't get out of control. Tom was face down, still clutching the satchel and Rocky was holding him there with one knee dug into his back. The straight razor was doing its own work, glinting amongst the oblique beams of light in front of Tom's sweaty face.

"Tommy, Tommy, Tommy... You're pretty well dressed for a waste of skin aren't ya?"

"I'm bleeding man... My face is all cut up."

Rocky turned his head back toward me.

"You hear that? Tommy says he's hurt... Maybe we should take him to the hospital?"

"Yeah, maybe we should call him a blue and white taxi to take him there... Y'know the ones with the lights on top..." I said, playing along.

Rocky grinned like an evil clown at my suggestion, then turned his attention back.

"Gimme the fucking bag you worthless sack of shit!" he snarled, moving the blade in closer to Tom's eye.

Tom let go of the satchel. Rocky picked it up and tossed it back to me.

"Make sure it's all there," he ordered.

I took out the cash and did my best to count it in the darkness.

"Get up, you fucking stool pigeon, before I surgically remove your eyelids."

I could almost see the vicious ripples of hatred emanating from Rocky as he grabbed Tom by the hair and forced him up to his knees, then up to his feet, then turned him around so he was facing me. The light hit him, showcasing a nasty scrape on his left cheek. There were still bits of gravel lodged within its contours.

"*You*, my friend, are gonna take a little ride with us."

He pushed Tom toward me with the razor still in his face for encouragement. I wasn't sure what the plan was at this point.

"Tommy's gonna come with us to Chinatown... He's gonna be a good little boy and buy some fucking wonton soup for himself... Aren't ya Thomas?"

He yelled that directly into his ear. Tom looked like he was gonna shit himself.

I remembered that Chinatown was part of the plan, so we could spend some of the stolen bills in the obvious spot and thereby make the Asian ruse all the more convincing.

"Wh—why Chinatown?" Tom whimpered.

"SHUT THE FUCK UP... ONE MORE WORD AND I'LL GIVE YOU A LITTLE BACKSEAT PLASTIC SURGERY."

Rocky pushed Tom all the way to the car, then got into the backseat with him, still holding the blade up to his face. I took my cue and hopped in the driver's seat, adjusting the rear-view so I could keep an eye on things. I finished counting the cash and put the satchel down on the passenger's side.

"The money's all here," I confirmed.

"Good... Let's take a drive, shall we."

I threw the car into reverse and backed out. My hands trembled on the wheel. I knew that anything could happen at this point.

Anything.

I pulled out and down the alley, then turned west onto Esplanade and headed straight for Yonge street. The tension inside the car was building like a jack-in-the-box. I looked up into the rear-view and saw Tom leaning back against the seat as far as he could—his chin tucked into his neck and his eyes shifting aimlessly from side to side as Rocky glared at him over top the razor. I reached back with my left hand and locked the rear door, just in case.

"You picked the wrong guy to steal from, Tom, and that's all there is to it... You tried to jeopardize my trip..." Rocky's voice was getting progressively louder. "You don't *know* what this trip *means* to me do you?" Tom shook his head. "Well what if I told you this was my ride into the sunset... What if, what if this trip was my last, and because of that important fact I felt like I had *NOTHING TO LOSE*... If I slit your jugular right now I could justify it to myself, Tommy... All because you tried to stand in my way. That was a *very* bad thing to do. You need to be punished... *Raymond* here *says* so."

He took his action figure out of his pocket and held it up in front of Tom's bloodied face. Then he made it do a little dance along the blade of the razor.

"*You tried to keep me from my homeland, Tommy...,*" Rocky said, with the same scratchy voice he used when puppeting the scarecrow under the reading light. "*I'm gonna need to scare you now, Tommy... I'm gonna need to put the fear of God into yeeewwwww.*"

I glanced up into the rear-view again, trying to divine from Rocky's face what all this "final ride into the sunset" stuff was about. Tom looked like he was about to break into tears. He was crumbling fast. Beads of sweat were lining his brow and he was panting.

We got to the intersection of Yonge and Esplanade and I turned north toward Dundas. I was driving as smoothly as possible. Not wanting to draw any unneeded attention our way.

"*Tell me, Tommy... Do you think God would approve of what you've become...? Or do you think he sent me to punish you for your idiocy?*"

"Fuck man... I don't even approve of myself... I don't. I—I just do what I have to do to survive. That's all... I'm sorry man... I'm sorry."

His voice was a tremulous whine.

"*That doesn't sound very sincere, Tawwwwmmy... It's just not a good enough excuse.*"

Rocky glared into the mirror and spoke through gritted teeth as he said that last bit. We caught eyes. It gave me the heebie jeebies. I knew he was speaking to me as well. He was taking the opportunity to let me know how much he disapproved of my own bad choices. It was subversive and very effective. As we looked at each other a sudden flash of red drew my eye back to the road. An old lady dressed in a red coat was meandering across the street in front of the car, completely unaware.

"SHIT!" I yelled, as I yanked the wheel and swerved.

I got around her without much trouble, but it was a close call. I looked all around to see if any cop cars were in the vicinity. I checked all the mirrors and that's when I noticed Rocky's facial expression had changed drastically. He now looked deeply troubled.

"Drop me off at the next intersection *with* the money, or I'll take your friend's spleen out," Tom ordered, in a much more confident sounding voice.

I turned my head as far as I could and saw what was going on. Tom had a pocket knife jabbed against Rocky's ribcage. Rocky was still holding up the razor, but it suddenly looked much less intimidating compared to the urgent proximity of the knife.

"He's got my knife," said Rocky, sounding hopeless and deflated.

"That's the problem with having a knife, isn't it? If it happens to fall into the wrong hands you're in trouble," chirped Tom, with a cocky slant of a smile.

We were euchred, unless I thought of something quick. My mind was spinning out of control but somewhere within that tourbillon of panic it came to me. I kept looking back up into the mirror until I made eye contact with Rocky again. When I did, I mouthed the words to what I was going to do. He nodded, ever so slightly.

The next set of lights were about a hundred feet away. With no cars behind us and none in front, it was the perfect time. I stomped down on the brakes and the tires squealed in response. I felt Tom hit hard against the back of my seat. I eyeballed the mirror and saw a blurred image of Rocky on the attack. He capitalized on the situation like I knew he would.

We rolled to a stop at the intersection of Queen Street west. I turned around to see Tom melting down between the seats, losing consciousness—eyes rolling back in his head. Rocky calmly folded up his knife and put it in his pocket.

"Well done, Quinn... Well *fucking* done... He's down for the count. Keep driving and when he comes to we might have to tell him what his name is... That was the rushing-heart elbow by the way. It's a Shaolin Kung Fu move... Very effective," he said, with cool confidence back intact.

I turned west onto Dundas and headed for Spadina.

Spadina.

Have you ever walked around a city and wondered about the street names?

Or.

Have you ever contemplated the millions of gallons of human waste flowing through the sewers beneath you?

Or the thousand tears that've traversed urban faces to fall into hungry gutters. Or the premeditated blood that saturates the soil of inner city parks. Or the working class sweat that lubricates the machinery of progress. Or the gazillion stars obscured by artificial ambiance. Or the flirtatious glances from never to be seen again strangers. Or the moon and her gravitational tug on your libido. Or the fat raccoons enjoying the view from the foothills of human extravagance.

Or the music composed by kids wielding grimy electrical instruments in the meat lockers of prosperity.

Raunchy, punchy, pulsating music that pushes slowly on your insides.

Have you ever defined rock 'n' roll?

Rock 'n' roll is vibrating airborne sex. It scrubs the gummed up circuits of bio-electricity. It's a crystalline display of Mother Nature's elemental breasts. It's the pristine kiss of a killer. It's the pure nectar from the undulating hips of Isis. It's a wisp of silken hair and pheromones.

It's a pink tongue speaking beautifully hued language—the language of angels and holy whores. The language of a crisp Christ figure dancing a heartfelt fandango across the reflected love of a paradigm shift, as the elephant of abundance stands yonder smiling at the mingling souls on the horizon, rubbing up against each other to stay warm during an unfettered dawn.

There's a crow across the street, perched on a roof top.

The crow looks beyond the veil and laughs in my general direction. His feet decorate my eyes as I smile. He thinks I'm perfectly crazy. He thinks I know. He thinks we'll embrace the night together. He thinks we'll shine and flash and burn.

The crow and I need each other. He laughs when I cry. I hold him over the yawning abyss with a deeply lined palm. He sees what I can't. He sees the fracture and the budding beam of light as I reach for my supernova.

SPADINA.

It's a strange word.

I thought it was the last name of a famous society man. But no. It's exactly not that at all.

It comes from the Ojibwa people. The word is a rough English approximation of the Ojibwe word, *ishpadinaa,* which translates as, "A high hill or sudden rise in the land."

The Ishpatina Ridge is the highest point in the province of Ontario and it rises up over *Scarecrow* Lake.

Is this coincidence?

No.

It's more specific than that.

It's *convergence.*

The vermillion red of Chinatown started dotting the roadsides as we proceeded toward Spadina. Tom was still out cold on the floor as Rocky kept an assassin's vigil above him.

"Look what I found," he said. "A bottle of Quinn piss!"

I'd forgotten it was still back there.

"How's about we clean Tom's face up to make him a little more presentable."

I didn't dare say it to Rocky, but there was a teeny tiny little spot inside my heart for a fuck-up like Tom. I couldn't help it. I knew he was most likely the product of the system. He was probably first detained as a young offender and from there, had every last stubborn fiber of his innocence stomped out of him by government issued steel toed boots.

His cycle of freedom and incarceration would've gradually increased in frequency with each passing year until it reached the shrill decibel level of a common criminal, where every day is pierced by the sound of sirens that may or may not be on the hunt for a coyote that developed a taste for the farmers' sheep.

Using crack was merely an appropriate lifestyle choice for Tom. Its explosive high was the chemical equivalent of living in the moment— in the eye of the hurricane where everything is eerily placid for a few scant minutes before all hell breaks loose.

I knew from my own experience that Tom was addicted to an underclass hustle as much as he was to crack. He craved the frisson of his particular sub-culture. Every day demanded survival, where he was from. Every day kept him busy outrunning or outsmarting the sirens. But the sirens never rested. They called him from the inside if he was out, and from the outside if he was in. Relentless, they were. They wanted Tom enthroned on the saddle of the Babylonian Unicorn—the unicorn that stood statuesque and seductive on an inner city carousel, enticing young riders to spin and spin between the clutches of the state and the clutches of the street.

When Tom hustled amongst the crack shacks and shooting galleries, he never once felt the downcast clinical stares of the white-coated Minotaurs. He never once acknowledged the architects who thrive on the near-sighted antics of a lab rat.

"Aww... C'mon Rocky... Let's just drop him off somewhere and be rid of him. He's bad news."

"No. He needs his face washed with your piss."

Rocky found some napkins and proceeded to wash Tom's face like a doting mother. After a few minutes Tom came to and pushed himself back up onto the seat.

"Tommy... I cleaned your face for you."

Tom looked at the bottle, put his hands up to his cheeks and felt the wetness, then put his fingers up to his nose and smelled them. His face scrunched up, but he didn't dare say anything.

"We need you to be presentable for the folks in Chinatown... You see this?"

Rocky had some hundred-dollar bills in his hand and was waving them in front of his face. Just like he did to me when he first jumped in the cab, six or so hours previous.

"I'm gonna be *real* nice to you and give you this cash to spend... And you *have* to spend it here, Tom..." He pointed outside the window at the intersection of Spadina. "You *have to*... You *understand?* If you don't we'll come looking for you, and trust me we'll find you and finish you off... *You hear me?*"

I pulled around the corner and into a small parking lot behind a restaurant. I brought the car to a stop and turned around in my seat.

"Go in here and order yourself a meal. A big meal... Then find other places still open and give them your business. Buy stuff... Lots of stuff... We won't be far away. Oh, and one other thing. Stay the *fuck* away from the Munch... If you're ever seen around that place again you're a dead man... Got me?" I said.

He looked like he was about to say thanks, but before he could, the door was popped open and he was booted out by Rocky's shoe, onto the pavement. He rolled while counting his cash. His eyes were lit up. It was as if nothing had happened. The money was all that mattered. It was his god and god was healing him of his minor scrapes and bruises.

We watched him walk into the restaurant. He even turned around and waved at us with a big stupid grin on his face. We both shook our heads.

It was approaching midnight. Glenda had to be wondering what became of us. I remembered catching a glimpse of her looking out her window as I ran down the alley.

"Where's the phone?"

"It's right here, but I forgot to get a picture of Tom and you?"

"That's all right... I can do without."

"*What*?! *Quinn*... This is a trip to *remember*. It's sweeping in its cinematic scope. It deserves to be preserved."

He said that with slightly disingenuous eyes, but with enough fervency to compel me.

"Why is saying no to you so damn hard? You shoulda been a mayor for Christ's sake."

We popped our doors open at the same time, and headed into the all-night sanctuary of the New Ho King restaurant to get the picture.

"Well would you look at that! He's actually being a good boy and following orders," I said, as we opened the door and saw a waiter filling his cup with tea.

"He drinks tea... How cute is that," Rocky added.

We walked over to his table and sat down with him. He went from being joyfully immersed in the endless deep fried options of the menu, to looking like he was about to get sick.

"I—I'm doing what you guys said... I just ordered a dinner for five."

The waiter smiled, gave us a slight bow of his head and left.

"We forgot to get a picture, Tom. That's all... It's just for personal use. I'm not gonna show it to the cops or anything."

I moved over beside him so that he was on my right, and Rocky snapped the photo.

This is a great picture. Tom's clutching his money and looking incredibly ill at ease with his scraped up, but freshly washed face. And there's me with my ubiquitous shirt and my arm slung around him in a less than brotherly embrace.

Poor Tom.

I wonder whatever became of him.

Chapter 9

Where the driver and his ever surprising passenger get back on the highway and head for Detroit. The gateway of the border crossing looms in the foreground.

WE LEFT TOM to his meal for five, and went back to the car. Before leaving I grabbed two of his egg rolls and some of that sweet-and-sour sauce, for the road. I was hungry. I was also starting to feel the very first phantom pains of withdrawal. It'd been almost six hours since I took my last pill, and seven hours was the usual tipping point. The ugly awareness poked me hard in the ribs, like it always did.

You see, anyone who gets hardwired to opiates winds up living a life dictated by the turn of an hourglass. For me it was a ten or twelve hour pile of sand inside my glass. By the seventh hour, I could feel the morphine just starting to recede from the shores of Bliss Beach. By the tenth hour, the beach became noticeably colder. It was no longer tropical, nor was it subtropical. It was more like a northern coast of France beach, replete with bone-aching dampness and remorseless gusts of chilling wind, rushing in off blood-slowing seas to warn the ancient mariner of worse weather to come.

Beyond the twelfth hour I was doomed to shiver on frost bitten sand, desperately needing the chemical warmth of my little grey pill—grey as my skin. Birds of purgatory gathered and squawked at my grievous mortal breath billowing out before me. I had, at the very most, three or four more hours before I was locked in a fetal position, drenched in cold sweat, and feeling three times my age.

If I let things get *this* far I was pretty much fucked unless I could find a dealer who delivered. I was in no shape to go hunting for the antidote. I was in no shape to leave the apartment. I was in no shape to get off the floor. As my body and brain served up a rancid helping of cold turkey, I was officially doomed.

The time to find some more medicine had unequivocally arrived.

"I need the phone... I need to call Glenda."

"We can't go back there man... We need to hit the highway... It's four hours to the border."

"I know... It's just—"

I hesitated. I didn't wanna have to spell it out, but the rest of our trip depended on it. I needed more dope, and I wasn't about to ask Tom if he could score any. That would've been a gong show. He would've snapped into his hustler routine to lead us on a scavenger hunt of grotesque proportions. Showing us his turf and his game and his bros and hos. He may have even been Machiavellian enough to lead us into a trap, where upon he'd stick it to us with twice as much violence as we did him. I envisioned a baseball bat and a gleeful smile.

"What? What? It's just—" Rocky stopped himself as he clued in.

I hushed my voice as we reached the car.

"I need to find some stuff... Y'know. It's that time."

"Right," he said, through rolling eyes.

"Look. I would've just scored back in Grey but you yourself said there was no time for long shots. And going back to my dealer's place was totally out of the question... He would've known something was up right away. He's like a fucking shark, man. He can taste fear."

"I paid you up front though. You coulda just paid him."

"This isn't a movie, Rocky... That kinda shit never works out in real life... Besides, it's not about the money... He ain't hurtin' for cash... He only cares about getting busted, and there was no way of knowing if he'd already heard about the shit show that went down. Six hours was lots enough time for word on the street to get around. There's just no way I could've risked goin' back there." I looked down at the egg rolls and the bright red sweet and sour sauce in my hand, and suddenly wasn't hungry anymore. "Being associated with a murder scene in any way is no good for a guy with a list of priors like his... He'd much rather force me to take the rap... He totally would've hogtied me and kept me as insurance until he knew for sure things had cooled down."

Rocky didn't respond. He stayed quiet as we got back in the car and drove off. Then a few blocks from the New Ho King he picked up his satchel and started into the story that changed it all. The story that I knew was hiding inside of him because I'd been feeling its gravitational pull ever since we first got on the highway back in Grey Grove.

"Remember when I pointed to that spot on my head?" he said, as he pointed to it again.

Of course I remembered. It'd stayed in the back of my mind ever since.

"Yeah, what about it?"

I knew this was going to be big, so I quickly tried mentally preparing myself.

He went quiet for a bit. Like he was crafting his words and deciding upon an angle of approach before fully committing. I continued driving somewhat aimlessly through the Toronto night. I wanted to call Glenda but I couldn't. This conversation was far more important.

"You've been driving cab for how long now? A few years at least, right?"

"Yeah. About four."

"Do you remember a couple years back, picking a kid up from the east end and taking him downtown? For a few months it was a regular trip for you... Five days a week, kind of thing."

I combed through my ragged memory banks, but came up empty.

"No... I don't remember. It's too long ago. I guess... I remember switching to the day shift around that time, but that's all."

Rocky shook his head and shifted in his seat.

"You switched to the day shift because even back then you were feeling the need to clean up, weren't you?" he said, with the tone of someone narrating my life.

I looked over at him, trying to figure out what he was getting on about.

"Well, yes... And obviously it didn't work. But back to this kid... Did you know him or something?"

"Yeah. I knew him for a while. We were pretty close for a bit there... He told me about the conversations you two had... He said he liked you, and that's why he requested you whenever he called a taxi."

"Weird... I'm drawing a complete blank... You'd think I'd remember him too, because I'm not generally that chatty with customers. I must've thought he was interesting enough."

"Well this kid wanted me to personally thank you for what you did for him... He wanted me to tell you that you helped him face what he had to face every day he woke up."

"So... What exactly was he facing?"

"Well... He always got you to drop him off at the park in front of the courthouse down by the water there. But that wasn't his actual destination... He only got out there because he never wanted you to know where he was really going."

His mentioning the courthouse sparked a vague memory. The hazy image of a young guy in a baseball hat paying me, then shutting the door and walking away into the treed seclusion of a park, flickered behind my eyes like a super-8 film.

"I think I remember him now...," I blurted. "He always wore a baseball hat, right?"

"Yeah. The Detroit Tigers were his favorite team. But anyways, he used to sit in the park and think about things. Y'know... He'd think about life while watching squirrels chase each other around the trunks of trees as people walked their dogs... He'd do that for about half an hour before heading off to where he needed to be."

"So where was he going?"

"To the hospital..." He paused for effect. "Every day after talking to you, and then sitting in the park, he'd walk by himself down sterilized hallways past people in various states of decay to the radiology section of the building."

Rocky looked away, out the window. I stared at him for a bit before looking back at the road.

"He was diagnosed with a malignant intra-cranial solid neoplasm when he was eighteen... A brain tumour. That was two years ago now... He made it through the four months of his first radiation treatments, and then a few weeks after it stopped he had a follow-up appointment... The doctors told him he wasn't responding as well as they hoped he would.

"They gave him the news that every human being fails to fully grasp... They said that if the next four radiation sessions didn't prove more effective they'd try operating. They told him he had a 50/50 chance of surviving the surgery, and even if he did survive there was a good chance he'd have brain damage. He didn't know what to think at first so he just went along with it... I mean he was only a kid... And he had nobody he really trusted that he could talk to other than the doctors..." He turned his head and looked at me. "And you."

"He had no family or anything?"

"No... He moved out of his home at sixteen and never looked back... He had his reasons."

"Fuck... I feel extra shitty now for not being able to remember him," I said, letting out a breath of shame.

"He was very careful never to reveal anything to you... There's no way you could've known. He just wanted to talk with someone who didn't know who he was, or what he was going through... You were that guy, Quinn... And he never forgot that..." He took his scarecrow out of his pocket again and held it. "Anyways, a year and a half later when his last radiation treatments were done the doctors told him the grim news... They said they needed to operate. He agreed to it and they set the surgery date for... Well... For today, actually... He would've gone under the knife right around the time I hopped in your cab."

I saw a parking spot coming up on the right hand side. I pulled over and stopped as something flashed in my head — a face.

"Let me see your passport photo."

He took it out of his satchel and gave it to me. I looked at it with new eyes.

It was him.

"You're that kid aren't you?" I asked, through a nervous chuckle.

There was a long silence. Cars blurred streaks of red and white in my peripheral vision as I waited.

"I'm not gonna risk dying before I've lived, Quinn. Fifty-fifty odds aren't good enough for me... Besides, I vowed I wouldn't let myself die in Grey Grove. So I chose Wichita. I wanna smell the roses before I push the daisies, if you know what I mean."

I sat there studying his picture. The reason why he looked so different was now obvious: he was sick and the photo was taken before the ravages of his disease.

The veil had been lifted.

The wall between us—finally dismantled.

His secret, revealed at last.

I was no longer blind. The truth opened my tired eyes and tied up the loose ends of my mind. His horrible headaches suddenly made sense and his devil-may-care attitude made sense, and his unbreakable will to get to his destination made even more sense. But above all else, his immediate air of affability now made perfect sense. In hindsight, he'd exuded the natural confidence of a friend right from the moment he sat down in my cab and started counting out his money. Because in his mind, I *was* his friend. I just needed to remember I was.

As I sat there contemplating Rocky's terminal bravery, the next level of his design opened up before me like a Russian doll.

"So what I thought was a stroke of unbelievable luck today, was actually more to do with me being a part of a master plan," I said.

"How could I have known about the money you owed your dealer? That *was* luck, for you *and* me, if you believe in that sort of thing... And I do make oversights by the way. Not often, but I do... For instance, not seeing the key in the trunk wasn't very keen of me, was it?" He sat up straight. "I'm not perfect by any stretch of the imagination, but do you really think I'd risk getting into a cab with just any old driver after robbing a bank? No. I called and specifically requested you... But I told them not to tell *you* that... They hummed and hawed until I convinced them I was your cousin by describing you in perfect detail... Eventually they went along with it."

"Always the details, eh? You're pretty impressive."

"Thanks... But I was still risking a hell of a lot even though I knew you wouldn't recognize me... Almost everyone who hasn't seen me in a while doesn't recognize me. I kinda like it actually... I'm like a different person now..." He looked off into the night. "I knew you wouldn't recognize me, but I knew you well enough to know I could trust you... You're a good person, Quinn... You've got a heart of gold and your mind stays open. The world needs more like you. I don't care what your personal choices are when it comes right down to it. The way I see it, everyone's an addict in one way or another, anyhow." He looked past me at a couple getting into their car across the street. "We're all addicted to the oil in our cars and the minerals in our cell phones and the sugar in our food and the electricity in our walls. I'm no hypocrite and neither are you. You might not remember all those conversations we had, but I do... I remember every nuance. I remember when I could tell you were fudging the facts by the way you'd look away, trying to hide your face from my eyes... And that's essentially your problem right there... You're a sensitive type who tries to medicate the sensitivity away because it gets to be too much... It gets in the way, as a cabbie, right? So many broken people with broken lives and broken stories all wanting to open up to you because they sense something about you... They sense your permeability. And some of them take advantage... For you the drugs thicken your skin... Without them you feel too vulnerable. But your vulnerability, and the sincerity that goes along with it, was exactly what I needed during my treatments. You told me a lot about yourself... Not just by your words, but by what you left out... I read between the lines and figured out you had a drug problem way back then. When I was planning this trip, I factored it in just in case you still had one... And well, after hoppin' into your cab today it was obvious to me you did."

He grabbed his satchel up off his lap as I was overcome by the acuteness of his perception. I wondered how many other people out there I wasn't fooling. Then I dropped that line of fearful thinking when I reassured myself that other people just weren't like him. Rocky was a force of nature. His mind was a diamond that'd been forged within the unforgiving furnace of hard luck. At some point he must've resolved to master his own fate, and to that end, began gleaning small details, minuscule clues and tiny signs; the diminutive stuff that can point the way through when pieced together.

His parents were ripped away from him in kindergarten. He'd been diagnosed with terminal cancer at eighteen, and now he was facing the reality of an early death. And I couldn't help wondering what else he'd been through.

The fact that he'd moved out at sixteen from wherever he was living suggested something happened there as well.

As he held the satchel, he revealed to me yet another detail of his master plan.

"As you know, every cancer patient is prescribed pain killers and obviously I'm no exception... They give me a monthly script of morphine, but I don't take it on a regular basis... Only when the pain gets to be unbearable... I don't wanna die addicted to the stuff. I wanna be clear headed and see it coming. Anyways, the stuff I don't take I sell to people... I had to. I didn't wanna spend my final good days slaving away for an asshole of a boss. And the government of course only doles out the bare minimum. Not near enough to live comfortably and that's what I wanted... I deserve to live out my last *fucking* days in some goddamn comfort."

He loosened the buckle on his satchel. As he did, I remembered going through it while he slept in the passenger's seat. I remembered hearing a faint rattling sound that came from the front pocket where the money was. It made me curious at the time, but I reined in the urge to look by assuming it was aspirin or something, for his headaches.

"Remember when you said you didn't have enough dope to get us to Wichita, and I said not to worry because I had a plan?"

I nodded as he reached down into the pocket. My heart soared with each disappearing inch of his hand. Then something went very wrong. Very, very wrong. Suddenly his face went white.

"BLOODY HELL... OVERSIGHT NUMBER TWO. THAT MOTHERFUCKER IS GONNA DIE NOW! HE STOLE THE PILLS I HAD FOR YOU. TURN AROUND AND GET US BACK TO THAT FUCKING RESTAURANT!" he bellowed, while rocking back and forth in his seat.

I didn't say anything. I only reacted. I slammed the car into gear, pulled out and turned around, then pressed the pedal down.

As we retraced our path back to the New Ho King, my heart sank like a stone. I couldn't help it. I just knew Tom wasn't gonna be there. I must've unintentionally eased off on the gas because Rocky started in on me.

"*Speed the fuck up,* Quinn... For Christ's sake this isn't a game. This trip depends on us catching him... My *life* depends on it."

"You mean your death." I said, as I pushed on the pedal.

I'll never be okay with the fact that I said that to him right then. But I just needed to call a spade a spade. His refusal to undergo surgery just didn't sit right with me. It seemed like he wasn't willing to live life if it meant he'd be brain damaged after the operation. His fear of being compromised had obviously influenced his decision. But how could he not fear death and yet fear the alternative? It had to be his pride. He was proud of his intelligence, and without it he simply wasn't interested in living.

In a woeful twist, pride had turned one of the most rabid despisers of preciousness I had ever met—a little bit *precious*. It was a god awful conclusion to come to, but it was obvious to me. By saying what I said, I was simply acting upon an uncontrollable desire to push him off of his pedestal and wake him up. For his own good.

He turned and glared. I thought he was going to reach over and start choking me, but instead he broke down. He started crying like a little boy, all hunched over and shuddering under tidal waves of unleashed emotion.

"*You fucker... I need you right now and you don't care do you? Nobody ever fucking cares,*" he sobbed.

"*Rocky. Stop it...* Tom's not gonna be there... Remember when we went in to get the picture? Well now that I think about it he had a terrified look that said, *oh fuck they found out about the pills...* He took off right after we left, Rocky... He's gone... I just know it."

I kept driving back to the restaurant just to prove it to him. He kept crying.

"It's gonna be okay... I can handle this... I promise I'll get you to Wichita... No matter what!"

He looked up and over at me and calmed down a little.

"Really?"

"Yes... This is my problem, not yours... But it's more than that. I like you... I really do. I wanna do this for *you*... I have to."

My voice echoed inside my head because I wasn't so sure I'd make it without the morphine.

"I'll call Glenda and see if she can hook me up... She'll understand. She doesn't judge... She'll help us, no questions asked."

He wasn't crying anymore, but his chest heaved every now and then in the aftermath.

I pulled around the corner so that we faced the New Ho King. We both craned our necks to look inside but didn't see Tom anywhere. He'd vanished into the darkness of the Toronto underworld with a bunch of cash and a bottle of morphine pills.

Rocky sat back in his seat and let out a tight chested breath.

"I'll call Glenda," I said.

The phone only rang once.

"Quinn? Are you okay?!" she said, bursting through the phone.

"Yeah, everything's okay... I don't think you have to worry about Tom coming back around the Munch again... We took him out for a little ride."

"Did he break into your car?"

"Yeah, he had Rocky's satchel in his hands when we got to him... If he hadn't of been standing there in the alley going through it like a complete idiot we woulda been shit outta luck," I said, looking at the time on the dash. "But listen, I have a very important favor to ask of you..."

"What is it?"

Her voice changed immediately. Her tone became business like.

"You know my little problem... My little habit?"

"What about it?"

"I need something to tide me over, y'know? Something to see me through this trip."

The phone went silent on her end. I could hear Blunt Fiction still shredding away in the background.

"*Please*, Glenda... I wouldn't ask if it wasn't absolutely necessary."

"I know, Quinn... It's not that... I don't have a problem helping you out. It's just I can't think of anyone."

My body reacted to what she said. My heart pushed fear tainted blood to my face and ears. I felt embarrassed all of a sudden. I'd gambled and lost, and now the worst case scenario was staring me down.

Then a tiny ray of hope broke through the gathering clouds.

"*Wait* a minute," she added. "Where are you guys crossing the border?"

"Windsor."

"Perfect... I know a guy in Detroit who can help you out... He comes to the Munch three or four times a year with his bands. He runs a small punk label, and road manages his acts when they go out on tour. He's the kinda guy who has his fingers in everything if you know what I mean... If he can make a buck he'll gladly help you out and trust me he's very connected... He'll be able to find what you need... I'm sure of it."

My blood pressure relaxed with each word that escaped her lips.

"Do you have a phone number for him?"

"Yeah... Hold on."

She put the phone down. I looked over at Rocky with reassuring eyes. He nodded back.

The truth is though, I wasn't feeling reassured in the slightest. It was better than nothing and it alleviated my mounting dread somewhat, but I wasn't convinced it would work. I'd been on one too many quests for dope in my time that all started out full of promise, only to fade into the grey mists of ambiguity and then on into the blackness of miserable failure.

I was also very much aware of the fact that I'd be going through one of the busiest and most notorious border crossings in North America, while succumbing to the first merciless snipes of morphine withdrawal. By the time we reached Windsor I'd be navigating the initial stages of something that can turn the simplest act into a circus of the macabre.

Everything's bathed in a sinister light during the harsh and demented winter of dope sickness.

But I made my promise to Rocky and I had to keep it.

A man's word is all he really has.

"Okay... You still there?"

"Yeah," I said, with less wind in my sails than a few minutes before.

"His name is Oscar Ambrose... Call him when you're in Detroit. He doesn't sleep much so don't worry about waking him up... I'll call him and let him know you're on your way." She relayed the number to me.

"We should be four hours or so," I said, looking down at my shoes. "And thanks, Glenda... If this works you'll be getting' me back home. If it doesn't... I'm totally fucked," I chuckled.

"You wouldn't wanna have anything on you, or look too stoned when you go through the border anyway, Quinn... This is probably for the best."

"Yeah... I suppose it is."

"Good luck, Antony," she said, with a smile in her voice.

"Bye, Cleo... See you on the flip side."

I put the phone away as Rocky flicked on the reading light and opened up his tattered copy of *The Stone Angel*. I assumed he'd calmed down, because if he was anything like me, I could only read on a still mind. My mind had to be as smooth and protected as a pond set deep in a forest of tight pines.

I wheeled the car around and made the short jaunt to Yonge Street, where I then turned north and headed for Eglinton.

"So Glenda says she knows a guy in Detroit who can help me out."

He looked up from his book.

"Here," I said, handing him the piece of paper I wrote the name and number on.

Rocky looked at it and laughed out loud, shaking his head as he did.

"The guy's name is Oscar Ambrose? You gotta be kidding me?"

"Yeah... Why's that so funny?"

He just looked at me and rolled his eyes.

"If you don't know by now, Quinn, I'm not gonna say. Not yet anyway... I'll wait 'til we get there."

"*Okay*... Whatever you say..." I decided to change the subject, sensing he was about to go a bit weird on me again. "So how's the book anyway?"

"You've never read *The Stone Angel*?"

"No... I skimmed through it in high school for a project, but that's it."

He flipped through some pages, then cleared his throat, and in his best old lady voice, recited a few lines.

"I can't change what's happened to me in my life, or make what's not occurred take place. But I can't say I like it, or accept it, or believe it's for the best. I don't and never shall, not even if I'm damned for it."

He stopped and rested the book face down on his lap.

"If I were to meet Hagar in real life I'd give her a great big kiss. She'd hate me for it, but the thing is we'd get along because we think the same way... We both feel cheated by life... We've been through so much disappointment and betrayal that nothing can touch us, because we've finally realized that none of it matters... Not one goddamn bit does it matter... That's why I could rob that bank, Quinn. It's also why I can die in Wichita, *alone* if I have to..." He paused to step on some invisible clutch in his head, then changed gears. "The only thing that matters is whether or not you can see the new you standing in the future. The stronger, smarter you that all your enemies and vices can reflect back if you squint hard enough. You gotta read the truth in every mirror, Quinn... Not just the warm and fuzzy ones with all the great lighting."

He picked the book back up and started reading again. Then he stopped and looked out the window as we turned onto Eglinton and headed for the 401. I was just starting to piece together the sagacity of his words when he asked the question that would birth the story you're reading right now.

"You ever try writing anything?"

"I've written poetry here and there... So has everyone though."

"So you don't remember telling me you wanted to write a book someday? 'Cause that's what you told me on one of our drives down to the park."

I shifted in my seat. I didn't remember saying that to him but he was right, I'd entertained the thought on a few occasions.

"It's crossed my mind before."

He turned his whole body around sideways to face me.

"I'm giving you a story here, Quinn... This trip is gonna make a brilliant tale... I need you to make it into a book for me... It's the other reason I chose you... I need you to turn my life into an epic adventure so that I'm never forgotten! So that the sands of time don't bury me in oblivion... Can you do it? Will you do it?"

He took me completely by surprise. He forced my hand as he compelled my word. He was blatantly pushing for another promise. He had me cornered and he knew it. I wanted to resist him out of sheer obstinacy, but a curious thing happened. There was no resistance. It was as if he'd shrewdly calculated the in-spite-of-myself reaction that went on within me right then. Somehow he knew what I didn't even know about myself.

A voice wafted up from some cobwebbed corner of my creativity and answered his burning question before I could stop it.

"Okay, Rocky... I'll do it... I'll write it."

And that's it. That's how this book came to be; a simple promise defied my sensibilities and put me in charge of his legacy.

At the time, however, I was more than a little doubtful of my abilities.

"Good," he said. "Good... Now let's get on down to Detroit."

A sheepish grin sprouted across my face, because I couldn't believe I was now under the yoke of his dying wish. I was now his chronicler—his executor.

All I could do was keep driving through the night trying to get used to the idea. And sure enough, little by little, I found myself taking mental notes and putting literary spins on things that'd already happened.

Thinking about writing a book was a nice diversion for a bit, but it was no match for reality. The upcoming drive from Toronto to Windsor loomed like a four-hour race toward disaster as we merged onto the highway under a half moon that seemed to be hiding something in her shadow—something troubled—something anxious and wrinkled.

The moon has seen it all, hasn't she? She's watched the entire history of mankind play out like an ad-libbed tragic comedy on late night television. She's witnessed the rise and fall of ambitious empires. She's laughed at the self-important civilizations that've all crumbled beneath their own pompous weight. She's pushed and pulled on the never-ending succession of human generations, parading before her like self-righteous waves of flesh and bone. She's cast disapproving eyes upon wrongheaded cultures, born out of pathological questing for comfort, safety, predictability, and routine. She's watched us harvest the bitter fruits of our false paradises—our electric gardens of Eden.

She's reflected upon the unholy matrimony that saw us married to avarice.

And she's flat out refused to be surprised by the sky high divorce rates as billions of souls become divorced from the source. Divorced from Mother Nature by religious invention. By fear of the unknown. By gainful employment. By media spin. By racial pride. By limp sexuality. By the guessing games of scientific process. By envy and gluttony. By excessive sanitation. By thousands of store bought goods, all deemed essential for survival. And yet we survive very little because we're all slayed by the slightest change in our delusions—defeated by minuscule bumps in roads that send us skidding out of control under a crescent moon.

A moon that rests her chin on an upturned palm, lets out a vexed breath and surveys with cringing eyes, a wasteland of willful ignorance. Of purposeful blindness. Of tedium. Of futility. Of unnecessary suffering. Of dull perversion. Of trivial advancement. Of toothlessness. Of bloodshed. Of dumb death. Of reeking artifice.

With disapproving lashes the moon has blinked her way through a never-ending plague of spiritual myopia spread not by the fleas of rats, but by ridiculous crowds of humans that gather and mock the soft, tender voice of nature.

And the moon looks on. The moon looks on, but then finally she looks away. Unable to make any more excuses for the sheer idiocy of it all.

She turns away to gaze upon the galaxy like a hopeful child. Wondering if something redeeming has beaten the odds and blossomed within the twinkling blackness. Something beautiful and timeless. Something exquisite and refined. Something inspiring. Something true.

The moon had spoken to me. I kept looking back up at her as we drove. She was weary. I was weary. I needed to recharge somehow.

I decided to interview Rocky. I decided to learn more about him. After all, if I was to write his story down I needed to get inside his head. I needed to flow through his veins and ricochet around the chambers of his heart.

Rather than diving straight into the interview, I decided to turn the radio on, and think about possible questions while the music played.

Or maybe it'd be just one question—one essential question that'd connect the dots of his personality like the missing piece to a jigsaw puzzle.

Picture this:

As movers shuffle about above you, clearing your home of furniture and heirlooms, you lower yourself on bended knee to pluck an amoebic shape from its final resting place. It looks old. Whatever it is has gathered up the dust of life over many years, in the far corner of your basement.

In a small shaft of muted light you see disintegrating strands of fur from long gone pets. You see the faint traces of ashes from long gone habits. You see tiny lashes from the young eyes of long gone children.

You wipe it with your thumb, clearing away the exfoliated skin of lives that no longer brush by one another within the hallways of a once bustling family home.

For some reason you hold it up to your ear.

You hear a voice.

It asks you, "You've long since discarded my brethren, but now that you have me in your hands, can you remember where I fit? Can you reunite me with my purpose within the crucible of your mind?"

You think about those questions as memories grace the prism of your cheek.

Then it asks, "What was it all for?"

I switched the radio on and immediately a propitious smile shaped the corners of my mouth. It was Rocky Raccoon.

The syrupy voice of Paul McCartney filled the inside of the car.

He said Rocky you met your match. And Rocky said, doc it's only a scratch. And I'll be better, I'll be better doc as soon as I am able.

Rocky started tapping his foot along to the beat as he read his book. I waited until the final strains of the guitar had faded out before I turned the dial down and prepared myself for what I expected to be an interesting experience, to say the least.

I knew what question I wanted to ask him.

FOURTH INTERMISSION

I'm not sure if you caught it, but I performed the secret handshake with the bartender and ordered up a couple absinthes for us. Hope you don't mind. It's a lovely elixir that augments the senses quite nicely. Did you notice that couple leaving as we stood by the bar? Some things can't wait.

Chapter 10

Where the driver interviews his passenger, receives a phone call, and gets surprised at the border.

I WASN'T AS READY for the interview as I thought I was. I lost my nerve soon after turning the radio down and instead drove for the better part of two hours without saying a word. Rocky kept reading his book. I kept worrying. I could feel myself getting heavier and heavier with every silent click of the odometer. And to make matters worse, every little physiological nuance within me ballooned into a new withdrawal symptom. Even when I rationalized the hypochondria away, my mind simply shot me the finger and returned to the far more pressing issue at hand: getting across the border without being skewered by the authorities.

On and on my no-rest-for-the-wicked turmoil churned. And on and on he turned the pages of *The Stone Angel*, completely absorbed. Finally, I couldn't take it anymore. We needed gas again, so I used that to break his concentration.

"I know you're really into that book, but we need to get gas... And did you see that sign back there? It said 200 km to Windsor... We're gonna be at the border in less than two hours."

He responded without looking up. "Okay, stop at the next gas station then."

"*Rocky*... Put the book down for a bit would ya? We need to talk about what we're gonna say to the border guards... We need to get our stories straight, y'know? We need to make sure they match so there's no room for suspicion."

He dog-eared his page and closed the book.

"Number one, I'm terminally ill... Number two, my favourite baseball team is the Detroit Tigers and number three... My dying wish is to go see them play tomorrow."

"That's your story?"

"That's *our* story... Yes."

"Are the Tigers actually playing tomorrow?"

"*Yes*, Quinn. Details, details, *dee-taails*... Remember? I planned this bloody trip *right* proper... How easily we forget."

"Yeah, just as long as there's no more Toms to contend with." I looked over at him with chiding eyes, then added, "I should probably put the top sign back on the car so they know it's a cab as soon as we pull up."

"Good thinking... *Gooood* thinking," he cooed, as he opened the book back up.

"Can you stop reading? It's bugging me... I'm a dope sick nervous wreck over here while you sit there all relaxed... Can we just talk until we get to the border? It'll help take my mind off stuff."

He shut his book again, then put it back in his satchel.

"I'm dying of brain cancer... You're merely a self-imposed junkie... Remember that."

His comparison reduced me to an insect. I was suddenly as insignificant and annoying as a house fly. An awkward silence ensued.

"I'm sorry, Rocky."

He chuckled sarcastically.

"It's okay. We can talk if you want... What do you feel like talking about?"

"Well... If you really want me to write a book about this trip I'm gonna need to know more about you. I'll need some background information. And I'd rather get it before we hit the border, if you know what I mean. Just in case."

"Okay... So what d'ya wanna know then?"

I paused to choose my words.

"Can you tell me about why you left home so young?" I asked, sounding tentative.

He pointed up ahead at a sign. "Next service centre 15 kilometres," he announced.

I nodded my head at his diversion tactic and waited.

"It's not a pretty story, Quinn... It's a... It's an ugly little story about a thief and a young boy. It's a story about a poisoned well."

"I promise just to listen... I won't comment *or* judge."

"All right... Gimme a smoke then."

I took out two cigarettes, lit them both up and passed one over. He took a big drag, inhaled deeply and started into his confession.

The interview had commenced.

The Interview

Rocky:

As you know, my parents were killed in front of my eyes when I was five. I was barely outta diapers when the officials swooped in and found me another home. A good, safe, normal, wholesome home. And it *was* a good home, too. It was the home of my aunt and uncle. My dad's brother. They couldn't have kids of their own so it was a win-win situation. It was everything an orphaned kid coulda asked for. I mean, they *were* my relatives. So right off the bat there was a blood bond. I was also still young enough to be malleable, y'know. I was pliable— mutable. There was still time to reinvent me, so to speak. And that's what my uncle took to doin'.

He made sure I was brought up under optimal circumstances. Under perfect conditions. *His* version of perfect conditions, anyway. He was an earnest, soft spoken guy. And I believe he really did want the absolute best for me. He wanted me to flourish. He wanted to see me shine. And I in turn wanted to shine *for* him. In the early days he became very close to being my actual father and his wife played a doting, caring mom. It wasn't until later that things went all to hell. Even then, it was only partially their fault. When I think about it now, I know they can only be blamed for their blindness. For their ignorant trust in the man that ruined my second chance.

[He pauses to smoke for a bit.]

Not many orphaned kids get the kind of second chance I was given. My aunt and uncle were dedicated parents. They were attentive and giving and warm and just all 'round good people. God bless 'em. Their fatal flaw though, like I said, was their stubborn need to blindly worship. They were highly religious folks. They went to church twice a week. Not just once, but *twice*! And of course I went along with them. At first I was happy to be there. I got to go to Sunday school and do arts and crafts and stuff.

[Rocky suddenly looks wistful here. A smile develops on his face and he laughs.]

I remember making this caterpillar one time at Sunday school. It was green and red and made out of little pom-poms all put together in a row. I glued two Popsicle sticks to each end of it so I could move it like a marionette. I brought it home with me and put on a little show for my aunt and uncle. I still remember the storyline, too. It was about a lonely caterpillar who tries to make friends with a beautiful Monarch butterfly. The caterpillar tells the Monarch that one day they'll be the same, but the Monarch just laughs and flies off. Then of course, a few months pass, or however long it takes and the caterpillar turns into a magnificent Monarch as well. He's flying through the meadow one day, trying out his new wings and sees the other butterfly that was too cool to be friends with him, snared in a spider's web. And here's where the moral of the story comes in. Instead of getting revenge on the old Monarch by leaving him to be eaten by the spider, the new Monarch helps him escape. When the old Monarch is free, the new Monarch reveals who he actually is, but the old Monarch is unable to accept the truth. He refuses to believe that any Monarch has ever been an ugly little caterpillar, and laughs once again before flying off without even saying thanks.

[Rocky pauses, as if he's waiting for me to catch up to him.]

Do you know what the moral is?

[I just shake my head.]

Never expect anyone to be thankful for your good deeds, but more importantly, never expect anyone to believe the truth.

[He stops and looks like he's had some kind of epiphany.]

Actually, just never expect anything from anyone ever, period.

[He grabs another smoke and lights it up.]

So anyway, I grew up going to church more than the average kid. I also graduated from Sunday school, straight into the boys' choir on account of my melodious voice.

[He sings a couple lines of some song I don't recognize.]

I excelled in the choir, you see. I was so good I got to be up front as a soloist. It made me proud to be good at something. But it was there at the front of the choir where I found myself face to face with the man that ruined it all — *The Ruiner*, we'll call him.

[He goes silent for a bit, smoking furiously and looking out the window into the darkness of the passing countryside.]

Rocky (cont'd):

It became obvious to me later on that The Ruiner had done his homework. He'd gone to great lengths gathering personal information on all of his boys. It was just my luck that I'd been recently elevated to head choir boy, which I found out later on meant I was his favorite for the time being. I'm pretty sure he had a crush on me from the get go. It was the weirdest thing in the world to realize when you're just a kid. Trust me. You see, most parents don't give their kids enough credit when it comes to discernment. They dumb kids down in their fearful minds and turn them into little idiots. The reality is most kids can tell almost immediately when someone is treating them oddly. And The Ruiner treated me like an heir to the throne. He always hushed the other kids when I was talking, which I have to admit, endeared me to him because I was pretty shy for a long time. And this goes back to him doing his homework, doesn't it? He was always having meetings with the parents, stroking their tender egos by talking their children up. He was a master manipulator. Like all diddlers are. *Fucker*! He deserves to be thrown to the *hogs*!

[Hatred overtakes Rocky at this point. It's unsettling to watch. He goes from calm and collected to seething in the blink of an eye. Veins pop out of his temples. Then just as fast he reverts back, and continues his confession in his previously detached state.]

The Ruiner must've had some kinda diddling manual he'd committed to memory, because he kept all the parents close with his incessant meetings, detailing the brilliant progress of their perfect children. He had them so fucking hoodwinked it was sickening. It was pure putrid evil being conjured up right under their noses. He had his filthy fingers on the pulse of all the necessary wrists. Shackled wrists. And they believed every last disgusting lie that passed between his polluted lips. Nary was a question asked. That would've been sacrilege. All he had to do was say their kid sang like an angel and was set to be featured in the next Christmas recital and they were putty in his cold hands.

You *must* know how church is, don't you? It's a goddamn dog and pony show, Quinn. It's the furthest thing from being spiritual you could possibly suffer through. It's nothing but a bunch of Joneses keeping up with other Joneses. All dressing up in their finest costumes to prance about the pews like a bunch of bastards on a catwalk. Fuck, I think I'm gonna make myself puke just thinking about it.

[He rolls his window down a bit for some fresh air.]

But things didn't start to get *really* bad until the one on one vocal sessions started. First he held them in the basement. How fucking creepy is that, eh? He'd take whatever boys tickled his fancy down to the fondling room, as I came to call it. That's where it all started. Right there under the altar. Right there under the life-sized crucified Jesus. Right under the asses of all those complacent sheep. All those parents who were unwilling to listen to their intuition and take action for fear of looking ungrateful. I mean, *come on*. You can't tell me there wasn't a cesspool of negative energy constantly swirling about inside that church. It was like a tornado of filth. I could feel it as soon as I walked through the big double doors. Every single time... Anyways, after the basement it was the cottage and then —

[He stops here. Actually, it's more like he freezes up. I can tell he's horrified by his mental imagery.]

Quinn:

Are you okay? You able to continue? If you can't I understand.

Rocky:

Yeah, it's okay. I'm good. Where was I? Oh yeah, the *cottage*. At his cottage he had this sailboat. To this day I still can't stomach the sight of them.

[He finishes up his second cigarette and immediately lights up a third].

Rocky (con't):

[As I prepare myself for the worst part of his story he suddenly changes his demeanor entirely.]

I can't do this anymore. It's bringing another goddamn headache on.

[He starts rubbing his temples.]

The only thing more I'll say about his sailboat is that it was expensive looking which means The Ruiner was getting paid pretty well by the church to molest little boys. You know what they say about the tithe, right?

[I shake my head.]

In Malachi 3:10 it says, "...bring the full tithe into the storehouse, that there may be food in my house. And thereby put me to the test, says the lord of hosts, if I will not open the windows of heaven for you and pour down for you a blessing until there is no more need." Keep that quote in mind and then know that the church where all this shit went down served an upper class congregation of about 300. That's a whole lotta money in the collection plate when you consider the tithe is supposed to be one tenth of your income. It makes you wonder how much of it went into The Ruiner's sailboat, eh?

[We pass another sign that says five kilometres to the next service centre.]

When I was on his boat I was stranded, Quinn. I was helpless.

[He hunches over as a spasm of pain shoots through his head.]

All I wanted to do was jump in and swim to shore, but I couldn't because I never learned how. I stayed on that evil fucking boat and I don't think I'll ever forgive myself for it. I stayed until he was finished, and I was destroyed. Too destroyed to do anything. I was a zombie. And that's when he got into my head and convinced me it was all my fault. For a long time I believed it. I believed I was to blame for putting on the swim suit he bought me and for what he did below deck.

[He brings his head up and turns to look at me. His eyes glisten in the darkness. But there's something else, a small trickle of blood is under his nose.]

Quinn:

Rocky! You're bleeding... Your nose is bleeding.

[I dig out some old napkins and hand them to him. He touches his face and looks at his fingers, then takes the napkins.]

Rocky:

Thanks, man.

[He holds the napkins up to his nose and keeps them there.]

I get lots of headaches, but I've never had one that made my nose bleed. That's probably not a good sign is it?

[He laughs a nervous laugh and continues.]

You know what though? After that day I swore to myself I'd learn how to swim and that's exactly what I did. Every day for a whole summer I went down to Crow Lake...

[Grey Grove is on the shore of Crow Lake.]

And I jumped off the pier, and forced myself to make it back to the rocks. By the end of August I was a pretty good swimmer. Actually I take that back, I was a damn good swimmer! I *fucking* did it, Quinn. All by myself and without a life jacket I did it! And after *that* triumph I started teaching myself other things. I taught myself how to get over my shyness and stand up to people. I stood up to my uncle and aunt, and told them point blank I was never going back to church as long as I lived. I didn't tell them why, because I just knew they wouldn't believe me, but that's what I did. Not too long after that I cut the cord once and for all. The day I turned sixteen I packed my bags and moved out of the house without even saying anything. I just picked up and left. I took a job at a grocery store, got myself a cheap apartment and never looked back. They didn't know what to think, but they accepted it. They had to I guess. For two years I was *fucking free!* Free as a bird. Then three days after my eighteenth birthday I went to emergency, because I had a migraine that wouldn't go away. Turns out it wasn't a migraine at *all! It was a lovely little brain tumour!* What a birthday present *that* was. *Fuck,* if I didn't have bad luck I'd have no luck at all.

[He goes quiet as the turn-off for the gas station comes up on the right. I get the feeling the interview is over and I'm almost glad for it. I feel drained. I can only wonder how *he* feels. He wipes his nose and sees the bleeding has stopped. But I can tell he's still in pain. Then he mumbles one last thing.]

Friends and adversaries. Family and strangers... Those are the only two full length mirrors you'll ever need, Quinn.

We turned off the highway and headed toward the electric lights in the distance. A few raindrops pelted the windshield and a thin blanket of fog hugged the ditches. I remember rolling my window down to breathe in the air. I like the smell of fog. It holds a supernatural fragrance that never fails to fly me away to a world where velvet gloves and feathered masks and strange dances around violet fires mimic the rhythm of the spheres.

I inhaled deeply, letting it dissolve into my blood through cool misted bronchioles. Rocky was doing his best to fight the pain he was in. I felt useless to help him. I felt like I was sitting in the long and wicked shadow of the interview; bound and gagged and blinded by the opacity of its darkness. I didn't know what I should say or do.

I decided to try and distract him.

"For being an old workhorse this car sure is good on gas... We just drove 400 kilometres, and we still have almost a quarter tank."

"As long as it gets us to Wichita," he said.

"Soldier... I call him Soldier."

For whatever reason, saying that perked him up. He stopped rubbing his temples, and looked over at me. Then he squinted at the dials on the dashboard.

"You call this car, *Soldier*?"

"Yeah. I don't know why really, it just seems to fit. It's taken me a lot of places, and made me a lot of money without needing much attention. If cars can have hearts, this one's got a big one."

He started humming a melody I knew. Then he opened his mouth and let his choir boy voice fill the car with instantly recognizable lyrics by Coven:

Go ahead and hate your neighbor, go ahead and cheat a friend. Do it in the name of Heaven, you can justify it in the end. There won't be any trumpets blowin', come the judgement day. On the bloody morning after. One tin soldier rides away.

I've always thought this song was haunting. It pulls no punches. I mean, it's basically up in your face screaming the truth at you no matter who you are, where you're from or what religion you subscribe to.

It's a dyed in the wool punk song.

It's a song that lays it on the line and makes no apologies for slapping any offending hypocrisy right out of your ears.

It should be the global anthem — if we can ever unify, that is.

Rocky stopped singing and chuckled to himself.

"They used to call Model Ts, Tin Lizzies," he said, through a waning smile. "And if I remember correctly the first one came off the assembly line at the Piquette plant in Detroit on August 12th 1908 — "

"August 12th is my mom's birthday," I interjected.

That put him into a pensive silence. He stroked his chin.

"Very interesting. Very... Ho-ly crap. That's it! I can't believe I didn't see it before."

I had no idea what sort of tangent he'd gone off on this time, but I felt pleased my distraction tactics had worked; he didn't appear to be suffering anymore from his headache.

"See what?" I asked.

"I'll tell you later on when I have the rest of the characters. And trust me, I'm almost there now. I mean *we're* almost there."

"What characters? And *why* later? You said that before too. Is there some kind of surprise waiting for me in Wichita? Cause I hate surprises."

"No... Never mind. It's just something that's been building since... Well, since I hopped in your cab today. Don't worry though, it's a good thing. A *very* good thing."

I shrugged my shoulders and left it at that. The gas station was up on the left.

I slowed down and pulled in, making a mental note to check the fluid levels of the engine and the air pressure in the tires. Soldier was the best car I'd ever owned, but it was only as good as my maintenance would allow. Besides, we still had more than half the trip to go before Wichita was even on the radar.

There'd be no more unnecessary surprises.

Not if I could help it, anyway.

The gas station was deserted, save for the attendant. Even from where I stood beside the pump I could tell the girl inside the kiosk was painfully cute. She had long, bone-straight, red hair that glistened under the fluorescent light. Her profile was perfectly patrician.

I took the nozzle off the hook and stuck it in the gas tank. She looked up at me, then reached over and pressed a button. The pump turned on with a click and a hum as I shivered violently in the damp night.

It was an ominous shiver.

Admiring her beauty couldn't save me from my heavy handed fate.

My descent into cold turkey had officially begun.

The chills had arrived first, as per usual. And like tolling bells of truculence, they warned me of the assault and battery just around the corner.

I had about three hours, if I was lucky.

There was absolutely no way in hell we could be detained at the border. Everything had to be in order when we pulled up: passports, compliant eyes, open faces, fixed hair, agreeable tones of voice, and of course, our story.

The dying young man at his first and last Tigers game, story.

Off in the far corner of the lot I noticed a set of coin operated vacuum cleaners. A light bulb went off in my head. I finished filling the tank, put the hose back, and then tapped on Rocky's window to see if he wanted anything to eat or drink. He rolled it down and squinted up at me.

"You want anything from inside?"

"Umm… Just get me the same stuff as last time."

He looked over at the pump to read the price as he reached into his pocket and pulled out a few crumpled twenties. "Here," he said, handing me the cash.

"You really watch what you eat, eh?" I joked.

"Yeah, I make sure it's all junk food. One of the benefits of knowing you're gonna die soon is you stop caring about your body. It gets relegated to the level of rental vehicle. Think of it like this, Quinn... Right now I'm on a scavenger hunt, and I need to find all the clues in order to get to the right terminal, so I can catch the right flight. Nothing else matters."

I wasn't expecting such an enigmatic response.

"*All righty* then. Junk food it is. Be right back."

I walked to the aluminium door of the kiosk and pulled it open.

"Good morning," she said.

I smiled at her as I started picking out the necessary items. I could hear her ring the stuff in as I grabbed it off the shelf. When I was done I put it all on the counter and handed her the cash. Her lip gloss flirted with my line of sight as I did. I'm sure that's not what she intended, but like I said, she was impossibly gorgeous. It was probably as much of a curse as it was a blessing, at least that's the vibe I got from her. It was like she knew she was pretty, but it bored the hell out of her. Her nails were painted, but they were short and chipped, and she wore a faded denim jacket over a thick grey hoodie so that it shrouded her delicate features.

"You need a bag?" she asked, as she handed me the change.

Her eyes were as green as Bermuda grass. They stunned me into silence. Either that, or I thought she was telepathic. I can't remember if I actually *did* entertain the idea of her beautiful telepathy, but it wouldn't have surprised me because getting sniped by odd little thoughts like that was par for the course when I was croaking for my next dose. I think they were smoke signals being sent up by my stranded-on-a-desert-island brain.

"So... No bag then?"

"Huh? Oh, Sorry... No, no bag." I laughed at myself. "I was somewhere else there for a second."

She gave me another flash of those emerald almonds. I smiled and looked off behind her.

"Are those vacuums working back there?"

"The one on the right is."

"Okay, thanks. Have a great night."

"You too. And keep your head outta the clouds," she said, with a glossy smirk.

I left feeling good. She made me feel good. Her warmth stayed with me as I walked back to the car and saw Rocky with his hand up to his ear. Closer up, I realized he was talking on my phone. I picked up my pace and rounded the back of the car, then rushed to the door and yanked it open.

"Okay, whatever you say Frogster," was all I heard before he hung up and looked at me.

"That better not of been who I think it was," I said, sounding panicked.

"He called himself Frogman and he wanted to talk to Eskimo. I asked him who Eskimo was, and he got kinda angry with me. Then he said *Eskimo* better show his face soon, or he'd release the hounds. Whatever that means... I'm guessing it's not a good thing."

"Why the hell are you answering my phone? For *fuck* sake, Rocky. Frogman's the dealer I owe the two grand to. He uses code names for phone conversations, because he's extremely fucking paranoid *and* sadistic...Now I have to call him back."

"Sorry, man."

I wanted to continue being mad at him, but it just wasn't in me.

"Don't worry about it... I was putting it off. I shoulda called him a long time ago."

I started the car and drove over to the vacuums.

I asked Rocky if he was feeling up to vacuuming out the car. He told me he just needed to drink some pop and eat some chocolate first. Maybe it was the after effects of the interview, but him saying that choked me up a little. I reached over and gave him a brotherly hug from the side. It was a little bit awkward, but I didn't care. It was a genuine spur of the moment gesture of fraternal affection, and it wasn't like he recoiled or anything. It was kind of funny actually. I remember thinking he reminded me of my old dog, who after too many hugs would curl up the corners of his snout into a vaguely forced smile.

I popped the hood and set about checking Soldier's fluid levels.

It was right after I'd wiped the oil stick with my fingers, and then without thinking wiped my fingers on my pant leg, that—

Sorry to interrupt. But I feel obligated to let you know that I've kept those jeans all these years, because the oil stain and the woman-from-the-car-wreck's blood still decorate them like badges of honor. I even wear them every now and then if I'm doing messy work. I wear them with a deep respect and reverence for stains — for reminders.

People get stained by life.

Rocky got stained, and he in turn left a stain on me.

Dear Rocky,

If you can hear me, or if you can read these words I'm typing, I hope you made it. I hope you're standing there with that slightly maniacal look in your eye, holding a sign up that says, *I'm With Stupid*, when it's my turn to arrive.

Your Brother In Arms,

Quinn J.

Thanks, for letting me put that in there.

Now back to the story.

So after wiping my oily fingers on my jeans and topping Soldier up with his regular quart of 10W30, I got a text message from Frogman:

Eskimo you better not be sloughing me or I'll send out the hounds. And who the fuck off'd Cupcake?

I read it over a couple times, before shoving the phone back in my pocket.

Rocky did a stellar job on Soldier. He didn't cut any corners. He even created striated patterns in the velour upholstery. He also got rid of my bottle of piss, and the bloodstained wiper packaging.

His extra care forced an inner grin that briefly warmed my blood in the aftermath of Frogman's threat.

Briefly.

Back behind the wheel my fears, once again, descended like filthy vultures. The upcoming border crossing, Frogman's way with words and my imminent descent into cold turkey all conspired to make short work of my sanity.

I felt hopelessly possessed by negative forces. I imagined myself as an inmate in a padded cell with his hands over his ears, trying to block out the voices. And the voices were all yelling at once, screaming the secret and terrible meanings to every nursery rhyme I'd ever heard.

I was, after all, quite permeable when I was approaching sobriety, and not in a good way. Sometimes I felt like I had no skin. I felt like a walking medical illustration of the nervous system—raw, bloody, and exposed to the ubiquitous whims of common cruelty.

The Equation of Common Cruelty:

(Of course, cruelty develops in many ways, but this is the common variety)

Normality => Self-Regulation => Repression => Frustration => Tyranny => Cruelty.

Repressed humans need to be cruel, don't they? At least that's the impression I get.

Tyranny and cruelty are the universal tools of the frustrated and the trump cards of the terminally repressed; they come naturally to anyone relying upon an unbroken mirror for validation. Like bad cologne they waft forth from those who shun the mosaic.

But more about the mirror mosaic later.

We merged back onto the highway with a clean interior, top sign back on, papers in order, speeches written, and attitudes adjusted.

Rocky wasn't about to take any chances and he told me so:

"Quinn, whatever happens at the border just remember the robbery doesn't actually exist yet." He looked at the digital clock on the dash. "Not for another four or five hours, anyway. So just keep a lid on it. Keep your cool. They don't know anything you don't tell them, and I'm not just talking about what you say. I'm talking about your facial expressions and your movements. You need to be relaxed... Muster every last bit of your sangfroid, because the more bothered you look, the more they taste blood. It's all fucking predator-prey dynamics."

Rocky's take on hassle-free border crossings made me think of something.

It was another run in with the cops, back in Grey Grove.

I had parked the cab and was venturing into a heat-score apartment to get some much needed dope. I knew I was breaking another cardinal rule, but I was desperate. I knocked on the door and about five minutes later I hear, "Who the fuck is it? Stand back so I can see you."

I stood back as the dead-bolt clicked, the chain got removed, and the door opened. Inside, about ten people were all smoking crack. The room was infused with that unmistakable sweet chemical smell. Not one of them even looked in my direction. I remember seeing a nice looking young girl sharing a pipe with her boyfriend, or maybe her client. She exhaled a huge cloud of smoke and looked over at me with gargantuan pupils as she unzipped his pants. Right there in front of everyone she plied her trade with absolutely no shame. Nobody but me paid any mind. I couldn't take my eyes off of her. I mean, this girl knew what to do. I was impressed, and shocked, and embarrassed, and turned on all at the same time. She kept going, and going as the guy took hits off the pipe, and then all of a sudden it was the money shot.

"Stop the shenanigans would ya… Warn me first," she said, as she straightened herself up, and caught eyes with me once more. I looked away. Her gaze now held a secret vulnerability that moments before had been sacrificed on the altar of addiction.

To this day the word shenanigans reminds me of cops, crack, and fellatio.

It wasn't long, of course, before she got right back on the pipe like nothing had happened. I was just getting ready to ask about buying some pills when another knock came at the door. The guy who was so cautious ten minutes prior, for some reason, didn't bother to ask who it was this time. He pulled the door open and standing there were ten drug squad cops. They immediately barged in and screamed at us to kneel down and put our hands behind our backs. I was shitting my pants as they did their pat downs and searches. I had my last half pill in the coin pocket of my jeans. The cop searching me checked everything, including my wallet, but totally overlooked that little pocket. I walked out of there a palpitating free man, swearing with each weak kneed step to change my ways. But, of course, I didn't.

To this day I still get an adrenaline rush when I think about it. I even think I get a little bit aroused. Strange how the mind affects the body like no time has passed.

The drive to Windsor seemed much shorter than any other part of the trip. And yet it was the longest stretch of driving I'd done up to that point. Why was that?

The answer has everything to do with context.

If I'm walking through the desert on my way to an oasis, time slows down. It'll seem like a small eternity before my destination wavers on the horizon, and another small eternity before I'm cupping cool water to my parched lips.

If however, I'm walking down the street on my way to a nightmare job I should've quit a long time ago, but didn't because I'm too worried about being able to afford all the creature comforts that mitigate the state of bondage I find myself in, then time will speed up. Way before I'm ready I'll find myself reaching out to grab the virus-laden handle of a door that mocks my cowardice with its distorted glass reflection of my embittered face.

We pulled into Windsor and navigated its empty streets until we were cruising alongside the Detroit River, on our way to the international tunnel.

"What about the money? They may not know about the robbery yet, but that much cash will make them suspicious, won't it?" I asked, as I neurotically checked my face in the rear-view.

"*Deeetaaaails.* You're allowed to bring exactly ten thousand dollars across this border. One penny more and they'll confiscate everything."

I nodded my head and resumed my mental housekeeping. Suddenly, the straight razor flashed in my mind. I handed it to Rocky, and told him to put it in the bottom of the glove box.

A sign came up on the right that directed us toward the tunnel. We were minutes away from the only compulsory exam of our journey. There were other tests, but none of them were as daunting because they weren't allowed to simmer as long within our imaginations.

I remember glancing at my new red shoes as we rolled down into the darkness of no return.

From here to Detroit, forward was our only option.

CHAPTER 11

Where the driver and his passenger get processed.

THERE ARE ACTUALLY PEOPLE out there who can remember being forced through their mother's vaginal tunnel.

The tunnel that connects Canada to the U.S.A., between Windsor and Detroit, is the second busiest border crossing between the two countries. The busiest being the Ambassador Bridge that spans the grudge-laden river just downstream.

Grudge-laden river?

Allow me to explain myself.

For 10,000 pristine years, the job of the Detroit River was to convey water from Lake Huron to Lake Erie, and thereby ensure the unimpeded drainage of the largest freshwater basin on the surface of the earth. After the colonialists arrived, however, her job description quickly changed. And over the span of a couple hundred years her reputation shifted from one of indispensability in the realm of water conveyance, to one of indispensability in the realm of trade conveyance. In short, she became a very big dollar sign in the ever-industrious eyes of the English and French conquistadors.

So why then exactly is the river grinding her axe? Well, I think it's because she's still very upset about being raped, pillaged, and poisoned for most of the industrial revolution.

Put it this way: during the industrial revolution, talking about her in terms of her ecological merit was about as socially acceptable as letting go a great big rancid fart in a stuffy board room.

Money trumps environment.

It always has and *still* does in most countries. And so it did in North America, up until Rachel Carson's *Silent Spring* came out in

1962. At that time, all the pink-faced tycoons and shipping magnates shut up for about three impatient seconds as they held their stock exchanged breath, and waited to see if what Rachel espoused would actually catch on with the general public.

And of course, it didn't.

At least not in any notable capacity until about thirty or forty years later. Only then did the river finally get attended to by folks who honestly cared.

Back in the dirty old days, however, the river was an unofficial septic tank. In fact, much of the garbage and sewage from Detroit's and Windsor's industrialized growing pains and subsequent bowel movements ended up floating amongst the rivers curling whitecaps, and for a long time the entire shoreline from Lake St. Clair down to Lake Erie was so thoroughly polluted that recreational use was scoffed at. The toxic buildup became so offensive at one point that thousands of migrating birds were murdered by marauding slicks of oil and reeking pools of human shit.

And what of the fish?

At one illustrious point in the history of North American industrial progress, the oxygen levels in the river were so low, and the mercury levels so high, that it was suicide for any aquatic creature to navigate its defiled depths. I'm positive a discordant chorus of dying perch and pike saying: "So long and thanks for all the fucking rubbish," could be heard by any child that dared dunk their head.

That same child invariably ended up with a double inner ear infection, and serious skin ailments.

But back to the vengeful nature of the Detroit River.

Since being dredged out in the middle to create a shipping lane for huge tankers, she's had a steady appetite for unaware swimmers of all ages. She's downright hungry for humans, and with her manmade drop-off and raging undertow, she's all the better equipped. She snares dozens of unassuming humans every summer.

As we drove beneath her cold rushing waters, I bowed my head and paid my respects. I knew she still held the balance of power. And I secretly hoped she might hear my thoughts and float us through the infamous gates of Detroit, unviolated.

Down through the soot-covered walls of the tunnel we coasted. It was dreamlike in its slow but steady procession of automobiles and trucks. The ones that passed us going the other way all seemed like successful graduates to me. Their engines purred with a Doppler tinged victory.

All at once we rounded a small corner, went up a slight incline and arrived at the gates. There were only two being used. We chose the one on the right. In front of us were three other cars waiting to be processed.

"I probably should've inquired about this earlier. But you don't have a record of any sort, do you?" Rocky asked, with an annoying ease in his voice.

"No. I should be the one asking *you* that question. Do *you?*"

"Deeetails." Was his now ubiquitous refrain.

"Right. *Deetaaails*. It's not like we can turn around anyway. They'd probably fucking shoot us if we did. I knew a girl whose mom worked as a border guard and she told me some things. She said her mom had the right to shoot people if she ever felt threatened. They *do* carry guns you know."

Rocky scoffed at that as he rolled his window down a little.

"I know exactly what they're allowed to do. Let me put it this way. There ain't much they *aren't* allowed to do."

"Exactly... She said the rights we normally take for granted aren't even considered at borders. If they happen to get a hunch about us, no matter how ridiculous it is, we're fucked. There's not much we can do but jump through the hoops they hold up."

"Quinn... Imagine for a minute you have 3,000 people to examine in a given day and your job is to find the guy smuggling drugs, guns, cash, or people for the sex trade. The ones committing these crimes aren't bloody well labeled. They look just like everyone else. Actually, most normal people would say they look a little like you and me."

"*Great...*Thanks for the encouragement." His perfectly placed pinprick of doubt overcame my centre of balance and snapped me into survival mode. "Grab my registration papers outta the glove box would ya. I wanna have everything ready."

"Relax... Just relax. Look them in the eye, and don't offer up any information they don't ask for," he said, as he handed me the papers.

I took them and noticed my tremors had upped their amplitude; so did he.

"How're ya feelin anyway? You gonna be able to hold it together 'til we get to Ambrose's place?"

"I don't have much of a choice, do I?"

"Just try not to show your hands too much. Okay?"

"Yeah, sure. That's *fucking impossible*," I said, through a nervous yawn.

"Don't sweat it. If shit goes down I have the ace up my sleeve. I'm the dying kid who loves their baseball team. Americans are suckers for that sorta thing."

"I'm actually glad you're dying right now. I'm truly fucking demented."

"Hey, no worries. The pleasure's all mine. And I've even got a doctor's note to prove it," he said as he patted his satchel. "It's a signed printout of my official diagnosis."

I looked at him and exhaled. I knew he might just be right about them. A little romantic tragedy was definitely part of the American mythology. But I wasn't crazy enough to count on it.

The fact is, we were flying blind and the weather was about to get heavy.

The cars ahead of us weren't stopped for long. But they all had Michigan plates, so I didn't get my hopes up. Instead, I watched how the guard conducted himself as best I could from the angle I was at. And this did get my hopes up. He was a portly fellow with sleepy eyes and a ready smile. I counted half a dozen good natured grins tighten up the edges of his jug chin.

I was just beginning to lighten up—just beginning to feel relief wash over me when a hatchet faced man walked out of the main building over on the right, and made his way to the other guard's booth. I had a bad feeling immediately. Something told me we'd arrived just in time for a shift change. As the car before us pulled forward through the gate, the friendly guard stood up from his chair, gathered some stuff and then disappeared out a small door in the back. Seconds later, Hatchet Man sat down and turned his chiseled profile toward us. There was absolutely no warmth in this man's face. He was cold calculation, through and through. *Don't fuck with me*, screamed out of his pores and pierced my wishful thinking like a hail of hollow-point bullets.

"Did you see that?" I asked, without turning my head.

"Yep. Just go with it. Whatever you do don't let him get to you 'cause that's exactly what he wants. He'll dine on your fear like a dictator if you let him."

"*Why?* Why couldn't we have pulled into the other line up or showed up a few minutes earlier?" I said, with an existential whine.

Right then the green light in front of us lit up, telling us to move forward. An iron spear of hot panic punctured my gut as I took my foot off the break and rolled the car toward the interrogation window.

"Here we go," I said, without moving a single muscle in my face.

"Remember eye contact," Rocky whispered.

We squeaked to a stop in front of his bristling authority. He was a paragon of intimidation—a definite candidate for an executioner in a past life. I was sure of it. A black hood and a bloody axe would've tastefully complemented the methodical manner in which he rolled up his sleeves and surveyed the scene before him. *Rolling up sleeves is never a good sign*, I thought, as I squirmed in my seat. I couldn't help but notice how his thick forearms advertised a set of icy blue veins the size of night crawlers.

He took a heavy silver pen out of his shirt pocket and pressed it into a pad of yellow paper in front of him, before raising his eyes to meet mine. Fighting the urge to look away right at that moment was one of the hardest things I've ever done.

"Good morning fellas. Passports please," he said, while looking at his watch.

His tone of voice was a chain link fence topped by razor wire. His eyebrows, two pestilent black caterpillars accentuating an eager mask of malevolence.

"Good morning," we echoed, in perfect unison, as I handed him our documents.

He looked back at his pad of paper and jotted something down. It bugged me. What could he have possibly surmised about us within such a short period of time?

"Jack's taxi, huh?" he mused. "And what city's that from?"

"Grey Grove. Southeastern On—"

"I know where it is," he said, cutting me off to focus his attention on Rocky, who was turned sideways in his seat so as to be facing straight on.

"I presume you're the one who hired this cab?"

"Yes, sir."

"And where are you headed?"

"Detroit. So I can see my first Tigers game tomorrow."

"I asked you where. Not why or when."

"Sorry, sir."

"Are you carrying any controlled substances, any weapons, any fruits or vegetables with you this morning?"

"No, sir."

Hatchet Man ticked a few items off on a list and punched some information into his computer. He must've entered our names, because he was reading from our passports as he typed. A suffocating silence ensued as he analyzed what popped up on his screen. Whatever it was, inspired him to make a clicking noise with his tongue. He sat there for a few seconds, then turned to sweep us with a pair of reptilian eyes that scorched the last strongholds of my optimism.

"Do you have a criminal record?" he asked, looking at Rocky.

Rocky said no. Then it was my turn.

"What about you." He paused to read my name. "Quinn Jacob. Do you have a criminal record?"

"No," I said.

Something in his face changed with my response. It was a fleeting look of satisfaction—a brief glimpse of the cat that ate the oblivious canary. He must've caught himself though, because it vanished just as fast as it formed.

Something wasn't right.

I could feel it. I looked over at Rocky without craning my neck, and saw him squeezing his scarecrow in a white knuckled fist. Hatchet

Man had resumed typing. As he clicked away I went over all my answers, trying to deduce the exact nature of the trouble we were in. Then the typing stopped.

"You know, Mr. Jacob. When a border official asks you a question you really need to think about your answer. *Before* you speak."

He started tapping his pen. I didn't know what to say, for fear of saying the wrong thing again. I remained silent.

"For instance, when I ask you if you've ever been in trouble with the law. You better think good and hard about your response. Do you understand what I'm telling you?"

He was masterful at putting the screws to youthful folly. The invisible monkey wrench he wielded with his words tightened up my already dry throat so that when I said: "Yes, sir. I do", it came out sounding like a squeaky whisper; he savoured the sound of it with two deliberately slow blinks, and another icy mockery of a smile.

"Excellent. So why did you fail to mention your history with the Grey Grove police department?"

Rocky's knee pumped out the rushed rhythm of impending disaster. His heel kept a time signature reminiscent of Charlie Parker hopped up on Benzedrine. As for myself, I think at this point I was pretty much hovering outside my own body. I was a spectator watching a blood sport unfold.

You know how pictures get developed in dark red rooms? Well, as I sat there with my senses scurrying about like rats on a sinking ship, the gist of what was being laid on me slowly gained relevance. All at once, I remembered the incident that hadn't even blipped on my radar, until now.

The day I turned eighteen I stole a box of condoms. It was my first and only offence, and because of that I was offered *diversion*. Basically, I was let off with a fine, and a promise of writing an apologetic letter to the proprietor of the store; which I did with as much remorse as I could manage.

Diversion kept me from a criminal record, but it didn't prevent me from getting fingerprinted down at the cop shop. When I asked why I had to be fingerprinted, I was told that theft under 5,000 dollars automatically required it, even if no record resulted.

Theft under 5,000.

Brilliant.

Steal a pack of gum or maybe a riding lawn mower—it's all the same to the judge with stock options at Walmart.

So you see, when Hatchet Man asked if I had a criminal record I answered to the best of my knowledge and said, "No," because I didn't *have* a criminal record. What I did have, much to my surprise, was a fingerprint file that flashed on the computer screen if my name was punched in.

Woops.

I choked down the bitter pill that'd coagulated in my throat and tried advocating for myself.

"I don't have a record, sir. I was let off under the diversion program for first time offenders."

Me saying that forced an audible cringe from Rocky. Hatchet Man pounced.

"You think this a joke?" he said, glaring past me.

"No, sir. I don't. Sorry, sir," Rocky said.

I looked over and got slayed by the evilest eye I've ever seen. Rocky wasn't impressed. He looked murderous. I knew exactly what he was thinking too. He was thinking I was no better than crackhead Tom, because I'd committed the sin of jeopardizing his "ride into the sunset."

I was standing in his way.

I was blocking his light.

Then Hatchet Man slammed the storm door down on my little pity party.

"You should've told me that in the first place, Mr. Jacob. Now. Would you kindly pull your vehicle around the other side of that building over there. Leave the keys in the ignition and proceed in through the main doors."

I rolled up my window as Hatchet Man let a freezer burned smile betray his face. His schadenfreude was magnetic. I had to tear my eyes away from his as I pressed down on the pedal.

Hoping to draw a little compassion out of Rocky, I explained as we drove that the entire incident resulted from a young man's chivalrous pursuit of his first performance. "I was merely trying to have sex with a girl. And safe sex at that," I said.

He shook his head slowly.

"Well she better've been worth it?"

Rocky's tone was doom laced.

"For what it's worth, she was."

I hadn't thought about her in a long time. But I had nothing better to do so I got down on bended knee and swept the dirt off her marker.

She was dead.

She was hit by a train three days after we were about to consummate our passions.

It happened in twelfth grade.

I would never have known she had eyes for me if it weren't for the way she turned away one day, slow as a search light, after I caught her looking at me. I remember feeling her heavy stare on the side of my head. She was looking for survivors in an institutional wasteland, and I was very much alive.

She sat beside me in geography class. She wasn't that pretty, but something about her provoked my vivid fantasies on a regular basis. Eventually, she picked up on it, because during class on the day of my eighteenth birthday she passed me a sketch of two people engaged in a rather intimate and unambiguous position. On the back it said, I'm ovulating so you'll have to use a condom. As my face turned crimson I managed to add underneath, when? Before handing it back to her. She leaned over and whispered in my ear, "Lunch hour at my house... My parents are at work."

I can still feel her warm breath.

I didn't really believe her until she caught up to me in the corridor and said cheerily, "So do you have any?"

Only then did I realize she meant business, and so I responded with as much machismo as I could conjure.

Of course, it came out all wrong.

I opened up my virgin mouth and testified, "For sure I do... I go through like two packs a day."

It's not like I was trying to be funny. I was merely doing my best approximation of what a real stud might say. She burst out laughing as a rush of embarrassment tightened up my cheek muscles. She laughed, and laughed and then all of a sudden went totally straight faced and said, "I've been having dreams about my death for six months now... There's certain things a girl needs to do before she dies, and one of them is you."

She was completely serious. I could tell by her eyes and the way she stopped chewing her gum. I felt like a fastball knocked out of a stadium.

In the span of a heartbeat, I fell in love.

I regained my balance as I refused to let the opportunity slide through my hands.

"Where do you live? I need to go home to get them. I can meet you in about 20 minutes."

She flashed an illegal smile and told me her address. Then she kissed me. As she pulled away I looked into her eyes and saw a strange beautiful sadness. It was deep and seductive. I blinked a few times to keep myself from being hypnotized. Then I smiled back and dashed off to the drug store up the road.

I didn't have a cent on me, but I wasn't about to let money get in the way of my sexual tutorial.

And of course we know what happened next; I got arrested and missed my first chance.

Three days later she was hit by a train while crossing a set of tracks with her headphones on. Somehow, I've always known she was listening to her favourite song.

We never even held each other, but she's still my first love.

We came to a stop in the parking lot of shame. I didn't turn the car off right away. I couldn't. I was still in shock. I was waiting for some smarmy director type to knock on the windshield and tell us we'd *absolutely nailed* the scene. There was no way this wasn't some bad Hollywood movie destined for the bargain bins of the world.

My denial kept my hand away from the steering column as Rocky finally broke his silence.

"If it turns out the lady I tied up at the foreign exchange managed to get help, we're done for. The cops would've given every border crossing in the province the serial numbers."

"They're not concerned with you, Rocky. It's me they wanna rattle so it's up to *me* to make sure things stay contained. I'll do my best to keep the attention away from you."

My trembling hands mocked the false confidence in my voice as I looked out and saw two guards walking toward the door of the building. They were laughing to each other as they closed the distance between us. It was just another day on the job for them.

"Here they come," I warned.

"Listen… If things get bad I'm not goin' down easy. I'm not gonna die locked up in Grey Grove. I wanna die free. So it might get messy. Just remember I know what I'm doing. I'll tell them I took you hostage, okay?"

How was I supposed to respond to that nihilism? The implications were castrating. My vocal chords seized up and left me nodding my head like a marionette.

Finally, I gathered up the necessary strength to shut Soldier down. I turned the keys back, but left them in. It was our cue. I gave Rocky one last glance of camaraderie before we opened our doors and stepped out to meet the guards.

They were as tall as trees. Their eyes were small bitter apples that tempted our insubordination as their guns gleamed behind black leather holsters — ready to punctuate any *necessary* use of force.

We didn't exchange words because the routine was a mute mechanical dance. We simply walked by them, and marched ourselves toward the door — a door to be exited by one or both of us, depending on how the dice were rolled.

The only thing that gave me any real hope at all was that Frank hadn't sung to me. Not yet, anyway. I knew it was a long shot, but at least it was something to cling to. He didn't warn me about every little thing, but the big things usually attracted his wherewithal.

I held my breath as I entered ahead of Rocky — into the air-conditioned sterility of law and order.

It was half past four in the morning when I sat down on a cold vinyl seat and waited for the hands of fate to shuffle through my papers. I remember thinking that only bad things happen at four in the morning.

The place was empty of anyone not in uniform and the air conditioning was up too high. The chill forced me to hunch over a little and hug myself to keep warm.

As I shivered, it became very obvious that I was officially on the roller coaster ride of full-blown morphine withdrawal. I was cresting the first big hill, but I knew I couldn't dwell on it so I busied myself by looking around the room. I saw one of those number dispensers. We were the only two there so I didn't think it was necessary to take one, but the symbolism wasn't lost on me. As I flanked Rocky under the harsh fluorescence, I got the distinct impression that my number was up. I thought about taking one just to see what *number* it was. Maybe it'd be the sum total of my karmic debts—a numerological clue that could show me the way out of the mess we were in.

At the exact moment I looked down at my shoes, my name was called.

"Quinn Jacob. Please approach wicket number nine with your hands visible."

I looked over at Rocky, then stood up to face the guard who called my name. He was just as impervious looking as Hatchet Man. My legs turned to rubber as my palms grew moist.

I stepped forward.

"Good morning, Mr. Jacob. Your passport please."

I managed to wipe it off on my pant leg, but it shook up and down as I handed it over. He took note. He also took note of my t-shirt. He wasn't amused.

When you're suffering through opiate withdrawal, all of your senses become hyper-acute. This is because you've spent months or even years dulling them, and when they return to normal, that *normal* suddenly seems superhuman. Unfortunately for me, this particular border official was enjoying his morning coffee and the smell of his breath singed every hair in my nostrils. It was revolting. I tried not to breathe, but it was so powerful I could taste it. As he inspected my identification I gagged a little. He looked up with a down turned mouth and narrowed eyes.

"Pardon me," I winced. "It's been a long drive."

"So you've had some trouble with the police in your past and you failed to mention it? Why is that?"

I rested my elbow on the counter to support myself.

"He asked me if I had a criminal record and I said, 'No,' because I don't... It was a shoplifting charge from ten years ago that I was offered diversion for."

Saying that much at once was excruciating. I had to keep swallowing, because my salivary glands were preparing for an imminent geyser of vomit.

"Are you trying to be smart with me?"

"N—no, sir. I'm not."

Just then the guards who searched Soldier came back in. One of them held a plastic bag with something heavy inside. His smile was murderous as he walked over and placed it down in front of my interrogator, before retreating to watch the games from a distance.

"And what do we have *here?*"

"It's a straight razor. It's from my. It's from my grandfather."

I was failing fast.

"Were you not asked if you were carrying any weapons?"

"Yes, I was. But it's not a weapon. It's a keepsake... It's like a good luck charm."

"Looks like a weapon to me," he said, as he unfolded it and ran his fingers over the edge of the blade. "And a sharp one at that!"

"It's not... It's *really* not, sir," I pleaded.

"Excuse me for a minute, Mr. Jacob."

He walked back to a shiny black phone on a desk and picked it up. A few seconds later he was talking to someone. The conversation was short. I looked over at Rocky and saw him filling up with dread. He'd been watching it all from his seat. He looked extremely pale as he rubbed his temple with one hand and clutched his satchel with the other.

When I looked back at my interrogator, he was talking in hushed tones to a much older man with a silver crew cut, a white shirt and *superior officer* written all over his face.

This new superior officer nodded a few times, then walked up to an empty wicket and did the unthinkable.

He called Rocky up to the counter.

I watched Rocky stand up and take three steps before he stopped and put his hands to his face. He held them there for a few seconds, then pulled them away as blood shot out his nose and sprayed the floor in front of him. He collapsed. The guard who found the razor walked over with his hand on his gun and stood over him. I turned my head back and saw the white-shirted man leaning over the counter to see what was going on.

That's when I saw it.

I saw a detail.

It was a pen in the pocket of the superior's white shirt. And it wasn't just any pen. It was a pen with a Detroit Tigers logo on it.

I seized the opportunity.

"*He's got a brain tumour okay. And he's got a doctor's letter to prove it. He's dying and all he wants to do is see his favourite baseball team play tomorrow... The Tigers. He just wants to see the Tigers play, that's all... He's just a kid.*"

Right then something came over the room; above and beyond the immediate stillness and silence my calculated plea produced. I'll never know what it was exactly, but the entire place became brighter, as if by some ethereal light source existing within the very molecules of air, and as it shone the face of the white-shirted man suddenly changed. His expression softened and his eyes grew wide.

He took action.

"Get that kid some paper towel and make sure he's okay!" He paused and looked like he was fighting with himself. "Then...Then get 'em on their way. Tomorrow's gonna be a *good goddamn game* and he won't wanna miss it... Poor kid," he said, as he walked away and disappeared behind a heavy wooden door.

With that, my interrogator stamped my passport and looked up at me.

"That never happens," he said. "Next time just answer the questions the way you're supposed to... Now go check on your friend."

He gave me back my things and I rushed over to Rocky. He was conscious, but didn't know where he was right away. I fished his passport out of his satchel and handed it to one of the guards, who went and stamped it and brought it back.

I put my hand behind his head as he focused his eyes up at me and smiled a smile I'll never forget as long as I live.

Rocky's hemorrhaging stopped with some applied pressure, generously provided by the gloved hand of a guard. The entire roll of paper towel was used to stem the flow, the sight and smell of which was just enough to put me over the edge.

There happened to be a small garbage container within reach, so I grabbed it and heaved up the bilious contents of my stomach. As I wretched, I saw a vision of Glenda dropping my old shoes into her trash can. It was a silent movie about a promise being made.

I felt my skin start to crawl as I got up off my knees and steadied myself. I knew I was descending rapidly into the next level of dope-sick hell. We needed to hit the road and find Oscar Ambrose as soon as possible.

"Can one of you guys help me get him out to the car?"

Two guards nodded their heads and helped him up to a standing position, as another took the vomit filled garbage away.

"Is he gonna be okay? Maybe we should get him to the hospital?" said one.

I knew Rocky never wanted to see the inside of another hospital, but I asked him anyway. It was official protocol for their benefit only.

"Do you?" I asked.

"All I need is a smoke," he said.

That settled that, and we all made our way outside. The guard that found my razor pulled a pack of cigarettes out of his pocket and offered us one. Everyone lit up and puffed away in silence for a minute or so.

It wasn't long before I saw a mischievous grin curl Rocky's lip.

"I wanna thank you two gentlemen for being so kind to us. Do you mind if I get a photo of you and Quinn here, together?"

They both shrugged in agreement so I walked over and positioned myself on the left.

"Saaay Tigers," he said, as he snapped the fourth picture of our trip.

This might be my favourite one of the bunch. There I am dwarfed by two huge guards. We're all smiling as the U.S. Customs sign lurks in the background and my t-shirt calls them stupid. But the best part is what you can't see. The best part is the fact that Rocky's taking the picture while smoking one of their smokes, after what'd just happened. It's pure poetry. And who knows, maybe this picture is proof of divine intervention. Because the way that room suddenly got brighter is something I still can't fully describe to anyone who wasn't there.

After getting the photo we got back in the car and chain smoked until our front wheels rolled over the first square foot of downtown Detroit.

Oscar Ambrose's place was our next stop. If he couldn't help us, we were dead in the water.

We might've hit Detroit, but we were still a long way from Wichita.

FIFTH INTERMISSION

I see the Green Fairy has touched you. Your eyes are glistening and a rapturous smile has parted your lips. You look good in absinthe. Oh, and look who's back! The frisky couple has returned with coy smiles and drinks in hand to catch the grand finale. Could those also be glasses of absinthe they're holding? They are! They've decided to accentuate themselves with the same enchanted hue as you. I may just have to get another, myself...

CHAPTER 12

Where the driver and his passenger briefly exchange roles after a rendezvous in Detroit.

IT WAS 5:30 A.M. when we pulled into the circular drive of the Marriott Hotel at the Renaissance center, on the shore of the river. A full twelve hours had lapsed since swallowing my last pill and my nose was running, my skin was crawling and the hot and cold flashes had begun; the junkie flu was starting to rage. If I didn't score anything within the hour, I'd be unable to drive. Within three, I'd be curled up fetus style in the back seat suffering through the first hideous cavalcade of hallucinations, and drenching my clothes with pools of sweat as my body attempted to cleanse itself.

I found a parking spot behind another taxi, left the engine running, dug out Ambrose's number and dialed it. My fingers and toes and every hair on my head was crossed. Rocky remained silent. He knew how important this call was.

As I brought the phone up to my ear, I noticed a patch of sky visible between the high rises had turned from black to navy blue; the first rays of dawn had splashed across the atmosphere. Soon it'd be morning, and the last thing I wanted was to be junk sick in the harsh light of day. Cold turkey and sunshine don't mix. To a junkie, squinting into the sun is no different than facing the beam of a law enforcing flashlight; both exposed those fine compromising lines — those secret creases and crow's feet of slow suicide.

A voice put an end to the ringing.

"Oscar Ambrose here."

"Oscar! *Thank god.* Sorry for calling so late... Er, I mean early. Did Glenda get a hold of you? It's Quinn. Quinn Jacob."

"Well hello, Quinn. And yes she did, she called and told me everything."

"Everything?" I said, with a leading tone.

"She told me what I needed to know. I can help you out. We'll talk more when you get here. I live at 20511 Livernois Avenue. It's right near Baker's Keyboard Lounge."

"*Shit!* I forgot to grab a map of Detroit."

"Where are you now?"

"In front of the hotel at the Renaissance center."

"All right then... Look out the driver's side and you'll see a Michigan left curving off just up the road. Take that and drive until you hit Woodward... Turn right at Woodward, get into the left hand lane and keep going 'til you get to the roundabout. Follow that around to Michigan Ave. Merge on to Michigan and drive 'til you hit Livernois... It's a fair piece so don't get discouraged. When you see Livernois, turn right and drive until you reach my address. I live above the store I own called Lust for Life... You can't miss it."

"How long d'you think it'll take us? I'm kinda hurtin'."

"Fifteen minutes tops if ya don't make any wrong turns, and trust me you don't wanna make any. Just stay on the roads I told you."

"Ahh, okay... I guess I better write those down then. We already had one run-in with trouble back in Toronto," I said, as I motioned for Rocky to give me a pen.

"Detroit makes Toronto look like Mister Roger's Neighbourhood. The cops don't even go to certain parts," he added.

"*Great,*" I drawled. "See you soon... Hopefully."

I wrote down the directions and hung up.

Within the span of the phone call, the sky had turned from navy to a deep azure. My body was that much weaker as well.

The rising sun was blanching my life force.

It was a race against time all over again.

As we traced Oscar's directions, the city revealed its secrets. It was a drive-by strip tease. We looked but didn't dare touch.

Detroit: The most elegantly wasted city on the face of the planet.

Detroit: The undisputed champion of the Post-Apocalyptic Metropolis contest.

Detroit: The definitive manifestation of urban decay.

Detroit: Undeniable proof of sketchy capitalism.

Detroit: Creating and destroying middle class aspirations since 1948.

Detroit: The birth, death, and rebirth of the North American dream.

Back in 1948, the Paris of the west, as it was known then, designed its very own flag. On this flag are two statuesque women. One woman stands in the foreground and watches the city burn behind her, while the other woman does her best to inspire hope by pointing at a new city rising up from the ashes.

Detroit: The Urban Phoenix.

The Bennu, in ancient Egyptian lore, is synonymous with the Greek Phoenix. It's the sacred bird of Heliopolis, and as such, represents the soul of the sun. Bennu is said to derive from the word weben, meaning rise.

The Bennu is also closely linked with the flooding of the Nile. For it is said to have stood alone on the primeval mound that rose up out of the watery chaos of creation, where it cried out to mark the dawn of time.

Dawn is beautiful, because real beauty is a rarefied exposition compelled by the early morning sunshine of truth.

We just happened to be driving through the labyrinth of downtown Detroit as the nascent blue of dawn unfurled itself like a hand-stitched quilt.

It was concrete convergence.

As I gripped the wheel and slowly succumbed to my dystopia, I felt the urge to cry out.

The mythology of the Phoenix was in my mind, so I cried out for rebirth.

I really did.

"Rebirth!" I shouted.

It startled Rocky.

"What the hell, man? You all right?"

"Yeah, I'm okay... Feelin' a bit ragged is all. Need a change," I muttered.

In spite of everything, I was okay. I could feel something regenerating within me. The spirit of Detroit was spurring me on. I looked down at my shoes again and then back up at the abandoned corridors of a bygone Babylon and felt kinship. I felt embraced. I felt home.

On July 11th, 1805, a fire swept through Detroit, burning everything to the ground, save for one building. On the city flag there are two Latin mottoes commemorating this disaster that read Speramus Meliora and Resurgent Cinerbus.

The first one translates as, *we hope for better things.*

The second, *it will rise from the ashes.*

Detroit did indeed rise from its ashes, but only briefly. Because one hundred and forty years later it was razed by a different kind of fire—an existential fire that was sparked by the race riot of 1943, and heavily stoked by the civil rights riot of 1967. In the aftermath of these two uprisings, racial integration within the city came to an abrupt halt as all the fear-struck whites moved out of the downtown core and settled into the suburbs.

Tragic irony is a brutal game.

For everyone knows that Detroit was the final stop on the Underground Railroad. It was the last bit of American soil to be kicked at by fleeing slaves before crossing over into Canada, and because of this the city came to represent freedom and equality.

Right here would be the perfect spot to suggest that there's nobody freer than he who rises from his own ash.

Just like Detroit, I had my very own fire and internal rebellion.

The fire was my father's sudden death when I was twelve years old. I watched as the world I grew up in was reduced to smoking rubble in the wake of a massive heart attack on a spotless kitchen floor.

The internal rebellion was my deleterious mid-twenties decision to let myself spiral down into the unmarked mass grave of drug addiction.

The question was, did I have what it took to dig myself back out? Could I rise? Could I rise all the way?

In Detroit I could feel the power of resurrection all around me. The irrepressible will to rejuvenate danced along the sidewalks and down the alleyways to an upbeat Motown rhythm. I felt the closeness of freedom. I felt my shackles loosening. I was about to take my first tentative step into the Promised Land.

If Detroit could do it, so could I.

And make no mistake, in spite of the odds Detroit was doing it again.

Economic recessions and Wall Street greed may have killed off her automotive manufacturing sector, condemning her to bankruptcy, but let's not forget who we're dealing with.

She simply adjusted her strategy.

She's a creature of rejuvenation, after all.

At the turn of the millennium, she began attracting grassroots opportunists from all over the world with her rock bottom real estate prices and vacant but extremely fertile inner city land; now slowly being repurposed for huge communal gardens that overflow with fresh fruits and vegetables. Her world class bounty of neglected architectural gems has also been snapped up and transformed into cooperative work spaces that spawn new and ethical enterprise.

Springtime in Detroit. Again.

And I was definitely ready for my next spring.

My winter had long outstayed its welcome.

The river and the city must've been looking out for us because we made it to Ambrose's store without getting rolled by thugs or jacked up by the cops. The only downside was, by the time we reached his place my body had resorted to its most basic form of punishment.

The moment we pulled into his parking lot my bowels began to liquefy.

Every junkie winds up with a compacted bowel at some point in their ignominious career, due to the dehydrating effects of opiates. It happened to Elvis. And maybe the pope was a junkie too, because it happened to him.

Ever heard the expression, drier than a junkie's fart?

Anyway, when the body starts to reawaken, in the absence of morphine or codeine or Oxycontin or Percocet, one of the last and most grievous things it will do is flush out its backed-up colon.

I felt a hot geyser head south as we sat in the car. On account of it not being my first dope-sick rodeo, I knew I had a few more minutes before detonation.

"Fuck... I need to find a bathroom," I said through gritted teeth, as I picked up the phone and hit redial.

A terrifying gurgling sound emanated from deep inside my gut and Rocky suddenly agreed with me.

"*Jesus!* What the *hell* was that? You weren't kidding were you?"

I shot him an uncomfortable eye as Ambrose picked up.

"Hey Oscar, we're here... Can we come up?"

"The green door to the left of the store. It's open... C'mon in."

"Perfect. Be right there."

Lust for Life wasn't your average retail establishment. It was an adult video store, and by the looks of it Oscar had branched out into the accessory market. The front window was a carefully arranged collage of glossy photos advertising everything from neon dildos to pocket vaginas. A life-sized picture of a firm Dominatrix in a rubber cat-suit holding a bull whip filled out the inside of the door.

It was a blunt marketing move on his part.

"I think I'm gonna like this guy," Rocky chirped, as he opened his door.

"Good. I'm glad... Now let's get inside, before I need a new pair of pants."

I hopped out the car and walked rather stiffly to the green door. Rocky was ahead of me with his head turned, still feasting his eyes.

"You ever read the book 'Sixty Yards to the Outhouse' by Will E. Makitt?" he asked, as I clenched my ass cheeks together.

"That's just plain unfunny," I said.

He opened the door and I brushed by him to make my way up the stairs. When I got to the top, I stopped and pulled myself together as best I could. Then I stepped up to the door just as it swung open. In front of me was a short, stocky balding man with thick limbs and a salesman's smile.

"Welcome my friends... Any friend of Glenda is a friend of mine. C'mon in and make yourselves at home."

Rocky was shoulder to shoulder with me and smiling back.

"I don't mean to be rude but can I use your bathroom? It's urgent."

"Sure... You must be Quinn?"

"Haha. Yes I am. The one with the problem."

"It's down the hall and to your right. No worries."

"Thank you," I said, as I squeezed past him. "I might be a while."

Rocky came in and shut the door but kept quiet.

"Quinn... Take this with you. It's all I could find... It's the real deal so be careful. Don't over amp on me."

Oscar handed me a fold of tinfoil. I knew immediately what it was. It was heroin. I'd only done it once or twice before because it was scarce back in Grey Grove, and even then the quality was always terrible. I had no idea how powerful this stuff would be, so in order to err on the side of caution I presumed it was pure.

"Thanks," I said, as I took it from him. "My tolerance is pretty high. I should be fine."

I continued on down the hall, stepped into the bathroom and shut the door, making sure not to lock it.

The mind is a powerful magnet.

Just holding the poppy powder in the palm of my hand was enough to stop the advance of my withdrawal symptoms. What was gearing up to be a posterior explosion of volcanic proportions, suddenly abated with the thought of getting high.

I sat down backwards on the toilet so I could use the top of the reservoir as a little table for my operations. I gingerly unfolded the tinfoil and there it was, China white. I'd never actually seen it before. It was like powdered magic to me. In Grey Grove the smack was all cut to shit and invariably wound up in your hand as a tan coloured mockery. I think I licked my lips as I reached into my back pocket, pulled out a Benjamin, rolled it up into a tight tube and without taking my eyes off my Asian mistress, tucked it under my left thigh. I got out my straight razor and carefully separated out half a pinkie fingernail's worth—my usual fail safe amount.

My moment had arrived; the only moment I craved. My moment of Persian mercy. My moment of pain killing truth. A moment of awesome that leaves one, and all draped like crushed velvet curtains, off the beveled edge of consciousness.

My regal return to Lotus Eater Isle was at hand.

I took the rolled-up hundred dollar bill out from under my thigh and held it up to the incandescent light. It was unobstructed. My bliss was unobstructed.

I descended upon my medicine with hungry passages.

I sniffed up the tiny pile of crystals into my right nostril and waited for it to breach the membrane and invade my brain stem.

I counted down in my head.

Ten.

Nine.

Eight.

Seven.

Six.

Five.

Four.

Threeee.

Twoooooo.

Onnnnnneeee.

Ever so slowly, I filled up with an ancient sense of well-being.

I felt my seasickness leave me like an exorcised daemon. It started in my feet and evaporated all the way up to the crown of my head, where it tapered off into oblivion, coiling back up into my neurons to lie in wait like a karmic viper.

I slouched a little as all the tension left my muscles. I took a breath in, then let it escape through assuaged lips. I smiled that imperturbable, ashen-faced heroin smile and maneuvered myself down onto the cold tiled floor, so that my back was against the wall. Snippets of conversation drifted in from down the hall and danced on the rims of my ears.

All was right in the world.

All was good and right.

Even my feet were relaxed. They were extended out in front of me in a lazy "v" shape. The red of my shoes exuded a scarlet aura as

Glenda returned to my thoughts. She was standing there in her charcoal trench coat, reading me like hard boiled fiction.

I wanted to tell her I was only doing what I had to do to get back home, but I knew she knew that. And her eyes weren't asking me why, anyway. They were asking me *when*. They were asking *when* I'd be ready to take up the fight, and neutralize the saccharine lure of a false rapture.

I attempted an explanation, but she just smiled, and receded back into the light from whence she came.

I let my head drop down and rest against my left shoulder. Then something caught my attention. I looked over at the dark space under the bathroom door, and saw hundreds of tiny soldiers marching toward me.

The strains of a familiar melody tickled my ears as they advanced:

"*Around and 'round the heroin bush,*" the tiny sergeant sang, with all the might he could muster.

And in a crisply militant call and response, the troops answered with, "*The junkie chased the neee-dle.*"

This was chanted over and over again until they were right up close, at which point they stopped and formed a front line. The sergeant moved forward on a black horse, holding aloft a red banner. The banner said something, but the writing was so small I had to lean in to read it. What looked like tiny hieroglyphs, gradually rearranged themselves into the English language.

Destroy The Image, it said.

"Destroy the image," I repeated. "Destroy the image... De-stroy the im-age. Des-troy thee im-age."

As I turned the mantra over, and over in my mind the soldiers raised their guns, and fired a three round salute. Then the door opened and Rocky was standing there. His mouth was moving, but no sound came out.

Slowly, ever so slowly, his words faded in.

"Quinn! I *fucking* knocked three times, man, what the hell? You're high as a kite aren't you?"

I wanted to answer him, but the thoughts in my head never hit my lips. I avoided his glare. I looked down at the floor and noticed the tiny army was gone. I looked all around, but they were nowhere to be seen. Then I felt myself being pulled up from the floor. Rocky stood me up against the wall and slapped my face. He turned around, twisted the faucet on, cupped some water and threw it at me.

The icy liquid worked.

"Okay. Okay… I'm here. Stop it would ya."

He gave me a nasty look.

"You stupid fucker. You coulda died in here. You're lucky the door was unlocked."

"I—I did that... I'm naaw tha sstupid," I slurred.

"Oh, yes you are… But Wichita awaits, my friend. Come with me, and we'll talk to Oscar. He's got some exciting news."

He put my arm around his shoulder, and helped me down the hall.

I remember being sat down on a black leather sofa. There was raunchy punk rock blaring out of some speakers as a video played on a large wall mounted screen. I was having a hard time keeping my eyes open for more than a few minutes.

The heroin nods were in full swing.

"Do you have any coffee? Quinn's medicine was a little strong I think."

"How 'bout a quadruple espresso. Bolivian style," Oscar quipped.

"Sounds good... Sound good to you, Quinn?"

My eyelids were like two sandbags. Holding them up was impossible so I looked at him through a series of blinks.

"Yeah. Suuure."

Oscar left the room and came back a few minutes later to sit down between us.

"This'll perk ya right up," he said.

He was sitting on the edge of the couch, hunched over with his elbows on his knees as he pulled a drawer open on the coffee table in front of him, and took out a mirror. He grabbed a small baggie out of his pocket and flicked it a couple times as he held it up.

It was more white powder.

"Coffee won't touch the stuff you just did but this will. This'll ring your bell loud and clear."

"Cocaine, right?" said Rocky.

"That's right. Bolivian marching powder."

"Are you sure it's okay for him?"

"A couple bumps and he'll be ready to take on the world."

He emptied the baggie out and started chopping the chunky contents up with a bank card. When he was done there were six lines ready and waiting. He licked the plastic edge of the card before putting it back in his wallet, then turned to me.

"Here," he said. "You go first."

I managed to peel myself out of the corner of the couch, and lean forward. I sniffed up two of the lines, one in each nostril, then sat back, and waited for it to burn through the opiate fog.

"Thanks," I said.

"No problemo. Your friend Rocky here makes some pretty fine vidz."

He pointed at the screen on the wall. I looked up and realized for the first time it was Rocky in the video that was playing. I remembered him telling me about his YouTube stuff involving the masks he made, back when he first hopped into my taxi.

Only twelve hours had passed since then.

I laughed to myself at the absurd distortion of time. There was no way it'd only been twelve hours. It was a lifetime already—a scintillating collection of unforgettable vignettes.

I felt my eyes widen as the cocaine slammed into my brain. My gums and teeth went numb. I was no longer nodding. I was *awake*.

Rocky snorted his up, and almost immediately started chattering.

"This video is good. I tried to capture the essence of humanity here. Watch this part... *Watch*!"

He was standing on the edge of a Walmart parking lot. Every now and then a car would pull into an empty space or back out of one as families pushing shopping carts passed by in the background. He stood there staring into the camera for a minute or so, not moving. Then he reached up and peeled off the first mask. He'd been wearing a smiling old man face. But underneath was the face of a sad middle aged woman. Again, he just stared at the camera for a bit before peeling off the woman's face to reveal that of a placid young boy.

This went on until he'd been through half a dozen faces: male, female, young, old, black, white, angry, happy, and sad.

Finally, he removed the last mask, and underneath was a faceless face. There were no features at all. He stood there again for a bit, before bringing up a black marker with his right hand and drawing a set of eyes, then a nose, then a mouth. On the forehead he wrote one word.

Image.

He walked up to the camera and turned it off.

All three of us sat there not saying a word after his video had finished. The silence was filled by the synaptic firings of my brain. I was disturbed more than moved, and I liked it.

Rocky jumped up and started pacing back and forth in front of us. I could see the gears spinning behind his eyes as he trod the carpet.

"Why all this focus on image?" I asked him. I was still thinking about the hallucination I had just minutes before on the bathroom floor.

I also remembered the quote he recited from *Eye of The Dragon*. The one about destroying the image to defeat the enemy.

He stroked his chin.

"Image is everything, right? Isn't that what everyone says?" he mused, as he stopped walking, turned abruptly and pinned me to the couch with his eyes.

Before he could continue, Oscar piped up.

"I know a thing or two about image," Oscar said, as he rubbed his hands together and wrinkled up a magnificent forehead. "I've managed a ton of bands in this city and the ones who go the farthest aren't necessarily the best... It's all about style, you see. And style is eighty percent sex appeal. The rest is raw nerve... If you ain't got those two things, you don't have a hope in hell. Sex is big business my friends. Lust for Life is a gold mine, trust me."

Rocky nodded his head at Oscar's theory, then proposed his own.

"The scarecrow works completely on representation... I bet if you really look at the most successful bands you've managed, they all stand for some kind of subculture or ideology or trend."

"Yeah, as a matter of fact... The most popular band I ever managed was a skin-head outfit. I didn't agree with their bullshit, but they always played sold out shows. They made big money until the singer killed some poor immigrant in a street fight. Stupid fucker's been in jail for ten years now, but back when they were hot I pretty much lived off the percentage I took."

"Image... Image... Image," Rocky droned. "It's the *root* of imagination. Craft an image, design your symbol, and you got it made in the shade... But!" He clapped his hands once for punctuation. "You could wind up tied to a poison rocket."

He walked over to the coffee table and picked up the mirror. It was a little vanity mirror.

"Does this mean a lot to you, Oscar?"

Oscar shook his head and looked a little self-conscious.

"No. Got it at the dollar store up the road."

"Good. I'll give you a hundred bucks if I can smash it."

Oscar laughed. It was a nervous laugh, choked off by dollar signs.

"A hundred bucks? Sure dude. Smash away."

Rocky took the mirror and held it up in front of both of us. First Oscar, then me. He lingered in front of the hard evidence that was my face. Dark caverns clawed at my eyes as bloodless flesh bemoaned.

I couldn't hold my own gaze. I looked away.

He gave me a nod as he held it up over his head and let it drop. The shattering sliced into my ear canals.

He picked up the pieces and laid them on the table one by one.

"Now look into the mosaic," he said.

Rocky handed Oscar a hundred-dollar bill. Oscar smiled and took it, then leaned over and looked at himself holding the money.

"I see dollar signs," he said, with a chuckle.

"Your turn, Quinn," Rocky ordered.

I hunched forward to see a dozen different sections of my unhealthy face. Rocky pounced.

"Those shiny little tiles are your mirror mosaic." He hesitated, like he was hoping or maybe half expecting me to guess the rest of what he was about to say. But I was too engrossed in the ravaged reflections staring me down. I heard him sigh before he started back in. "Amidst a thousand reflections we create each other, for if I'm a small part of your mirror mosaic then you're a small part of mine. We're all shiny tiles reflecting back to each other our ideas and images of one another, which makes up the divine providence of context and detail. And as long as we stand far enough away to take in the entire mosaic, but stay close enough to heed the details, we benefit from its natural checks and balances.

"However, the second we get in too close, and fixate on just one reflection because we decide we like it the best, because it makes us feel better about ourselves. Well that's when the trouble starts... We lose balance... We get sick... We get cancer of the imagination, because we're no longer in the mosaic, and that's when the poisonous growth starts. That's why we gotta be relentless in our hunt for growth fueled on singular ideas, and images. Capitalistic growth that secretly feeds on fear while hiding behind the illusion of protection. I call it the Great Breakwater Bamboozling because we get tricked into isolating ourselves from nature by building breakwaters in our minds. Breakwaters built on viral ideologies." He paused to search for more ammunition in the battery of his brain, then threw his hands up, and smiled big. "And pretty much any crap that promises to save our souls... You know the stuff I'm talking about...

"The rancid chicken soup and sugar pills peddled by fearful shepherds. Those meddling bastards who size up the fragility of life, cook up vaccines, and sell them as secrets to success. Then, of course, they sit back and count their coffers as the virus sickens yet another generation of young hopefuls." I saw him glance at the clock, and swallow hard. "There's not one fucking secret out there we can't *see* for ourselves, all in good time, all in good faith... But if we settle, and fixate out of weakness, we wind up bamboozled." His eyes glinted like black ice under a streetlight. "It's all very simple, Quinn. When you fixate, you forsake the grace of your shiny tiles."

He stopped, with eyes still blazing. And although I was held in rapt attention, I found myself feeling strangely awkward, not knowing what to do or say in the wake of his diatribe. To be completely honest, my drug-hobbled intellect was simply out of its depth. I couldn't seem to make heads or tails of what he'd said. All I remember taking away from it, at the time, was that it sounded inspiring, and yet vaguely paranoid.

As I sat there trying to decode his words, the pressure to engage him in some kind of philosophical discussion was relieved by another one of his videos that started playing behind him. He turned around to watch it with us.

Actually, hang on a second.

I can put it on right now and close caption it for you, as it plays. It's my favourite one of his.

Just a minute…

Okay. Here we go.

This one has him standing in a bathroom with the camera pointed at himself.

"What is your fucking problem?" he says, looking past the lens.

The camera pans to a mirror he's standing in front of. Somewhere within the pan he's made a seamless edit so that his reflection is wearing a daemonic looking mask.

"Problem fucking your what is?" answers the daemon.

Camera swings back to him.

"WHO THE FUCK ARE YOU?"

Camera swings back to the mirror.

"YOU ARE FUCK THE WHO?" bellows the daemon, in a guttural voice.

Camera swings back to him.

"You don't exist," Rocky says.

Camera swings back to mirror.

"Oh, yes I do," hisses the daemon.

Camera jerks back violently, to him.

"THEN PROVE IT!" he cries.

Camera turns very slowly back to the mirror. There's a background sound of stretching latex. When the lens finally frames the mirror we see a skull instead of a daemon.

"Fear makes daemons of us all," the skull says.

Camera pans one last time so that it frames the back of Rocky's head.

"Then I'll *rip* the fear right out of my own brain!"

He reaches up and starts digging into his temple with his fingers. Because of decreased depth perception it looks quite real. A squishing and ripping noise ensues. He pulls and pulls until finally his fingers re-emerge with a black sphere. He then pivots on the spot to face the camera, masked as a boy of about thirteen. Nothing is said as he holds up the sphere and throws it at the mirror, smashing it. He walks forward, turns on the tap and starts washing his hands as pieces of the mirror in the bottom of the sink show sections of his youthful face.

Camera shuts off.

When the second video finished Rocky took his seat back on the couch beside Oscar, who was chopping up a few more lines on the surface of a CD case. Again, we were all silent for a bit as the imagery and dialogue moved about our brains like some dark electrical current tripping switches.

Then Oscar offered Rocky his share.

"That's some pretty radical stuff you got goin' on, man... I like it... I like it a lot." He pushed the case over and Rocky lowered his head. "You ever thought about puttin' a soundtrack to any of this stuff? You know, like something suitable. Something edgy and cool. Like one of my bands for instance." He paused as Rocky sniffed up the powder and leaned back against the couch. "The CD you just looked at is by one of my newest acts. They're up and comers, trust me. They're gonna break large, and you my friend could ride that wave if you wanted."

Rocky leaned over again and took another look at the jewel case.

"They're called Corvus? I like the cover."

"Yeah man... Corvus is the scientific name for ravens or some shit like that. That raven you see there is actually the lead guitarist's pet. You should see the thing... Smarter than most humans. It can play tic tac toe... I kid you not!"

That put a great big smile on Rocky's face.

"So you mean you wanna use my YouTube stuff for a Corvus video?"

"Well yeah. They're about to release their debut album, and ohhhh man does it kick ass. It's face melting hardcore, dude. Your videos would be a match made in heaven. Or hell... depending on your personal preference."

I was thinking symbolically when Oscar shot me a satisfied grin. The words that flew from my lips were numb replicas of a school project I'd done back in ninth grade.

"Did you know it was a legendary Babylonian raven that inspired the Greek myth of Corvus?" I said. "He sat on the tail of a serpent and was sacred to the god of rain and storm."

"Niiiice," Oscar chimed, as he passed me the blow.

I looked into the raven's eyes as I filled my nose.

"The music I played along to your first video there... The one you did in the parking lot. That was them... Pretty fuckin' tight, huh?"

Rocky stood back up and started pacing in front of us again.

"Okay... I'll do it. I can give you the password to my channel and you can download them all from there."

"I don't need your password, just email me the files when you get back home or whatever. We can work out the arrangement then."

"I'm not goin' back home. And I won't have access to a computer where I am goin'... If you're serious about this, we have to work it out now."

Oscar rubbed his hands together over the urgency of Rocky's response, as a look of serious business etched itself between his eyes and mouth.

"I like a decisive man," he said, as he searched through the drawer in front of him and pulled out a sheet of paper. "I've got a general contract right here... All we have to do is fill in the blanks, and you'll be famous. Trust me."

I thought things were moving along too fast. It didn't seem right to me and I said so.

"Rocky... Think about what you're doing here before you sign off on anything. Read it over a few times."

Oscar took his cue and threw himself into neutral, biding his time. Rocky just shook his head at me.

"Quinn, you know the score... I wanna be remembered. Besides, those videos barely have any views on YouTube. This'll get 'em exposed and maybe even make some cash for whoever I wanna leave it to."

"Leave it to who?" questioned Oscar, as he put the contract down and leaned back against the couch.

Rocky had said too much for his own liking. I could see it in his face.

"It's nothin'," he countered. "I've got a younger sister that needs money. She's got three kids and her chump husband just left her."

He shot me a look and I played along.

"She does need help... All right, all right, just read it over," I repeated.

"It's a licensing agreement. He maintains artistic control and takes a twenty percent royalty... The band takes forty, and I take forty. You can walk if you want, but this is a win-win situation... It'll be your big break."

Rocky kept pacing, then stopped in his tracks as he looked at the clock on the wall. It was going on 7:00 a.m.

"We gotta move, Quinn! I wanna be in Wichita by sundown... Where's the pen?"

Oscar smiled.

"Like I said. You're a man after my own heart. Congratulations," he announced, as he thrust a pen forward with one hand and held the other out for shaking.

Rocky shook it, then took the pen.

"Before I do this, I have a favour to ask of you."

"Anything, man... Anything at all."

"I've got some money that needs to be cleaned up... if ya know what I mean."

Once again, that look of serious business washed over Oscar's face.

"You know how to bargain, I see," he said, through a cautious chuckle. "I don't get into the shady stuff too often, but I got friends who can deal with it. How much you talkin?"

"About nine grand, but I'll give you half that if you can do it for us right now."

"Yer gonna give me a *fifty* cut!?"

"That's what I said."

Oscar struck a meditative pose. I just sat there watching, knowing how crucial the next few moments would be.

"All right... I'll do it. I've got five grand in the store safe. You sign and it's a done deal."

"Show me the money first," demanded Rocky.

Oscar smiled and stood up.

"Be right back, boys."

He padded off down the hall, then went out the door and down the stairs. Rocky and I both sat there not saying anything. We knew the rest of the trip depended on getting the money.

Coin laundries would be pretty scarce along the lonesome highways that stretched out between Detroit and Kansas. And after 9:00 a.m. or so, the serial numbers on the stolen bills would be circulating far and wide, over police wires.

CHAPTER 13

Where the driver and his passenger make their mad dash to Wichita, pick up a hitchhiker along the way, and see how thoroughly life can imitate art.

WHILE WAITING FOR OSCAR, I remembered the heroin was still in the bathroom, so I shuffled off to get it.

I carefully wrapped it back up in the foil and scolded myself for misjudging its strength. On the way out the door, I stopped in front of the mirror to check my nose for traces of powder.

Doing this brought his video right back to the forefront of my mind.

Is it really that simple?

Does fear really turn us all into daemons?

And if so, what kind of daemon was I?

These three questions ran through my mind as I beheld my fear-fuelled and drug-addled reflection.

Then I remembered another thing Rocky said to me near the start of our trip, "I see a bunch of you, but one's killing all the others."

For a second I felt like smashing Oscar's mirror, but then I saw a bar of soap sitting there. I took the soap and drew a big X over my face.

"I won't let you rule," I whispered. "I'm many more than you."

Just then I heard the sound of heavy footsteps coming up the stairs, followed by the squeak of an opening door. Oscar's voice drifted down the hall so I turned off the light and went out.

"Here's the forty-five hundred... Can barely even read the numbers on these babies," he said, as he handed it all to Rocky.

Rocky stopped pacing to count the money. For the first time I noticed a blood stain on his shirt, a souvenir from the border crossing.

"You got blood on your shirt."

He looked down at himself, but shrugged it off and kept counting.

"Hey! I've got a shirt for ya," Oscar said.

He darted over to a large cardboard box and pulled out a black t-shirt with a red stenciled raven's head on the front. Rocky looked up and smiled as he peeled off hundreds.

"It's Corvus merch," he said, as he tossed it over to me.

I caught it as Rocky finished counting.

"It's all here," he confirmed.

I traded Rocky the shirt for the money. As he changed I glimpsed his bare chest and back, up close. Every one of his ribs and vertebrae were visible. I looked away.

Oscar went and got the contract from the coffee table and came back.

"Sign this and leave me the nine grand, and you'll be on your way to... Where're you guys headin' again?"

"Wichita," I said, as Rocky took the paper and signed on the dotted line.

After finishing his signature with a purposeful flourish, he went back to the couch, grabbed his satchel and returned with the other seven thousand.

"Gimme the two grand you have, Quinn."

I did and he put it all together, then handed it over to Oscar who counted it out one more time with the speed and dexterity of a bank executive.

"You Canadians and your Monopoly money," he smiled, while licking his thumb and sliding it over the last bill. "It's all here. Now... Can I interest you in anymore of that marching powder, for the road?"

I looked at Rocky. He shook his head.

"Naw, we're good to go. But thank you. You fixed me up... I'll be able to make it home now."

A job-well-done grin spread over Oscar's face.

"Like I said, a friend of Glenda is always a friend of mine... By the way, I'll call her and let her know everything's cool with you."

I was planning on doing that, but he seemed pretty eager for the accolades, so I went along with it.

"Tell her I'll drop in on the way back," I said.

"No problemo amigo."

Rocky turned the contract over and wrote something on it.

"Here's my YouTube password and my bank account number... If any money rolls in from this deal, wire it to me."

"Sure thing! And it will... Trust me."

For a split second I saw Rocky's eyes grow skeptical. But they softened quickly with the return of his trademark mischief.

"It's been a pleasure, Oscar... Do you mind if I get a picture of you and Quinn together?"

"Not at all," he said, as he looked down at my shirt. "And just so ya know, you can call me stupid 'till the cows come home. But don'cha *dare* call me late for dinner!"

He laughed and winked at me, then walked over and draped his thick arm over my shoulder.

Rocky snapped the fifth picture of the trip.

This photo is the one I look at when I wanna remind myself of how bad I let things get. I was death warmed over by a coke and smack speed-ball. Not to mention I hadn't slept or eaten a proper meal in well over 24 hours.

My eyes were two panhandlers begging for change.

Lucky for me, change did finally come. It didn't arrive as quickly as I'd hoped, but eventually it graced my decrepit doorstep and knocked—drawing me from the depths of my hovel, with open arms.

I think I'll take a break from writing and go watch some more of Rocky's videos.

I do it every now and then when I feel the need.

Brb.

Hear that sound?

It's a drum stick on a table top.

So I just watched everything on Rocky's YouTube channel, then put on "Sides of You"—the Corvus song that accompanied his parking lot video. And while I was listening I remembered the drum stick Oscar gave us right before we left him.

We were all standing outside in front of Soldier, saying our goodbyes and shaking hands and stuff, when Oscar blurted: "Hang on a minute. I've got somethin' for you..."

He yanked open the green door and took off up the stairs, then came charging back down with the stick in his hand.

"You see that night club over there?" He pointed and we both turned to look across the street. It was Baker's Keyboard Lounge; the place he referenced back when I asked him for directions to his place. "That's the oldest jazz club in the world. Been goin' since 1934... Art Tatum, John Coltrane, Oscar Peterson, Cab Calloway, Nat King Cole, Ella Fitzgerald, Chic Corea, and Fats Waller all played there." He paused as he ran his finger over the splintered wood. "Now... Take a good look at this stick."

He handed it to us. It was grey with age and pretty chewed up.

"Looks real old," Rocky said.

"It's from the 1930's. At one time that there stick was held by the late great Harry Dial, who used to drum for Fats Waller. You familiar with Fats?"

Rocky shook his head but the name rang a bell for me.

"Wasn't he in the movie *Stormy Weather*?" I asked.

"He was, he was... Which, by the way, is considered to be the greatest African American musical of all time." He nodded his head as if to convince us before continuing. "Fats Waller was one of the first great Jazz Cats. He played a mean piano. One time he was actually kidnapped from a gig by gangsters and taken to a party. When he got to the party he realized he was playin' for Al Capone... Can you imagine that man!? Anyway, he died in Kansas City well before his time... But even still, most of the standards you hear nowadays are attributed to him." He stopped talking and admired the stick in Rocky's hand, looking like he was second guessing what he was about to do. Then he shrugged it off and followed through. "I paid a lot of money for these sticks, Rocky, but I'm gonna give you this one as an act of good faith. Think of it as a symbol of our new partnership."

Rocky took the stick and tapped his head with it.

"Does it have good luck?" he mused.

"Well it's sure got somethin'. You *know* it."

I dug my keys out of my pocket. The jingling sound advanced the moment.

"All right boys... Drive safe and stay on the main roads 'til yer outta Detroit."

"I was gonna ask you which way we should go... We need interstate 94," I said.

"Just take eight mile here over to interstate 75. That'll take ya straight down to 94... And here. Before I forget. Take my card."

I took it and gave it a once over. On the front it said, *Oscar Ambrose Management*. On the back it had his address, phone number, and email. The email contained a different name, joeread@gmail.com. I assumed he must've changed his name to affect a little more panache. I was gonna ask him why he chose Oscar Ambrose, but didn't wanna get wrapped up in a long winded anecdote.

I stuffed the card in my pocket, walked to the car and hopped in.

From the driver's seat I watched Rocky and Oscar shake hands. Then Rocky jogged back and took up his station beside me.

We waved goodbye as we pulled out onto the road.

The bright blue dawn was calling us onward.

We got out of Detroit with 4,500 freshly laundered dollars and a 1930s drum stick once wielded by a legendary jazz drummer. Rocky was sporting a new t-shirt and I was sufficiently medicated.

All we had to do was follow the asphalt vector we were on, straight down to the flat fields of Kansas.

I was ready and willing as the cocaine tickled my veins and the Michigan air tousled my hair.

I drove for almost three hours.

Somewhere close to the state line of Indiana I remember looking over at Rocky. An evergreen treeline was cascading along behind him. A mirthful smile sealed his lips and his head was thrown back a little. He looked classic somehow. He looked timeless. It made me wanna take a picture of him, so I picked the phone up off the seat and just as I did it started ringing. He looked over as I looked down to see who it was.

It was my mom.

I rolled up the window and cleared my throat.

"It's my mom," I announced.

An aw-shucks expression angled his eyebrows as I answered.

"Hi, mom," I said, in the breeziest way possible.

"Well hello, stranger. Would it kill you to pick up the phone and dial my number every once in a while? Maybe once a week? Heck, I'll settle for once a month."

She sounded relaxed, but just underneath her casual veneer was the usual mix of disappointment and sadness.

You see, I wasn't the kind of son who kept his mom's regular counsel; but that's not the worst part. The worst part was, I managed to rationalize my neglectful behaviour by blaming words—cumbersome words that "flew in the face of real connections," or so I told myself. Somehow I became convinced that I was incapable of clarity. I began to feel constantly disingenuous, even with my own mom, and this, in turn, made me disgusted with all forms of conversation.

In simple terms: I was afraid to break her heart by telling her the ugly truth about myself.

So what did I do?

I gave up and made the erroneous decision to scale down my communications altogether. Basically, I resorted to empty formality. I did what most people do—I picked up the phone and called her at the predictable times, Christmas, and birthdays, and such. Of course, this grievously selfish decision backfired, because it kept me from staying abreast with the one person in the world who truly loved me unconditionally. It also allowed me to slip through the cracks unnoticed—down into the abyss of addiction.

Had I maintained regular contact with my mom, she would've been alerted to the fact that I was drowning. She would've made the harrowing journey into my personal hell to do her very best at saving me.

For a long time I just didn't get the wisdom behind small talk and chatting about the weather.

Dignity can be found in the smallest gesture.

"I know mom... I'm sorry."

A transport truck roared by us in the other lane.

"Are you at work?"

"Yeah... I am." I paused to pick my words carefully. "I'm on a long drive. It's a big call and it's lots of money, which I need, as you know. Right now I'm about to cross into Indiana. On my way to Wichita."

I waited for her shock to pour through the phone.

"Wichita? Quinn! You should've *called* before you left!"

"I know, mom. I know... I'm sorry."

She launched into a tirade of safety issues that all involved not letting people know when I was going out of town on a job.

Then Rocky tapped my shoulder. I turned to see him mouthing the words to what he wanted me to say.

"Frank. Ask her about Frank," he mimed.

I just looked at him and shook my head, trying to ignore him, but he kept at it. Every time I turned away he tapped me again. Finally I gave in.

"Hey mom... Can I ask you a question? It's a bit of a strange one."

"Sure. Go right ahead, hon."

"You know how I was supposed to be a twin?"

"Yeees..."

"Well... I was wondering if you'd picked a name out for him?"

There was a brief silence. Rocky was leaning in.

"Your father and I decided that he would name one and I would name the other. I wanted to call him Francis."

"Francis? No wonder he bailed," I blurted through a laugh. "Why not Franklin?"

"You might be right there," she chuckled along. "But Francis was the name of your great-great-grandfather on my side. It was a traditional thing," she explained.

Rocky was nodding his head with an I-told-you-so slowness.

"What made you think about that?" she asked.

"Oh, nothing really. It's a long drive... You know how it is. After a while you start thinkin' about things you haven't thought of in a long time."

A silence ensued.

"Wichita isn't really that far from Omaha. You'll get to see the land that raised me up. It's still thick in my blood, you know." Her voice trailed off into a wisp of nostalgia, soothed by whatever memories she was reliving. Then she snapped out of it. "Be *safe* out there, Quinn... Call me if anything happens, okay? I'm your mom, *remember* that."

"I will... And I'll call when I get back... Love you."

"Love you too, hon."

We hung up and the first thing out of Rocky's mouth was a whistle. It was a deep and drawn out whistle; the kind people make when something significant has just come to pass.

Neither one of us felt the need to comment on the conversation I had with my mom. The idea of Frank being connected to me through some sort of familial soul group was something we'd already intuited.

We fell back into a hush. For another hour or so I drove until the inevitable happened: the cocaine ran its course, allowing the longer half-life of the heroin high, and my bone-crushing exhaustion, to overtake me once again.

We were passing by Gary, Indiana when the full weight of my eyelids started crashing down like steel doors. All of a sudden I was looking through a slow strobe light at a stop motion world.

"Rocky..."

"Yeah?"

"I'm wiped out, man. I gotta sleep or I'm gonna get us killed."

"What? Not an option," he barked.

"We need gas anyway... And there's a station comin' up."

He remained silent. Brooding. Then all of a sudden he perked up.

"Then let me drive... You have to let me drive. It's the only way we're gonna make it on time."

I should've seen that coming but I didn't. I was caught off guard and was thereby completely ineffectual to counter him. I tried cooking up an excuse but nothing presented itself. I was just too tired to think, so I caved.

"When was the last time you drove anything?"

"I had my driver's license for four years before they took it away on account of my tumour."

"Well, obviously they took it away for a reason," I said.

"You're not seriously gonna be the Ministry of Transportation right now, are you? Cause if you are you can go fuck yourself."

He was right. Who was I to stand in the way of a simple joy? It would've been a crime. I didn't have it in me to tie the hands of a kid staring death in the face.

"We'll switch at the gas station."

"YEEES! You're the best, Quinn!"

Hearing him shout that out right then was worth any problems that might arise on his watch.

We pulled off the highway and gassed up. It was getting close to noon. The sun was ascending in the sky and it was windy. The clouds marched across above us like colossal regiments of cotton.

I took my spot on the passenger's side as he climbed in behind the wheel and turned the key.

I stayed awake for as long as I could to make sure he was capable, and he was. He was quite good, really. He kept an eye on his mirrors, did shoulder checks before lane changes and made sure our speed was well within the limits.

It was enough to reassure me and I quickly fell into the deepest slumber.

The down-filled jacket of sleep hugged my shoulders and I fell into a dream.

Around and around I went.

Until the worm turned and my thoughts frosted.

I made my way through thick forest, navigating undergrowth and whistling smoke.

The crunch of branches under foot kept odd rhythm as cicadas improvised and brave beams of sun warmed the clay.

I walked and walked.

I drank in the succulence of May and tasted the sugar of her sap.

The air grew humid.

Vapour filled my ribcage as I glimpsed the edge of reason.

A clearing was presented.

I forged my way and stepped out onto wild strawberry, squinting in the new light.

I saw a lake crowded by crooked firs.

I made the shoreline pilgrimage.

Off to my left a heron bird stood statuesque, blinking.

To my right an ancient dock stretched out upon curling waves.
It called me.

I went.

I counted my steps to its nadir.

At thirteen I stopped to dangle my shins in water.

My frost melted and dripped down the inside of my thigh as a black speck skirted the horizon.

I watched it dance.

Then it changed direction and started toward me, expanding as it came.

I dismissed my fear.

A raven.

It called out with a voice soaked in thunder as a cumulonimbus veiled the sun.

Hovering above with colossal wings, it sheltered me in shadow.

Its eyes were liquid mirrors of relentless precision, and I saw the many within.

Two platinum claws clutched a distant future.

Cued by the thrust of a black beak, I opened my mouth to quench an abyssal thirst.

Drops of mercury laced my tongue.

A spiral wind appeared.

Feathers responded and the raven was gone.

As I watched the bird shrink back down to a black dot on the horizon, a girl's voice faded in from somewhere. She was laughing. Then she said something. It sounded like my name.

Then Rocky's disembodied voice drifted by, "Looks like he's dreaming."

I rubbed my eyes and opened them. I looked around. Rocky was still driving.

I turned my head a little more and saw a girl in the back seat searching through her knapsack.

My eyes lingered on the girl for a bit. Her soft features, full mouth, and willowy physique made her easy to look at. I guessed she was no more than nineteen or twenty. Her hair was pulled into a side ponytail that grazed her collar bone like silken charcoal, before reaching down to shield her left breast. She wore a fern green button-up shirt, a denim jacket frayed at the cuffs and collar, and black rimmed prescription glasses. I was studying her chocolate eyes when she looked up at me.

"You're awake!" she said through a smile.

Rocky looked over.

"Good dreams?" he asked. "You looked like you were drinkin' something."

My mouth was dry. I could barely swallow.

"Is there any water?"

"I've got some!" said the girl. "It's unopened. You can have it… Here."

She fished a bottle out of her knapsack and handed it to me.

"Quinn, this is Rhonda… I picked her up outside of Joliet about fifteen minutes ago… She's hitchin' all the way to Hollywood."

Rocky adjusted the rear-view. I checked the clock on the dash. I'd been sleeping for just over an hour.

"Thanks for the water, Rhonda."

"You're welcome. Call me Ronnie if you want… Ronnie Lee."

"Pleased to meet you, Ronnie Lee," I said, after a big gulp. "That's got a nice ring to it."

"She's not related to Bruce by the way," Rocky interjected.

"Bruce who?" I asked.

"Bruce Lee! Cripes, Quinn… Who'd ya *think* I was talkin about?"

I laughed and turned back toward Ronnie.

"He's a big Bruce Lee fan, if he hasn't already told you."

"Yeah, he told me," she chuckled. "While you were sleeping, we were going on about the movies he could've made nowadays. With all the computer effects."

There was a brief lull in the conversation and my curiosity quickly filled it.

"So what makes you wanna go to Hollywood?"

She leaned back against the seat as a faraway look took hold of her.

"I'm gonna be an actress… Joliet isn't the place for me to do that. I mean it's nice and all." She paused and leaned forward with her arms on the tops of our seats. "Actually, have you ever seen *The Blues Brothers*?"

"Yeah! Great film. Belushi's the best," I said.

"Remember how his character's name was Joliet Jake Blues?"

"So that's where it came from?"

"Yup... The opening scenes were shot at our prison. And quite a few popular TV shows have used it too... As a matter of fact, when I was six my parents took me to see some filming there and well... That's what happened to me. I got bit by the bug, as they say."

"I guess we should add *The Blues Brothers* to our list of great road movies," Rocky noted.

"Totally... Can't believe we didn't think of it."

Ronnie was still leaned up against the back of our seats. Her hands dangled from delicate wrists in my periphery. I couldn't help turning to glimpse them because hands had always fascinated me; they spoke. Hers were smooth instruments that tapered off into white tipped nails of natural gloss. They added to her already substantial list of charms.

I knew instinctively her allure would be both a blessing in the west coast audition rooms, and a curse on the open roads that led there.

"So what made you wanna hitchhike? It's a risky venture these days."

"Maybe so. But what's life without a few risks," she countered, before leaning back.

I saw Rocky smile at her from the rear-view. She smiled back. I wondered if maybe they'd hit it off while I was asleep. It felt that way to me. It was like they were comfortable with each other already.

"You know we're headed to Wichita, right?" I asked.

"Yeah. I'll just hop out at Springfield and go south from there... And thanks for picking me up by the way!"

"How could I not," chimed Rocky. "We were the only car on the road. I couldn't leave you stranded like that."

"Well thanks. When I get famous, I'll look you guys up and invite you down to my beach house in Malibu!" she joked.

"If you can find me," he said, as he shot me a look.

That was enough to tell me he hadn't divulged any secrets to her. Not that I thought he would. But pretty girls can make guys do some strange things, and for all I knew Rocky might've been one of those guys.

Maybe he was capable of changing his plans entirely?

Maybe if she asked him to follow her, he would?

I looked over and immediately felt ashamed for silently doubting him.

Then I started thinking maybe I should doubt him—for his own good. It was like a small part of me wished he would hook up with her. She was intelligent and adventurous and pretty much gorgeous. And there she was in our car. Her presence had to mean something, or at least I wanted it to. Because the closer we got to Wichita, the harder it was for me to accept the fact that Rocky was giving up—that he was basically finding a place to die.

Maybe they'd fall in love and she'd convince him to have the operation he needed?

It was too many maybes though, and time was running out. Springfield wasn't far away.

I decided to take the wheel back so they didn't have to use the rear-view as an interpreter. Maybe looking directly into each other's eyes would germinate something more intimate.

I laughed at myself for thinking these things, but I couldn't help it.

My growing sadness was forcing my hand.

We pulled into a rest area just north of Bloomington; about an hour from Springfield. The wind pushed against hickories and maples, and the distant western sky looked a shade or two darker than the rest.

All three of us got out and stretched our legs. I headed off to the treeline to take a leak as Rocky leaned up against Soldier and continued talking to Ronnie.

When I came back she had a different look on her face. She looked befuddled—less sure.

"You two ready to go?"

They looked at each other and nodded and we all got back in the car.

"We're gonna drop her off at the train station in Springfield. Okay?"

Rocky said that as he took the cash out of his satchel.

"Sure," I said.

He turned around so he was facing Ronnie.

"Your parents are obviously worried sick even though they let you go. I know they woulda bought you a ticket if they had the extra cash, so I want you to take this."

He counted off a thousand bucks and tried handing it back to her.

"I can't take your money. I've been planning this trip for months and the hitching part was gonna be the proof that I'm brave enough to own my dream. You know what I mean?"

"That's exactly it, Ronnie. I don't want anything getting in the way of your dream. Do you realize how many fucking creeps and perverts are gonna be trolling these highways from here to Hollywood? You're a pretty girl, and you're all alone. You need to get there safe and sound so you can knock 'em dead."

I did a shoulder check before pulling back out onto the highway. I saw her lower her head. She was torn, I could tell.

"I'm a pride drunk Leo, Rocky. I can't accept your money... I'm sorry. I need to do this on my own."

Right after she said that, and without looking at me, he placed his left hand upon my shoulder. Then in the most peculiar tone, he uttered something that made absolutely no sense at all to me at the time. As a matter of fact, it wasn't until the entire journey was over and I had many quiet hours to slowly piece everything together, that I came to terms with the full depth and breadth of the words he spoke.

"And so the Lion makes her cameo," he said, with calm eyes scanning the horizon. Then just as quickly, he snapped into a state of extreme agitation. He shifted in his seat a few times and rubbed his face with his fist. "If you don't take this, I'm gonna let it fly out the window," he said, as he grabbed the handle and fitfully rolled it down.

I looked over at him, not knowing if he was for real.

"What'll you do when you get there," he challenged. "You're gonna need a place to stay aren't ya? Hitchhike if ya want, but please take this money. Hide it real good and when you get to Hollywood use it to rent a room or whatever. Deal?"

He was holding the wad of cash up so that the wind was threatening to rip it out of his hand. I heard her take a deep breath.

"All right," she said, as she pulled on her ponytail. "I'll take it. But I'm still gonna hitch. I have to."

She accepted the money, then quickly stashed it away in her knapsack like she didn't wanna have to look at it. Rocky smiled and turned back around to face the highway.

"There's something else you'll need," I said, as I reached into my pocket. "I've been driving cab for five years and I've never once gotten behind this wheel without a little protection. Just like Rocky said, there's lots of weirdoes out there..." I held up my straight razor. "Take this. Technically it's not even considered a weapon, but it'll ward off any trouble that crosses your path."

She took it from my hand and looked it over.

"It's nice," she said, as she opened it up.

"My grandfather was a barber. It was passed down to me."

"I—I can't."

"*Pleeease*, just take it," begged Rocky.

She shook her head, then folded it back up and put it in her pocket. Just then, a few drops of rain hit the windshield. I looked up at the sky and saw that the darker clouds from the western horizon had moved in a little closer.

"Looks like we're in for some rain," I announced, as I flicked on the wipers.

"They're having some pretty nasty storms to the west of here. Just this side of where you're headed, actually. I saw it on the weather channel before I left today," Ronnie said.

Rocky laughed as he rolled his window all the way down and stuck his head out for a couple seconds.

"Bring it onn!" he yelled, up at the sky.

When he was back in his seat, he wiped his face with his shirt and smiled with defiance.

We had a half hour before we hit Springfield; from there we'd be turning directly into whatever nature had in store for us.

We needed to make a right turn just south of Springfield, so we drove through the city on our way. It was a calculated move on my part because we could've saved time by going around. The thing is, I knew Rocky was hoping to pass by the train station, and so was I.

I was far too cynical to believe Ronnie could thumb it all the way to Hollywood without having at least one serious run-in with a predator.

The rain was coming down pretty good as we pulled up to the main intersection of East Jefferson Street and North Ninth. I put the wipers on high and looked around. Tucked in beside the traffic signal was a small sign for the Amtrak station. I nudged Rocky with my elbow and pointed with my eyes. He looked up and nodded. Ronnie was busy getting her raincoat on so I hit my signal and turned.

We were there before she even realized what we did.

"With this weather I don't wanna drop you off on the highway. Go in here and wait it out. It's only 5:30 so you got lots of time before dark."

She looked up.

"You *guys!* I should've known. Because I'm a girl you think I can't handle myself, right?"

"It's pouring rain... Just go in and see how much a ticket is. I know it's pretty cheap," said Rocky.

"I'll have you know I'm a brown belt red stripe in Kung Fu... Do you really think I'd make this journey without the necessary skills?"

Rocky's face lit up.

"Hey! I used the Shaolin rushing heart elbow on a guy back in Toronto... Knocked him right out!"

"Niiice. Bruce would be proud," she drawled.

I pulled into the parking lot and stopped, as they launched into a discussion of different striking patterns.

"Okay then, here we are," I said gently.

They stopped talking and just looked at each other. Knowing that the moment of truth had arrived; Rocky seized it and pleaded his case once more with his eyes. She put her knapsack on her knees and paused, looking at the front doors of the building.

"Fine. I'll go in until the rain stops. And... And I'll see how much a ticket is."

"Promise?" asked Rocky.

"I promise."

I saw him relax his entire body with her affirmation. Then he checked the time on the dash and swallowed hard before speaking.

"Then I guess this is it, Ronnie. Quinn and I gotta keep truckin'. I wanna be in Kansas by sundown."

She looked a little shocked, but let it pass. I picked up the phone.

"Hang on a minute here. Let me get a picture of you two together," I said.

She moved in closer and leaned up against the back of Rocky's seat. She put her thin arm around him, then leaned in and kissed the side of his head.

I snapped the sixth picture.

This one makes me wonder about the blind cruelty of life. There just seemed to be so much potential between them.

If it'd been another time and place, would he have been interested in, or even pursued her?

I actually worked up the nerve to ask him that question as we left the station. His response was saturnine to the extreme. He shook his head and muttered: "Why would I wanna weigh her down with all my baggage. She's got a shot at life, I'm at the end of mine... I'm an old man, Quinn. Far too old to be chasin' dreams. That's your job."

Despite my illustrious taxi driving degree in worldliness, he managed to make me feel like an incurable naïf right then. I shut up. Nothing more was said about Ronnie.

In fact, nothing more was said between us for quite some time.

As water hissed its way through Soldier's fading rubber treads, we got back on the highway and headed toward the state line of Kansas.

He took *The Stone Angel* back out of his satchel and started reading again.

I set about silently trying to ready myself for the end of our journey— for the end of our time together.

I knew it wasn't gonna be easy and I knew it wasn't far away.

Nothing's ever easy when the heart gets tangled up with the mind.

I drove for an hour and a half in steady rain. Rocky read his book while I thought about all the different ways our trip could end.

The bad endings I put out of my mind.

The good, I kept.

The ending I liked the most had Rocky surprising me at the very last second by telling me to take him directly to the main hospital in

Wichita, so he could check himself in. I was still with him, of course. I helped him up to a front desk where a nurse took phone calls and looked busy. When we got to her she lifted her head and said, "Can I help you?" Rocky answered, "Yes, I'm scheduled for surgery tomorrow morning." The nurse responded by typing in his name and smiling a friendly mid-western smile, before getting up to show us to his room. His room was quiet, and clean, and he immediately took to the bed for some much-needed rest. Before drifting off to sleep he told me the best brain surgeon in North America worked in Kansas. Then he explained how they'd been corresponding online to work out the details of an arrangement that had his operation being done for free, "if he could just get himself to Wichita."

If only.

Around 6:45 p.m. we closed in on the state line of Missouri. I remember it well because right at that point Rocky finished *The Stone Angel*.

"Done!" he announced, as he clamped it shut, touched it to his forehead and looked up.

"Missouri. The *show-me* state, eh..." Rocky read the sign and chuckled to himself. "You ever heard the expression, Missouri loves company? Or how 'bout... Put me outta my Missouri!"

He made me laugh. I was still laughing a few minutes later as we approached a bridge.

"You know what river this is?"

"No," I said.

"Why it's the great Mississippi, Quinn... The Native Americans called it the father of waters."

I stole a quick glance down at the rolling waves as we crossed over. On the other side a sign said, Welcome to Hannibal.

"Did you know Hannibal's the boyhood home of Mark Twain? It's also the setting for his greatest books."

"For Huck Finn?" I asked.

"Yes indeed... Up until Huck and Jim set sail that is."

That got me thinking.

"Wouldn't *Huckleberry Finn* classify as another great road movie?"

Rocky smiled as he turned his head back to feast his eyes on the legendary muddy water.

"For sure it would. It might even be the best road story ever told!" He turned back around as the river faded into the distance behind us. "Actually no..." he said, changing his mind. "I take that back. The best road story ever told is *Don Quixote*... You ever read it?"

"Not yet... Isn't it like an epic or something?"

"It's 980 pages of medieval adventure. Quixote changes his name to The Knight of the Sorrowful Face, and him and his partner Sancho travel all over looking for noble battles to fight... Quixote is rather insane though, so most of the battles are farcical. It's funny as hell."

"I'll have to get it out of the library when I get back."

When I said that, a shot of anxiety coursed through my body as the reality of leaving Rocky behind and returning to Grey Grove to settle my debts crushed down upon my consciousness. I fell silent under the weight of it all. Rocky must've been feeling the pressure too because he quickly returned to his own inner world.

The rain started coming down even harder as we passed by Mark Twain State Park. I squinted into the distance and squirmed a little in my seat. What I saw didn't look inviting at all. The entire visible section of sky was a grim shade of greenish-grey, flecked by a terrible blackness.

I was about to mention it to Rocky, but when I looked over he was gripping his scarecrow again and wielding a thousand-yard stare. I decided against it.

I clenched the wheel a little tighter and drove on.

I kept the speedometer hovering around 140 km/h. I knew if we were gonna brave a bad storm, then we were better off minimizing the braving time with sheer speed.

I also knew I'd need every last fibre of my focusing power to get us through.

But the sky's magnetic pull undermined my concentration, and every five minutes or so I found myself looking up in awe at a slowly unfolding malignancy of cold ambition. It was like nothing I'd ever laid eyes on before, because somehow the whole knotted mass of turmoil was backlit by a pristine sunset. The contrast was nauseating.

By 8:00 p.m. the rain had become a snapping wet sheet in the wind.

We were nearing ground zero when we passed a sign that told us we were 60 miles from Chillicothe.

"Bet ya didn't know Chillicothe was the stomping ground for a couple of serial killing seniors, did ya?"

"Nope... News to me," I said, as a lash of rain studded wind struck us from the side and rattled the car.

"Ray and Faye Copeland. They were the oldest couple ever to be sentenced to death in the United States. Sixty-nine and seventy I think they were... Ray lured drifters to the farm and used them to pay for cattle with bad checks he wrote. When they were no longer useful, he'd put a single bullet in the back of their heads. Killed five people before someone found human bones on their property and called the police."

"Money makes people do some pretty evil stuff," I said.

Rocky turned the scarecrow over, and over in his hands before continuing.

"Y'know that last town we drove by?" he asked.

"You mean Hannibal?"

"Yeah, Hannibal... It made me think of the movie *Hannibal*. You know the one? It's the sequel to *Silence of the Lambs*... You really get inside Lecter's mind in this one, and you know... I gotta say I like him. I really like the guy."

He was beginning to make me feel a little uneasy. That dark, unknowable quality was back in his eye and he was talking with a wistful, almost reverential tone about killers. At least that's how it sounded.

The infernal skies might've influenced my perception a little, I suppose.

"D'you remember the scene where Hannibal holds up the piece of broken mirror and tells the Mason Verger character to cut his face off with it?"

"Umm... Yeah, I think so." I hadn't actually seen the movie, but I wasn't about to say so. Something told me just to go along with him on this.

Out of the corner of my eye, I saw him start to rock back and forth. It pushed me over the edge completely. I was officially disturbed as he continued ratcheting up the tension.

"Mason's tweaked out on drugs so he takes the mirror and starts doing it. Hannibal watches and smiles that frosty smile of his." He paused to rub his temple. "You know why Hannibal told him to do that?"

"Not really, no."

"Because Mason is a waste of life. He's a playboy who does nothing but go to parties and stick his dick in things. He gets by on his good looks and money... But Hannibal of course, sees through his mask like he does with everyone he meets, and in an act of divine compassion suggests a simple and permanent cure."

I didn't really think what he was describing could possibly qualify as compassion. Nor was it likely to be confused with divinity. But I let it go in favor of asking him if that was where he got his idea for the broken mirror video he made.

However, just as I was about to speak, three things converged at once:

1. A huge bolt of lightning screamed across the sky in front of us.
2. Rocky grabbed his head and doubled over in pain.
3. The lyrics to a song started coursing through my head.

When the wind blows and the rain gets cold, you know it's time to go. He knows it's time to go.

I knew the song well because it was one of my all-time favorites. It was "Moonlight Mile" by the Rolling Stones. But the words weren't right and I knew what that meant.

Frank was calling.

Rocky whimpered. I looked over at him as he looked up at me. He was deathly pale and his nose was streaming down with blood again. He pulled back his lips into a smile, revealing a row of scarlet teeth.

"I need to lie down. I feel dizzy," he murmured.

I immediately stepped on the brakes, pulled over to the side, hopped out and ran around to help him into the back. When he was comfortable I returned to the driver's seat, three quarters soaked.

"Keep driving!" he ordered.

I did as he said. I put Soldier back into gear, checked my mirrors, and then looked up at the road ahead. There wasn't a single car in either direction for as far as I could see.

But something else seized every last goose-bump of my attention.

"What the *fuck* is that?" I shouted.

At the extreme end of the highway, a wounded cobra with a flared hood of nimbus cloud writhed about in pain as the sun peeked over the continental shelf to bid us farewell before falling away. Dying rays of amber and saffron danced upon the aft face of this sky snake, weaving into its tightening coil of violence a delicate mix of shimmering hues.

It was the most beautiful and most terrible thing I'd ever seen, in that order.

As I sat there watching, mesmerized as I was by its swiveling spine, a loud popping sound emanated from directly above. I glanced up into the rear-view and saw the top sign bouncing down the road behind us, smashing against the pavement into smaller and smaller bits as it disintegrated into nothingness.

I took my foot off the brake, hit the gas, turned the car around and started racing back the way we came.

"What the hell are you doing!?" Rocky bellowed, from the back seat.

"I'm saving our lives. Take a look out the back!"

He propped himself up, turned his head and saw for himself what was chasing us. He sat there staring in silence for a few seconds, before erupting once more.

"Stop this fucking car right now!"

I pretended not to hear him. It just didn't make any sense to me so I figured his headache was making him delirious. I kept driving.

Then I felt the cold blade of his pocket knife press into my throat.

I looked up into the mirror. His eyes were two fully dilated apertures of anger, ready to vaporize anything in their path. I could feel his breath on my neck as his knife threatened to open my jugular.

Yet I flat out refused to stop.

If he had death on his mind I wanted no part of it. My life was royally messed up, but it wasn't beyond repair. I wasn't ready to die. Not now. Not with him.

"Don't test me, Quinn... I'll slit your goddamn throat right here and watch you bleed out. You'll stop driving eventually."

I could feel the car getting rocked from side to side as we hurdled down the highway. But my foot didn't budge. The gas pedal was all the way to the floor and the needle was buried.

Then Frank sang once more.

When the wind blows and the rain gets cold, he knows things you don't. He knows things you don't.

The words were different this time. They made me wonder. They made me wonder just enough to doubt myself.

What things did he know?

Slowly, I eased off on the gas.

"That's better," he cooed, in my ear. "Now stop this thing and let me out."

I pumped the brakes and pulled over as he took the knife away from my throat.

"There's thirty-five hundred in my satchel. I want you to give Glenda a thousand. You can keep the rest... Ya hear me?"

I nodded as I kept one eye on the advancing funnel of debris in the rear-view.

Then he dropped the knife and screamed in pain.

"Ahhh fuck. My *head!*"

He fell back against the seat and wiped the next hot stream of blood from his face with the raven on his shirt.

"You okay?"

"Stop worrying about me, Quinn. I'm already dead. When I get out of this car, I want you to floor it. I want you to get the fuck outta here as fast as you can. Don't look back!"

His voice got drowned out by a daemonic groan of wind.

"What'd you say?!"

He leaned up against the seat again and spoke directly into my ear.

"I said, when I get out I want you to floor it and not look back! And here. Take this... I want you to have it."

He handed me his scarecrow as the car was ramrodded by a spiteful gale that pushed us a full five feet back out onto the road.

"Why are you doing this Rocky?"

"Because I'm sick of being a scarecrow. I'm sick of being sick. I'm sick of being everyone's reminder of death. I taught myself to swim and now I'm gonna teach myself how to fly. I wanna..." He looked down at his shirt. "I wanna be a raven. I wanna fly above it all and perch on the tallest motherfuckin' tree there is—" A violent cracking sound stopped him mid-sentence. We both jerked our heads to the right to see a tree get ripped out of the ground and sucked up into the sky. "Ravens like shiny tiles too. I'm gonna find me an emerald mosaic!"

The noise was almost deafening at this point. The windows were threatening to shatter and the hood was clamoring up and down like a hypothermic jaw.

"Your lace is untied, Quinn… Do it up! Those shoes have to get you home." He pointed down at my left foot. "And don't fall asleep in the poppy field."

"What the hell are you talking about?"

"The only character I wasn't sure of was Toto. But it finally came to me. It's Frank… Frank is Toto!" he said, through a laugh of disbelief. "I mean, why do you think he never warned you about walking into that murder scene?"

I shook my profoundly confused head.

"Because if that hadn't happened you'd never have taken this road trip with me. We create each other, Quinn. And together we created a story… *This* story," he said, calmly looking back at the anarchy getting ready to swallow us up.

Suddenly it all dawned on me: my red high-tops, and the scarecrow, and Kansas. And who knows what else. The remaining clues would all arrive in their own good time; that is to say, they were coaxed into focus by fingers on a future keyboard, and a head deep in the rarefied air of the past.

As I sat there reeling in the wake of his vision, something drew my eyes back up to the mirror. He'd been watching me with a tacit look of approval threaded into his brow, waiting for a raw awakening to smoothen my face; when he saw it he let loose a grand finale of a smile, then leaned in, and whispered against the back of my head the last words he ever said to me.

"The supreme javelin thrower respects the smallest of final touches. He's mastered the release and perfected the art of letting go… I can let go now," he said, with deposition on his tongue. "I can let go because you've seen the details in the shiny tiles… *It's all there, Quinn. It's all right there in front of you.*"

He rolled the rear window down and a mean burst of air tore through the car. His satchel fell off the front seat. *The Stone Angel* spilled out onto the floor and started flapping its pages like wings. Beside it was his passport. I picked it up.

"Take this you—you *crazy* raven... Just in case you need it where you're going!"

He took it from me and winked, then climbed out the window so that he was sitting on the door frame. I grabbed his leg.

"*I'll meet you there, Rocky! I'll meet you there someday!*" I yelled, at the top of my lungs.

He stuck his hand back in and placed it on top of mine. Then ever so faintly I heard him start singing above the roof.

I could while away the hours
Conferrin' with the flowers
Consultin' with the rain
And my head I'd be scratchin'
While my thoughts were busy hatchin'
If I only had a brain
I'd unravel any riddle
For any individual
In trouble or in pain...

His voice faded out as he rose up into the air and floated, still half in the car and holding on.

Then he relaxed his grip, let go, and was gone.

I stepped hard on the pedal as possessive winds tried pulling Soldier and me up with him.

Tires squealed as vicious torrents howled like wolves.

I didn't let up, and I didn't look back.

All through the night I drove, smiling every now and then at the scenes parading by in my head—scenes Rocky had masterminded by choosing me, like he did, as his driver, and ultimately his chronicler.

It was now my duty to uphold the solemnity of a promise.

As the new clear calm of a once raging sky streaked by above me in trails of ancient light, the first venerating words formed upon the ridges of my salt stained lips:

We both had our secrets.

Without taking my eyes off the empty highway, I rifled through the glove compartment and found an old stub of a pencil. Then I reached into his satchel and pulled out *The Stone Angel*.

As the Missouri wind rushed in behind me, I steadied the wheel with my knee, struck the flint of his Zippo and by its soulful glow wrote those five words down on the inside cover.

And now?

Now here I am a full decade older than I was on the road to Wichita, looking at those five scrawled words.

It took me many years of failed attempts, bad beginnings, and broken narrative threads, but finally I did right by him.

Finally, I told his story for the world to read.

And perhaps, my own story too.

THE END

EPILOGUE

WITH A LITTLE HELP from the heroin I had left over, I arrived back in Grey Grove safe and somewhat sound. I made sure to finish it all before I hit the border, of course. I also made sure not to do too much at once.

I remember crinkling up the empty tin foil into a tiny silver ball and rolling it between my trembling thumb and fingers while looking down at my shoes.

I was parked at the edge of the Detroit River.

I remember seeing Glenda in my mind. She was giving me her come-hither stare with her hands on her hips and a tapping toe—waiting for me to make good.

Beside me lay Rocky's satchel. I went through it and found the latex eye of Bruce Lee. I put it up to my own eye and traced the resurrected edges of once polluted waves.

In that instant I knew I could vanquish my poison.

I rolled down the window and flicked the glinting silver sphere out onto the shoreline.

Minutes later a crow descended.

I looked over at the action figure lying on the passenger's seat and smiled, then checked my rear-view and started home.

I found a new appreciation for ravens and crows after the Wichita trip. My ears are now tuned to them. If I'm walking to the grocery store or the library to do some writing, and I hear their raspy laughter, I always look up.

I stand suspended in time beneath black wings, gleaning details and heeding tiny signs. Because above all things I've learned to respect the unstoppable steps and clear squinted eyes of survivors — the Rockys — the ones who use the flame of life to forge new links in ancient chains.

Chains that rattle through time and space.

Moved by rhythmic visions and shiny tiled grace.

AFTERMISSION

What an excitable couple. They're holding each other, teary eyed. I didn't think the ending was that sad? I've heard of people surviving tornadoes before. They get sucked up, flung about, and then dropped back down onto hay bales and things, completely unharmed.

I see you finished your absinthe. There's a great band playing across town. Wanna go?

ACKNOWLEDGMENTS

A debut novel is a team effort on every front. And I was lucky enough to have had my manuscript accepted by the visionaries at **BOOKTROPE** Publishing; where innovation and cooperation stand like granite pillars, supporting a vibrant and pioneering literary community. It wasn't long before I made the necessary connections that are needed to bring a novel to life. I would, therefore, like to thank:

Ken Shear (CEO at BOOKTROPE).

Katherine Sears (CMO and founder at BOOKTROPE).

Jesse James Freeman (Director of Community Management at BOOKTROPE).

Duke Miller (fellow author, all round good friend, and giver of invaluable advice).

My editor, **Stevie McCoy**, whose many savvy suggestions were incorporated into this book.

Michelle Hartz, who weeded out those eyeball-evading typos.

Anne Chaconas, whose vibrant energy and shrewd business acumen is exactly what this project needs.

Author photo by **Frank Melong** and **Stephanie Nash**.

And finally, **Majanka Verstraete**, who designed and created an absolutely perfect cover for this book.

To All Readers,

Without you, writing would be a truly lonesome undertaking. For although every writer must write for the sake of writing, they do so with aspirations of one day being read. There is, of course, a huge reward that comes from having your work appreciated and interfaced with.

I'm never without a book to read. When I don't have one on the go I feel lost. I feel anxious. I feel deprived of an escape.

Thank you for reading *Taxicab to Wichita*, and please continue searching out and discovering new writers.

Aaron.

*Please visit **aaronlouisbooks.com** for more information on the author.*

MORE GREAT READS FROM BOOKTROPE

Living and Dying with Dogs by **Duke Miller** (Literary Fiction) Living and Dying with Dogs is a journey from war to epidemic to famine. Your tour guide? A hesitant, unsure narrator with a unique and tragic understanding of refugees, war, sex, the past, and our bloody world.

The Dead Boy's Legacy by **Cassius Shuman** (Fiction) 9-year-old Tommy McCarthy is abducted while riding his bike home from a little league game. This psychological family drama explores his family's grief while also looking at the background and motivations of his abductor.

The Long Walk Home by **Will North** (Fiction) Forty-four year-old Fiona Edwards answers her door to a tall, middle-aged man shouldering a hulking backpack—unshaven, sweat-soaked and arrestingly handsome. What neither of them knows is that their lives are about to change forever.

Twist **by Myron Night** (Fiction) In the dystopian year 2075, Adam Twist, a down-and-out private investigator, ekes out a living inside the walled city of Wichita. Tornadoes stalk the ravaged landscape and lost children haunt his nightmares. When the rebellious daughter of the most powerful man in the city runs away, Twist must follow into the hell outside the Wall to find her.

Discover more books and learn about our new approach to publishing at www.booktrope.com